Misdirect

A novel
Fine Line Series– Book 2

Faking the truth is easier

Jennifer Conklin

Cover Designed By: Aaron Trudell

Publishing Assistance/Editing By: Tempered Ink

Font Designer Creatype Studio, "Porcelain," 2019, via creatypestudio.co

Font Designer Impallari, "Kaushan Script," 2011, via impallari.com

Font Designer Khurasan, "Tahu!," 2020, via creativefabria.com

Illustrator seamartini, "Moutain, Hill and Rock…" 2024, via iStockphoto.com

Photographer: Clix Photography, Author photo, 2022

Photographer Markus Novak, "Misty Mountains," 2018, via iStockphoto.com

Author/Publisher: Jennifer Conklin Author, LLC

First Edition: December 2025

Printed in the United States of America

jenniferconklinauthor.com

happydetours.com

ISBN: 979-8-9889850-5-1 (pbk)

ISBN: 979-8-9889850-6-8 (ebk)

To SM & CH.
Without your books (SM) and
your cinematic vision (CH),
I would never have started my literary journey.
Not only as an avid reader & movie buff,
but as a writer.
So, thank you both!

Table of Contents

CHAPTER 1

...in common now.

Shane Whitmore

MY JAW STILL ached from being sucker-punched and thrown into a car a few weeks ago. I got hit so hard I blacked out in the middle of my best friend's driveway. At the time, I didn't know what was happening. But I do now. And I'm still paying the price.

The clock ticked loudly as my therapist waited for me to respond. I couldn't help but look down at my wrists where they had been bound. My leg bounced, and I involuntarily grimaced at the muscle strain. It wasn't every day that a crooked cop messed with my family.

"Is there anything else you'd like to share?" Dr. Collier asked.

Share? No. This was the last place I wanted to be. I bit my bottom lip as more memories I tried so hard to suppress trickled in.

Dark. Pain. Hard to breathe. Trapped. With a hood over my head, my vision and sense of space were distorted. But I knew I was in a car moving fast. I forced myself to stop struggling and took a deep breath. Panic that had flowed freely now ebbed. Think Shane. Think. That's when I heard a noise.

"There was a low hum from the radio. Rumbling cars. We drove for a long time over what felt like patched-up seams. I had guessed the highway," I mumbled. *Headed somewhere I didn't want to go.*

"That was resourceful of you," my therapist gently added after a beat of silence. My brows furrowed as more of the memory faded into the present moment. Like I was both here and there at the same time.

Everything was pitch black, nausea rocking my insides. Pain electrified every nerve, forcing my body to shut down as the world faded away. Once I came to, my lungs burned as I gasped for air. How long had I been out? I tried to move, desperate to free myself. But it was useless. Cuffs held my hands together, skin nearly raw from the contact. The bag over my head was still too tight around my neck. I couldn't breathe. I couldn't—

My chest heaved. "Shane? It's okay. You're safe now. He's gone, and he can't hurt you anymore," Dr. Collier spoke in a low, steady tone.

"W-what?" My body trembled.

"You're in a safe place. He can't hurt you anymore, Shane." Memories. They're just memories. That was then, and this is now.

"I know," the answer spilled out of my mouth, saying whatever I could to appease my therapist. She set down her tablet, leaning into the chair as I willed my shaking to end.

"Are you okay to continue? I'd like to hear more of the story from your perspective if that's alright."

Anger threatened to emerge. I've regurgitated this story so many times, to so many people. It was like acid burning my tongue. Why? Because Dr. Collier already knew the story splashed all over the news. Tragedy of the week. Then here I am, a hot, shaking mess. I silently pushed it down like I've done with every feeling since that horrible night. If I'm being honest, I don't want to recall, relive, or talk about any of it. I don't need therapy.

"Well, at first, I was confused, mostly." That much was true. I allowed the nightmare inside again. "Steven, er… the man kept badgering me about someone named Wren. He wanted to know where he could find her. And back then, I had no idea who he was asking about."

"How did that make you feel?"

"Angry, I guess?" My brows furrowed. "I *knew* he grabbed the wrong person." *Actually, I was pissed that this happened to me.*

I glanced at the old clock on the wall, taking a deep, steady breath. I closed my eyes, trying to shift back into the memory.

The smell of cigars filled the air. An aroma I knew well from spending time with my elderly neighbor. He'd hire my younger brother, Kyle, and me to do odd jobs around his yard. Mowing the lawn in summer and shoveling snow in the winter. He was a widower, lonely, and loved to talk. I would sit with him on the porch after I finished my tasks and shoot the shit.

We had a ritual where he'd offer me a beer, and I would say I couldn't because my mother would disapprove. He would then pour half a cup and tell me to drink my refreshing lemonade. He'd belly laugh over his not-so-covert ruse, and I'd always play along.

We'd sit on that porch for hours, sipping our drinks as he smoked big, fat cigars, reminiscing about the glory days. I enjoyed spending my summer afternoons with him and hearing his stories. He lived a colorful life, and it made me yearn to live mine. He was also a good listener, never judged, and always gave the best advice. I didn't have a dad growing up, and he filled that void. When he passed last winter break, it was a bleak time for me.

Until Robin came into my life. I mean, Wren. It's still hard to use her real name after knowing her as Robin for so long. She was the light in the dark I desperately needed. I clung to her, letting her energy envelop me. She was new to our high school last January, and I immediately felt drawn to her. I couldn't pinpoint why, but I had to know her. Although reserved, we shared a common love. Running. That was how it all started. Besides school and soccer training, Wren encompassed the rest of my time.

Wren's betrayal, falling for my brother, cut like a knife. Our strained relationship when I returned from overseas only now made sense in hindsight. I had been away for two months. Two months! Back then, I blamed the weirdness on our time apart, never suspecting more. I once believed Wren was the light in my darkness. Instead, she kept me in the dark. I guess I never truly knew her before I left for training in Portugal last summer. And the demons that haunted her during our time together? They came out to play.

That hell came in the form of her stepdad, Steven. He was the one who came out of nowhere, blocked my car in Max's driveway, and punched my lights out. Once again left in the dark, literally and metaphorically.

Dr. Collier waited intently in her powder-blue wing chair. I shifted uncomfortably, signaling a response. "Shane, you mentioned he badgered you. What did he say exactly?"

"He kept insisting he had proof I was lying. That it would be in my best interest to tell him where she was. But again, I didn't know who Wren was, and he wouldn't offer to elaborate." Abruptly, that exact terrifying moment violently flooded back.

Our car finally stopped, confirming we were in the city. A pulse of hustling sounds wailed around me—sirens, horns blaring, and the squeaks of echoing brakes. Still blind, the man wrenched me out of the trunk and down a flight of stairs. He roughly flung me onto a chair and finally pulled off the hood.

My eyes squinted from the bright light shining in my face. He stood behind the glow to hide himself. You could tell he had an ego the size of a skyscraper by his stance. The basement walls radiated a musty chill. And the smell? I almost regretted being able to breathe again. I tried to shield my face, but my hands were still bound behind me.

"I'm going to ask again. Where is Wren?" Steven demanded.

"I honestly don't know who you're talking about. You have the wrong guy. I've never met anyone named Wren! I promise!" I hated remembering how pathetic I sounded.

"Don't play games with me, punk. Tell me where she is!" He grabbed my throat, fingers bruising my neck. You'd think this would scare the shit out of me. But all it did was piss me off.

I narrowed my eyes, steeling my resolve. "Even if I knew where she was? I sure as hell wouldn't tell you!" This answer wasn't my smartest move, even if it felt good at the time.

Steven hauled off and hit me so hard my nose spurted blood. "I'll ask you one last time. Where. Is. Wren?"

I sniffed the iron-laden crimson that dripped down my face, unsure how to answer as my nose painfully pulsed with each heartbeat. There was nothing I could say to him that would make him stop. I didn't have his answer.

I snapped back to the present as the searing pain in my knee throbbed just thinking back to the barrage of blows it endured. Reflexively, I rubbed my leg.

Dr. Collier's eyes flashed down toward my repeated movements. It seemed she could tell I was dissociating elsewhere. "Would you be willing to share how he reacted to not getting the answers he wanted?"

Vivid images of Steven wiping my blood off his hands on the side of his pants flashed. "He'd try to jog my memory."

"And by 'jog your memory', do you mean he would hurt you?"

I hesitated. "Yeah. Something like that."

"Do you want to expand on that?" *No, I don't want to expand on that.*

"There's nothing really to tell. He would rough me up a bit. That's all." I didn't have it in me to share gory details today.

"Dr. Collier, I get that this is your job. You want me to open up and share how that night made me feel. Determine if I'm doing okay. But I'm fine. And as far as Steven? He's gone. There's no threat anymore. I just want to move on and focus on soccer. I'm missing valuable training to be here today. And that? That makes me mad, if you really want to know how I'm feeling. So, no offense, I don't need to be here."

"I take no offense at how you're feeling. I welcome it. And to be completely transparent with you, this is voluntary. Yes, your mom is concerned, but I think you could truly benefit from our sessions. However, this is totally up to you. What you put into our time together is what you get out of it."

Awesome. My therapist pulled out the mom card. But I'm eighteen, I could choose not to be here, even though I knew Mom would be disappointed. Especially after everything that happened: my brother falling for my girlfriend, being kidnapped by a madman, and the shooting all happening within a few days. It seemed so unbelievable that if I hadn't lived it myself, I would've thought it was a plot for a Netflix movie.

"What if we made a standing appointment every week? If you want to come, you can. And if you don't? That's fine too." Dr. Collier queried.

"We can't afford that."

"Insurance will cover the sessions you attend, and I won't bill for any you miss. Sound fair enough?"

"I guess."

"At least consider it?"

I exhaled loudly, unsure about this therapy bullshit. "Okay."

"Great. I hope to see you next week, Shane." I stood up from the matching wing chair facing hers, smiling awkwardly as I walked out of her office.

There's a weight on my chest that always sits there now. It's constant. It knew I had to head home. Home to where I lived with my mom, Kyle, and Wren. The approaching winter holidays made that weight unbearable.

If Dr. Collier had asked me what I really wanted? I'd tell her I wanted to punch something hard enough to make it hurt. That I'd want it to feel my pain. But I couldn't say that to her, my mom, or anyone else. So, I'll keep saying what they want to hear.

Limping to my car in the cool December air, questions from my therapist reverberated in my head. There were too many emotions jumbling together, but one stood out above the rest. Sympathy. Sympathy for Wren. It felt weird after everything, but at least I could understand her motivations now.

Since the kidnapping, my days revolved around reassuring everyone that I'm fine. That everything in my life is fine. But it couldn't be further from the truth. It's been utterly exhausting, always having to pretend.

Wren and I had that in common now.

Kira Sky Bowman

It was hard to be sympathetic toward Robbie… er, Wren. But I tried. I, along with the entire school, knew about the dramatic events involving the Whitmore brothers and Robbie. I mean, Wren, *ugh*. Will I ever get used to calling her that?

Sarah was everywhere on social media, keeping us informed. She latched onto any nugget of information she could ascertain. I even brought Wren flowers, but I chickened out when it was time to see her. I ended up leaving them at the Hospital's front lobby desk… I do feel horrible that she had lived with such evil. But I wasn't ready to speak to her yet… or run into Kyle. I figured he'd be by her side during her recovery.

While Kyle and I didn't date for long, three months or so, they had all been a lie. Every single second of it. Our breakup still felt raw. Everyone, including my family, says I'm trusting and forgiving… but I'm finding it hard to be either one right now. My feelings are valid, but it doesn't make it hurt any less.

The relief of winter break finally began to settle. I could escape the endless whispers and chatter of speculation among hormone-ravaged teenagers. Having to relive the sting of heartbreak again and again was too much to bear. I ended up bowing out of the Winter Talent Show. My parents were disappointed, but they understood. It's not like my routine was riveting. I had planned to perform some lasso tricks I learned from my summers in Montana on my uncle's ranch.

Sarah, on the other hand? Yeah, she was downright pissed that I didn't show up. She had planned on singing and felt slighted that our entire friend group wasn't going. Except for Brody, but he had to go. It was part of the unwritten rules of boyfriend duties. However, she still gave me a good guilt trip. I found it amazing how that girl could turn any event or situation into being about her. Then again, that was our Sarah.

The Whitmore brothers and Wren hadn't come back to school since December. Plus, Robi… Wren was recovering from a gunshot wound, Shane from his kidnapping ordeal, and Kyle from the rest of the trauma. Don't get me wrong, I was thankful they were all okay. But I was also thankful to have a reprieve from everyone. Especially from Ro… I mean, Wren. And to be honest? I'm not sure if I'll be ready to see her anytime soon.

I was startled out of my thoughts when I heard a knocking at the front door. As I pulled the handle, the sharp sting of karma slapped me across the face.

"R-Wren?" I stuttered in surprise.

"Hi, Kira."

"What… uh… how are you?" My mouth felt dry as words scraped over my sandpaper tongue.

"I'm healing."

"What are you doing here?"

"I wanted to see you."

"You walked here in the bitter cold, while healing from getting shot, because you wanted to see me?"

"I didn't… walk here."

I scoffed. "Oh. I see. *He* drove you here."

"Yes."

"So, where's Kyle now?"

"He's in the car. He didn't want to upset you."

"And you being here wouldn't upset me?"

"Kira, I'm sorry—"

"For which part? Coming into our lives and turning everything upside down? Cheating on Shane with his brother Kyle, while he was still *my* boyfriend? For putting everyone in mortal danger running from your lunatic stepfather?" A torrent of pain smashed through my carefully built dam of emotions.

"All of it. I'm sorry for all of it."

"Please don't mistake my flowers at the hospital for forgiveness, Rob… aagghh, Wren. I will never forget what you did to me or Shane, and I will never forgive Kyle. He used me as his placeholder, and I'm worth more than that."

"You *are* worth more than that, Kira. I want you to take your anger out on me. Not him. He cares about you and has been miserable that he hurt you. Everything that happened is because of me. Please forgive Kyle."

"Does he know you're begging me for his forgiveness?"

"No."

"Then what does he think you're telling me?"

"That I'm making amends like I've been trying with Shane. Apologizing. He knows it's weighing on my mind."

"Does it?"

"All the time."

"Good." I tried to sound strong, but my shaky voice betrayed me. Still, she looked uncomfortable. I stood taller, squaring my shoulders. "Is that all you wanted to say?"

"The three of us have been cleared to return to school after winter break. That means every news outlet will be there too. I just wanted to give you a heads up."

"Well, thank you for your concern, but I'm doing just fine," I fumed.

"I should go. I truly had good intentions in coming here tonight. I hope deep down you know that. Have a happy New Year."

Wren descended the porch stairs, moving down the front path. I continued watching as she ambled slowly across the sidewalk toward the car. To him. I could see the exhaust billowing in the frigid air under the streetlight. My stomach tightened. He had parked in the exact same spot the night he blew up our relationship with his truth bombs. I swore I would never think about him again. Long for him again. But that was a lie.

I stood there in the doorway holding my shivering frame until their car pulled away. Last year, I had hoped for a happy New Year, too. But that's not what I got. And it's because I fell for Kyle Whitmore.

Wren and I had that in common now.

CHAPTER 2

...wished I were.

Shane

WINTER BREAK FLEW by, both a good and a bad thing. I asked Max to drive me to school since I couldn't stomach riding in the same car as Kyle and Wren. We were likely to have hundreds of eyes peeled on the three of us returning. I knew we'd be like celebrities, and the paparazzi were waiting to pounce. Like the literal paparazzi. Well, I guess we did take down a corrupt cop from New York City. Our little town and high school, just an hour and a half outside city limits, was now on everyone's radar. One silver lining? I'm on the radar too.

The calls were non-stop from top soccer recruiters around the globe. My coaches developed a training plan to highlight and refine my skills to prepare for spring. Even my coach from Portugal reached out, saying he'd be in the States starting late April. Apparently, he's been gathering a scouting team to come see me play. I've never known a better opportunity than this.

I was cleared to train with the caveat of attending physical therapy. But even though my heart was all in, my mind had other plans. No matter how much time I invested, my focus waned, especially when it involved my ex-girlfriend. Wren was a constant reminder of everything that imploded in my life. Every time I thought about her, it was like I was back in that therapy session. Or really, back in that memory.

When her stepdad kidnapped me, I honestly didn't have a clue who he even meant. Never in a million years would I have guessed that he was asking about Robin. I was trying to live long enough to convince him he had the wrong guy.

But he didn't have the wrong guy. He had the wrong brother. It wasn't me that Steven's lackey saw at the restaurant on Black Friday in New York City. It had been Kyle. I later found out that it was because I had stupidly used my own debit card to pay for lunch. That's how Steven found me.

Don't get me wrong, I'm grateful that Kyle wasn't kidnapped and that Robin was brave enough to rescue me. It all worked out in the end. I chuckled at that thought. *Worked out for whom exactly?* Because it wasn't me.

I'm alive but still dealing with the fallout. My girlfriend *and* my brother betrayed me, my ex lives with me while dating my brother, and I'm still trying to heal from the beating I received at the hands of a desperate maniac. I just can't make this shit up. Now add the pressure of going back to school, the paparazzi, and all the teenage gossip. It was overwhelming.

I woke up this morning knowing I needed to distance myself from both of them. Even if only for a singular car ride. I may have been able to avoid everyone on social media, but I would be voluntarily walking into the madness I wanted to do it my way.

"Shane. Are you okay?" Max asked from the driver's seat.

"Huh? Yeah. Why?"

"Because you keep cracking your knuckles over and over."

I jerked my hands down to my sides. "Just not looking forward to all the eyes and questions. You saw the news vans camped outside my house."

"You're a certified celebrity now. I always thought it would happen because of soccer, but—"

"Yeah. Me too. This sucks."

"I can pull around to the back and text one of the boys to open the door so you can slip in. There might be less of a crowd."

"Sure. It won't help, but sure."

Max drove behind the school, a throng of students instantly noticing his car. They didn't hesitate to rush after us. Max got me as close as he could without running up the sidewalk. I grabbed my backpack and made a mad dash for the door. I heard the crowd closing in, and as I diverted my attention for a split second, I caught the edge of the curb wrong. *Shit!*

My leg rotated in an awkward direction, knee searing with pain from the odd twist. Of course, it was the same leg that Steven used to help "jog my memory." I groaned loudly and hobbled the rest of the way. A teammate Max must have texted ushered me in and quickly slammed the door shut behind me.

My breathing was heavier than it should be for running such a short distance. I leaned over at my waist, trying to catch my breath while rubbing my right knee. Frustration and pain compounded alongside my stress. As I continued gasping, unable to stop. I realized I was drawing a crowd. A familiar voice began coaching me to take slow and steady breaths.

"In. Out. Shane. Keep breathing." I did as Kyle instructed, but seeing his face pissed me off. How was my brother here already? Then I heard her and felt her touch. Robin gently laid her hand on my back and hovered near my ear.

"In. Out. In. Out." She said in her feathery tone. Having her near used to calm me. But now? I wanted to flee. To turn off my feelings for Wren. But I couldn't. Even though I'm still mad at her. Mad at him.

It's only been a month since our lives changed. I try to act like I'm okay whenever I'm around them. Apparently, I'm not a good liar like Wren is.

However, at this moment, I wished I were.

Kira

Of course, school was a complete zoo as usual. Every day since the whole ordeal happened, I've gotten swarmed by classmates hoping I had learned something new. Not to mention all the broadcast vans waiting for Shane, Kyle, and Wren. The "Hero Trio" was what the news had dubbed them. Those lame headlines haunted every printing press. It felt impossible to escape.

I looked out the car window as my mom pulled into the drop-off zone. Students and invasive reporters immediately crowded the car, hoping any of the Hero Trio was present. The local police attempted to keep them at bay, albeit unsuccessfully.

I wanted to turn to my mom and beg her to pull away. But instead, I squeezed her hand and opened the door. I pushed through the crowd with some assistance from the authorities and made my way through the front. Unfortunately, the police couldn't follow me inside and save me from the students who were eager to hear gossip they thought I had.

I jogged down the hall to my locker. But when I turned the corner, I saw Sarah waiting right beside it. I didn't have it in me to deal with her the very first second of my arrival. I quickly darted down the back hall toward the locker rooms and gym. I hoped to hell I could get some fresh air. Unfortunately, by the time I realized who was at the end of the corridor, it was too late. I crashed right into my ex-boyfriend.

"Oof!" A loud sound forced itself from my throat. "I'm sorr..." I subconsciously began to say, abruptly stopping myself.

"Hey," Kyle said apprehensively, helping me upright.

"I didn't see you there. I was trying to..."

"Escape everyone. I get it."

I wriggled out of his grasp as my head jerked in the direction of gasps. "What's wrong with Shane?" I asked, watching R... Wren whispering in his ear.

"Shane was chased by the paparazzi. He's catching his breath. That's all."

"It seems like he's hyperventilating. Should we get the nurse?"

"No," Kyle snapped. "I mean, no thank you. He wouldn't want any more attention when he's like this. He just needs a couple of minutes, and then he'll be okay." His eyes pleaded.

Hypnotized by his gaze for only a moment, I shook myself back to reality, lamenting how many times I had wished that I'd be okay too. "I should go."

"Kira wait—"

"Don't, Kyle. Not here. Not now." I pivoted, scurrying away before Shane or Wren saw me. I decided in that split second that Sarah was my best option and bolted toward my locker. And just like a bad penny, there she was. Pacing and waiting for me.

"Oh my gosh, finally! Where have you been? It took you forever."

"I got stuck in the crowd up front." I find it's better to keep my answers short and sweet around Sarah. She usually did enough talking for both of us anyway. Some days it felt impossible to get a word in.

"But you came from the back of the school. Where were you?"

Geez, she doesn't miss much. Except maybe tact and subtle nuances of annoyance. "I took the long way around to avoid as many people as possible."

"Well, we *need* to talk. The 'Hero Trio' won't pick up my calls or return my messages, so you need to tell me everything you know. My other sources are tapped out."

"Don't tell me you're calling them that horrible headline?"

"Why? It's catchy."

"Sarah, I don't understand what you want from me. I haven't talked to any of them either." *Lies.*

"I don't believe you. You must know something. You were dating Kyle, and you were friends with Wren."

"Key word: *were*. Meaning, no longer."

"Come on. You can tell me. Brody saw you at the hospital, so I know you're talking to them."

Damn that Brody and his loose lips when it comes to his spicy jalapeño. "I brought flowers to the lobby. Trying to be nice. I didn't even see Wren."

"So, you haven't talked to anyone since the incident?"

"No." *Lies again.*

"Wow. You too, Kira? I didn't realize lying was a communicable disease, but here we are. Another *friend* who lies to me. I sure can pick 'em." And with that retort, Sarah stormed to the auditorium for the opening message. Our greeting for the second half of the school year.

Head throbbing before homeroom was a fun perk to my first day back. I opened my locker and threw my heavy backpack inside. It landed with a clunk against the metal bottom. The weight from extra library books was my distraction over break. But not one of them cracked open.

Instead, I wallowed in my bed trying to shut out the noise. Dad tried to enlist me for a few office chores, but I couldn't bring myself to leave the house. I wanted to fade into the background. And for a while I did. But now I'm thrust into the fray again.

Then there was Sarah. She was the cherry on top of my shit sundae. Immediately calling me out for lying, knowing she wasn't wrong. The very thing that I had admonished both Kyle and Wren for since finding out about them.

I'm a hypocrite now. Because lying to others *is* easier than the truth. Apparently, I'm not a good liar like Wren is.

However, at this moment, I wished I were.

CHAPTER 3

And the truth is...

Shane

THIS WAS THE last thing I needed today. Seeing Wren the very moment I entered and the very moment I couldn't keep it together. I knew we would eventually cross paths, but not in the first minute and certainly not like this. I had carefully crafted my façade at home, eager to achieve some type of normalcy. A reminder of my life before her. However, karma has never been on my side when it came to Wren.

As I gained control of my lungs, her fingers slowly slid off my back. I remained hunched, watching her step away. My head rose, seeing the pair staring at me in pity. It took everything I had to unclench my fists and swallow my desperate fury. I winced as my knee straightened, clenching my teeth while I wobbled. Kyle reached for me, but I smacked his hand. It was better for me to look past him. Toward the hall. Focusing on anything other than knocking him across the face.

When my eyes adjusted, I saw Kira spin on her heels and sprint off. Before I could call her name, she had turned into the main corridor and disappeared. That's just great. She saw my little "episode," and once she sees Sarah, well then that's it. The whole school will know.

A bright red haze clouded my vision, like the blood that had dripped down my face after Steven swung. My teeth clamped tightly, making my jaw vibrate.

Heat flushed my cheeks. *Aaggh. Steven is gone. He can't hurt me anymore! So why is the fear still here?* I shook out my hands and began taking slow breaths to halt another full-on attack.

"Are you ok?" Wren asked timidly.

"I'm fine. You can go now. Show's over," I snapped. I almost regretted seeing the hurt in her face. Almost. I didn't bother to look, but at some point, they left. As my muscles finally relaxed, an involuntary sigh escaped me. Max, who must have come inside in the middle of my attack, silently picked up my backpack. Without a word, we walked together toward the auditorium. He understood me unlike anyone else.

I met Maxwell Burkett in kindergarten. We immediately clicked and have been joined at the hip since. Besides my mom and Kyle, he understood me more than anyone else in the entire world. He also loved soccer, but it wasn't his whole reason for existing like it was for me. This guy had a seriously great work ethic and was our team's goalie since middle school for a reason. He's just not pursuing the sport professionally after high school. I don't think he's even sure about college or where his future is headed. But he likes it that way.

Max always had my back, no matter what, no questions asked. He's like a brother to me. The "incident" last month was no exception. I'm not sure how I would've made it without him. He's the reason I'm still somewhat sane. Max took my side without hesitation, even though he's also Kyle's friend.

He was traumatized too. Being unable to stop my kidnapping weighed heavily on him. I tried to reassure him that none of it was his fault. Deep down, I'm sure he knew that. But knowing everything I went through didn't always keep the remorse away.

"You alright?" Max asked, concerned, resting his palm on my shoulder as we stood outside the auditorium.

"Yeah. I'm good. Let's get in there and get this done with."

We found seats in the senior section as far from Wren as possible. I tried not to look, but I couldn't stop myself. The hold she has on me is unnerving. And annoying. I saw her tapping away on her phone and knew she was texting my brother. It still rubbed me the wrong way even though I know we're over, and she's with him now.

"There you are! I was looking for you," Sarah pulled me from my sulking into a huge hug. "I tried to see you, but your mom totally wouldn't let me. Why didn't you text me back? I messaged you like a million times."

"Yeah. Overprotective Mom. She really wanted us to have some quiet downtime. Focus on getting better."

"But…" she paused as the auditorium lights flashed. I was never so thankful for a boring message from the principal. Sarah turned to sit in the only open seat next to me when Max sat down first. "Hey! Dude, not cool."

Max shooed her away with his hand. Our peppery friend gave him the finger and sat in the row behind us. Max flashed a grin over at me, and I smiled. I couldn't help but shake my head.

Principal Harper launched his message about how wonderful the second half of the year would be. How we could choose to have the best finish. My body tensed. I wanted this year to be over. I wanted to leave this school, this town, and my home.

The place that had once grounded me was now a source of regret, anger, and lies. No matter how hard I pretend that I'm recovering, I can't hide the truth from myself.

And the truth is, I'm in pain.

Kira

I wandered the junior section, looking for a seat while avoiding Kyle at all costs. His best friend, Brody, waved enthusiastically toward me, patting the spot nearby. I hesitated, knowing Kyle would want to sit near him as well. I swiveled, scanning for my ex-boyfriend and debating whether I should linger.

"Kira! Over here," Brody called out. I ignored him, pretending I hadn't heard. "KIRA!" Brody exclaimed louder. I couldn't play dumb without drawing more looks from other students. But I hadn't seen my ex yet, so it had to be safe.

On cue, Kyle scooted down the row toward Brody too. He paused when he noticed me, then immediately turned and sat at the farthest seat from us. I exhaled. Awkward relationship musical chairs, anyone?

"Hey, Brody," I greeted him as he leaned in to hug me.

"How are you?" he asked, genuinely.

"Been better."

"Sarah said—"

"Can we please not talk about her or the Hero Trio?" I cringed as the stupid label slipped out of my mouth inadvertently.

"Sure. My bad."

Unable to stop myself from glancing at the seniors, I saw Sarah chatting it up with Shane. Her Cheshire smile made my stomach turn. Sarah was in Whitmore breakup heaven. Pouncing at the ready with poor Brody sitting next to me, none the wiser.

Suddenly, the auditorium lights flashed, and we settled into our seats. Principal Harper ascended the stairs, taking his spot behind the podium. He droned on about the second half of the year. I rolled my eyes because no matter how hard I tried, there was nothing I could do to make this year turn out the way I wanted. I bristled, my anger swelling again.

Brody's knee bumped into mine. As I looked over at him, I saw Kyle at the end of the row with his gaze trained on me. At first, I froze, unable to break free. My heart fluttered, and when I finally got my wits about me, I snapped my head back toward the stage. I chided myself for letting him still affect me even after everything that had happened. I had to remember that he was a liar and a cheater. My head was on board, but my heart still wasn't.

As my thoughts wandered, I found myself looking at the senior section again. Shane and Rob...Wren looked as miserable as I felt. It brought me a bit of comfort knowing I wasn't the only one suffering right now.

Sarah had called me back in December to spill about Kyle and Wren. I was shocked, to say the least. To hear it from her first, knowing she had already shared the news with everyone at school, caused me to retch. As she so eloquently put it, *"Bad news. Kyle's been cheating on you the whole time you've been together. With Robbie, no less."* The slight hint of glee in her voice was what really set me off.

I almost didn't believe her. There was no way I was that blind to his cheating. But as Sarah recounted every agonizing detail, things began to click. All the trivial things he said or did when around her. But it was what he didn't say that put the nail in the coffin. When Kyle texted me that night to go outside to his car, my heart sank. Sitting there, listening to truth after truth fall from his lips. I wanted to curl up and die of humiliation. I tried to stay strong, but everything within me broke.

I remembered every detail from that night. The crisp cold, the bright streetlight reflecting off the windshield, the car heater blowing with a hint of pine from his dangling air freshener. How Kyle wore a zippered hoodie and shorts in any weather. How my eyes stung with salty tears as he admitted he loved Robbie, stomping any remaining dignity. I remembered it all.

I also recalled the last words I said to him: "Then maybe... someday... we can be friends again." I'm not sure why I said it or how I managed to speak as fury and pain mixed within me. I fled from the car with blurred vision, running straight up to my room and slamming the door shut. My dad was hot on my heels and immediately knocked. But instead of answering, I raced to the window, watching Kyle drive away. He didn't stay. I really was his placeholder while he pursued someone else. I meant nothing to him.

I remember not being able to stop my sobs, gasping as I dropped onto my bed. Dad barged in and scooped me up. He knew exactly what had transpired without me uttering a word. To his credit, he didn't talk, lecture, or give sage life advice. He just held me quietly and let me sob. I was thankful for that.

"Kira?" Brody carefully shook me out of my reverie.

"What?" I asked foggily.

"The assembly's over? It's time for first period."

"Oh. Thanks." I felt a bit ashamed that I had totally tuned out the rest of the principal's *captivating* speech.

Grabbing my things, I ambled up the auditorium aisle, still sluggish from sorting through those old memories. Deep down, I knew I was better off without Kyle Whitmore. But no matter how hard I pretend, I can't hide the truth from myself.

And the truth is, I'm in pain.

CHAPTER 4

To distract...

Shane

THOSE FIRST FEW weeks back at school were a blur. I kept myself as busy as humanly possible. I was either in class, at training, at physical therapy, or hanging out with Max. Although Kyle and Wren didn't rub their relationship in my face, I couldn't bear to be home. Mom tried her best to act normally, but the air was thick with everything left unsaid. I've become an expert at dodging topics, especially anything involving my brother, my ex-girlfriend, and that night. I planned to keep it that way for as long as possible.

"It's been a while," my therapist, Dr. Collier, said cordially.

"Yeah. Mom found out that I wasn't coming in, and the look on her face… well, I can't stand disappointing her."

"Did she say that?"

"No, but she didn't have to. Her silence said it all."

"Could she be giving you space? So that you can decide on your own?"

"I guess." I hadn't put too much thought into it.

"So, you're here today because of your mother and not for yourself?"

"I don't know."

"Maybe we can start easy then. Tell me how your training is going. Is the physical therapy for your knee helping?"

"Yeah. They said I should be cleared any day now. No restrictions."

"Does that make you happy?"

I didn't mean to, but I hesitated. "Sure."

"You don't seem sure."

"It does. I just still feel… off."

"Physically. Or is it something else?"

"Oh! I wanted to tell you—I ran into Officer Markham the other day."

Dr. Collier paused, fiddling with her tablet's stylus. "Was it good to see her?"

"Yeah. She helped Robbie save my life. I owe her a lot, but…"

"But…?" My therapist left the word dangling for me to pick back up.

"But… I don't get it," I said, my voice rising. "Wren seems to handle the aftermath just fine, and she was the one shot, for fuck's sake! She's making college plans, living her life, and is madly in love with my brother." I chuckled wildly to stave off the stinging that formed near the corners of my eyes. *What is wrong with me?* I thought.

"Shane, everyone handles trauma in different ways. Some people distract themselves. Others put up a wall to mask the pain. But I promise you, it will get better. It's not easy, and it takes time. Unfortunately, I can't predict how much time that will be."

"I know. It just sucks."

"It does."

***

I sat in my car, debating whether to go inside my house. I felt like I was running on fumes after practice and therapy. The last thing I wanted was to "hang" with the family, especially when I knew Mateo is there too. I'd be the odd man out around both couples, again. I really like Mateo, and I think he's great with Mom, but I'm not sure I can stomach being around the happy twosomes this close to Valentine's Day.

I dragged my soccer gear up the front stoop and slowly opened the door. Everyone's attention snapped in my direction.

"Hi, honey," Mom greeted cheerfully.

"Hey, Mom."

"How are you? Did practice go okay?"

"Fine. Tired. Heading up to my room." I gave a little wave to the group and slinked upstairs, dragging my bag behind me.

"I saved you some dinner!" Mom yelled up the stairs after me.

"I'm not hungry. But thanks."

She didn't push it any further, but I could hear her quietly say, *I'm so worried about him.* I threw my stuff down next to my bed and pulled out my phone to shoot a quick text off to Max.

You busy

Nope

Pick me up in 20
Read 8:01PM

On my way

I could always count on Max to be there at a moment's notice. I washed up before sneaking downstairs. Thankfully, everyone was moving into the kitchen as I covertly made my way to the front door. Ready to make my exit, Kyle returned to the living room. I paused, our eyes locked, but he didn't say a word. He knew he owed me this much. I quietly closed the door and jogged over to Max's car as he pulled up to the curb.

"Where to?" Max asked.

"The city," I answered without missing a beat.

Max looked at me in surprise. "It's a school night, and we won't even get into the city until ten o'clock tonight."

"And?" I mocked.

"And... we have training tomorrow afternoon. You know Coach will kill us if we don't show."

"We'll be back in time for practice," I reassured.

"Do you want to tell me what's going on?"

"Not really. Are you in or out?" I raised a brow, challenging Max to answer.

"I'm in. Always."

"Good. Let's go."

As the streetlights zipped past us on our drive into the city, I leaned my head back, closing my eyes. I listened to Max butcher songs on the radio, my body melting into the seat.

My therapist said healing takes time. Well, I'm sick of waiting. I've basically been hiding from the world since everything happened, and I'm over it. Dr. Collier said we either put up a wall or distract ourselves when dealing with trauma. I got a second chance so I'm damn well going to live it.

I grabbed my phone and texted an old high school buddy who now goes to NYU. Maybe he had a lead on where to have a good time. And trust me, that's exactly what I needed to do.

To distract myself.

Kira

It was almost Valentine's Day, and I was miserable. Sarah often rubbed her relationship with Brody in my face, which was annoying, but I tolerated it. I tolerated *her*. In fact, I've been tolerating a lot of things that I never would have previously. I've become so passive, I barely recognize myself anymore.

I remember Kyle telling me he loved that I had my life all together. He praised me for having dreams and aspirations for my future. That I went after what I wanted. Back then, he was right. I did. But now? I felt like a shell of my previous self. Unable to trust.

That old saying about *keeping your friends close but your enemies closer* rang true for me and Sarah. She was my shield from the outside world. At least with Sarah, I knew exactly where I stood, and she has never lied to me. She wasn't always tactful, but she never lied.

"Helloo? Earth to Kira?" Sarah mocked me as the final school bell rang out in our chemistry class. I looked up at the clock, checking the time.

"My mind wandered. What did you say?"

"I asked if you wanted to come to dinner with Brody and me for Valentine's Day." She waited expectantly for my answer.

"Are you serious?"

"Yeah, why?"

"Because I don't have anyone to go with, that's why." I shook my head. Being a third wheel sounded like torture, but maybe it would be better than spending that night alone.

"Yes, you do. Ask Shane."

"WHAT?" She couldn't be serious.

"He's available now!" There's the *tactful* and truthful Sarah I know.

"That's the worst idea I've ever heard."

"Well, excuse me for trying." She turned with a huff and started to walk away. Against my better judgment, I gently grabbed her arm.

"Sarah, wait... I know you're only trying to help."

"You could be more appreciative of my friendship."

My jaw clenched, and swallowing hard, I decided to stroke her ego. "I should. You're a good friend. What would I do without you?"

"I know, right? Look, he may not be your first choice…" she began. *Or a choice at all, I thought.* "…but you told me that the two of you got along great whenever the four of you double dated. And he *is* a coveted Whitmore brother, so that's a win-win. What could it hurt?" *A lot, actually…* I grimaced to myself.

"I don't know, Sarah. It seems weird. What if he says no?"

"What if he says yes?"

"I'll have to think about it."

"Well, don't take too long. I'd need to change the reservations. Hey, gotta go. I have a student union meeting. See you later, Kira." With a flip of her fiery hair like a curtain call, she strolled down the hall.

Ugh. Why did I even agree to think on it? I already knew what my answer would be. There's no way in hell I'm asking Shane out on a date. The brother of my ex-boyfriend? No. Way. In. Hell.

Realizing the time, I hurried down the hall toward the auditorium. I was on the scenery committee for the school play that I'd signed up for before the "incident." And of course, being the pushover that I am, I couldn't shirk my responsibilities. I rushed to my meeting, passing couples holding hands, hugging, kissing, or excitedly talking about Valentine's Day. Without thinking, my feet carried me to my locker instead.

I yanked open the dented metal door, snatching my winter coat. I slammed it behind me and ran. Down the back hall, past the locker rooms, running faster than ever before. I needed to escape this miserably happy place.

To distract myself.

CHAPTER 5

I couldn't believe...

Shane

WE RACED BACK from the city. Max and I had lost all track of time. We ended up at my friend's dorm last night to sleep off our hangovers. I had no idea it had gotten so late until Max woke me up in a panic. I tried to gather my bearings as Max ran around the room looking for his keys.

The details of the party were fuzzy. I remember showing up at the frat house my friend invited us to, and that was about it. There are flashes of Max and me playing beer pong with raucous frat boys and sorority girls while dipping our cups into a garbage can full of alcohol. The music was loud, and the place was rocking. We drank, danced, and did a little flirting. The perfect distraction. If my throbbing headache was any indication of the evening we had, then it must have been epic.

My friend left a note for us to lock the door on our way out since he had class. I don't know how he attended a lecture after a night like that. I stumbled around grabbing my hoodie and phone just as Max found his keys. As we ran to his car, the brisk air felt oddly good against my pounding head. It was snowing lightly, a stark contrast to my bloodshot eyes, as we hopped in the car and took off. Max weaved in and out of traffic as we zipped through the streets.

Once out of the city, my thoughts cleared, and I realized with horror that I didn't have my gear.

"Shit!" I yelled.

"What?"

"I never grabbed my training bag," my head snapped toward Max.

"Oh, shit. We're not going to make it, Shane. Not if we have to stop first."

"We have to," I pleaded, "Or Coach will bench me." I grabbed my phone and shot off a text that I didn't want to send.

> *Bro need help*
> *Left my soccer stuff at home*

I put your bag in the locker
room this morning

> *Seriously*

Tripped over it in our room
Wren forged a note for school

> *Wow thnx*
> Read 1:37pm

No prob

I was shocked by what Kyle and Wren had done, to be honest. I haven't made it easy on them lately, but they came through for me today. That also meant they didn't tell Mom I was out last night or that I blew off school today.

"Hold up, everything's good. Kyle brought my bag to school this morning."

"That was cool of him," Max gave me a wry smile.

"Yeah. It was."

***

As Max turned the corner to school, a flood of cars started pulling out of the parking lot. Crap. Coach wanted us out on the field, ready to go, fifteen minutes after the final bell. This was going to be close.

Max became impatient, pounding the steering wheel as we waited for a slew of cars to get out of the way so we could pull into the parking lot. It was right by the locker rooms, the same door I had entered on my first day following winter break. Hopefully, we could shave off some time getting ready and onto the field.

Once parked, we sprinted for the building. I was able to run faster since Max was lugging his giant ass training bag over his shoulder. The back was usually locked, so we had to hope someone was nearby to hear us knocking. When I was almost at the door, it unexpectedly opened.

I couldn't believe my luck.

Kira

My tennis shoes slapped the linoleum so hard they drowned out every other sound around me. I sprinted faster, tucking my phone into my pocket, as I threw on my coat. The door loomed ahead of me, my escape in sight. I braced myself like a linebacker and smashed the push bar with every ounce of my strength.

First was the biting cold, then second, the hard crash of my body into someone else considerably larger. The momentum sent us to the ground with a loud thud. I was sprawled out on my stomach, my full weight on top of some stranger. We both groaned as I finally rolled off them.

"Oh shit. Are you guys, okay?" Max asked, holding the back gym door open.

Still unable to get any words out, I continued to lie there as little wet snowflakes landed on my face, melting quickly. I lamented the fact my escape from school had been thwarted by this... this escape thwarter.

"Kira!?" Shane pulled himself up. "Why the hell were you running?"

"Why the hell were *you* running?" I tried to sit.

"We're late for practice."

"Well, I was... I was..." *I couldn't tell him I wanted to avoid all the happy kissing couples.* "...looking for you."

"For me? Why?"

Come on, Kira. Don't be a coward. "To ask if you wanted to grab dinner. On Valentine's Day. With me."

"Like a date?" He looked so confused.

"It doesn't have to be. It could be two jilted friends eating dinner together on the most annoying holiday ever," I said in my best sarcastic Sarah tone.

His silence was loud.

"Shane!" Max jolted Shane out of shock. "We're late. Tell her yes!"

"Um... yes," Shane answered with Max's directive.

"Okay. Great. I'll text you the details," I muttered.

"Sure, great." With that, Shane pulled himself up and the two rushed past me into the building.

I sat there dazed that I had really done it. First, I asked Shane Whitmore out on a date. And second, *I asked Shane Whitmore out on a date.*

I lay back down on the ground and squeezed my eyes shut. *What am I doing? This is ludicrous.* It was a bad idea when Sarah suggested it, and it's a bad idea now.

"Hey, you, okay?" Brody asked, somehow appearing behind me.

Of course, it was Brody. He had a knack for showing up at all the right and wrong times. "I'm fine. Just lying here enjoying the crisp snowy air," I answered through closed eyes.

"I can see that. But why are you…"

I threw my arm up toward him, "Just help me up." Brody reached down and helped me to my feet.

"Nice bump on your head."

I reached up and gently felt my forehead. *Shane's skull must be made of concrete.* "Can you take me home? I think I need ice."

"There's ice here at school. I'll go get some."

"I don't want ice from here, please take me home?" I asked more forcefully.

"Sure. But how did you end up sprawled on top of Shane?" *How many others saw me tackle and accost Shane Whitmore?*

A burning embarrassment rose. "I don't want to talk about it!" I screeched.

"Okaaayy. Geez," we drove in silence, guilt creeping in. I wanted to apologize for snapping, but my head stopped me. The Shane incident was all I could focus on.

Brody pulled up to the curb. "That bump is starting to look gnarly. Do you need any help?" Brody offered so kindly. He really was a good guy, which makes his interest in Sarah that much more perplexing.

"I'm good. Thanks for the ride home," I said.

"Anytime. See you tomorrow."

Ambling down the narrow hallway to the small but functional kitchen, I grabbed a sunflower-printed towel and loaded it with ice. Sitting at the old wooden kitchen table, I noticed it had seen better days. There were years of abuse from childhood crafts and projects.

Exhausted, I rested both elbows while holding the cold pack to my forehead. I hadn't even remembered closing my eyes, but the next thing I knew, a hand gently shook me awake. My head slowly lifted off the wet towel, water pooling onto the table as I craned my stiff neck upward.

"Hey, kiddo," Dad said.

"Hi, Dad," I said, sleepily looking up at him.

"You alright?" he carefully rubbed his thumb over the lump.

"I crashed into... someone today after school."

"Ouch, must have been some crash."

"Yeah, it was, but you should see the other guy," I tried joking.

"How are they doing?" I hadn't given it a thought until Dad mentioned it.

"Um, okay, I guess. He got right up and went to practice."

"He didn't check on you?"

"No, he did. He was just late, so I didn't get a chance to talk to him."

"Who was the guy?"

I froze, unable to tell him another Whitmore brother hurt me. He still wasn't pleased with the first one. Add the fact that we were also going out on a date? On Valentine's Day? And that I was the one who asked him out? My mind raced a million miles trying to decide what I should or shouldn't say.

My dad's phone suddenly rang, "It's work. I've got to take this. Sorry, honey." He answered as he strode out of the kitchen. I exhaled loudly when he left the room.

I couldn't believe my luck.

CHAPTER 6

How did I get...

Shane

MY HEART POUNDED. I stood on the porch for what seemed like forever before I mustered enough courage to knock. Dealing with dads was out my depth, considering mine split before I turned one years old. Hushed talking and scurrying feet echoed from behind the door. Suddenly, it swung open.

"Hi, Shane."

"Hey, Kira. You look... really nice."

"Thanks."

"You ready?"

"Um, my dad wants to talk to you first," she sputtered out nervously.

Her dad? My voice threatened to crack. "Uh, sure. Of course."

I knew of Mr. Bowman, especially after the whole Kyle breakup situation, but I had never officially met him. He had made it known he was not pleased about how all of it went down between Kyle and Kira.

I slowly stepped inside and saw her dad waiting expectantly for me, a scowl planted firmly on his face. "Hello, sir. I'm Shane Whitmore," I said nervously, extending my hand. I had hoped it was a peace offering.

"Oh, I know who you are," he sneered.

"Dad!" Kira said pointedly, nodding her head toward me, widening her dark brown eyes at him.

The man extended his hand, "I'm Levi 'Gray Wolf' Bowman, of the Montana Crow Nation, and Kira's Dad."

"Dad!" she scolded him again.

"Very nice to meet you, sir."

"So, you're Kyle's brother?" Mr. Bowman asked with disgust. His daughter gave him another pointed look.

"Yes, but I'm not him."

"Let's hope," he replied sarcastically, finally releasing his grip.

"Dad, we have to go, or we'll be late for our reservation."

"Okay. But be home by ten."

"Dad—"

"Yes, sir. Ten o'clock sharp," I answered quickly. I wasn't adding any more fuel to the fire. Kira snapped her head toward me in protest but remained silent. I held out my arm for her in case the front path was slippery, but she didn't take it. I wasn't sure if this was a good or bad indication of how the night was going to turn out.

***

We pulled up to the restaurant after our silent car ride, spotting Sarah and Brody waiting for us at the entrance. I dropped Kira off, then quickly strode back to join them in the lobby after parking.

"Well, don't you look good," Sarah schmoozed, hugging me. She leaned back quickly. "Oh, and you smell great too! That makes up for being late." She had a way with backhanded compliments.

Perturbed, I snapped back, "Are we still waiting for a table? Looks like I'm right on time."

"Okay, snarky. I was only pointing out a fact," said Sarah. I rolled my eyes but let it go.

Kira ran her fingers through her hair, brushing her long bangs off her forehead. That's when I noticed the bruise. "Is that from the other day when we collided with each other?" I motioned toward the injury.

She reflexively reached up to touch the slightly raised purplish skin she had tried to hide. "Yeah, you have a really hard head, apparently," Kira said innocently, but Brody snickered. Sarah smacked him.

"I'm really sorry I never saw you," I said honestly.

"I know." We both stood there awkwardly, not knowing what else to say to each other. It was brutal. I don't remember it being this hard to talk to her before when she was with my brother.

I slowly rocked on my heels, glancing at the Italian specials posted near the hostess podium. My training diet was rigid, so I had limited choices here. But oh, how I dreamt of cheat days while in Portugal.

There was this gorgeous little restaurant right by the coast. Mom and I would meet up once a week, and I would always order seafood. It was the freshest seafood I'd ever had in my entire life. The pasta with the crème sauce was heaven on a plate. I genuinely looked forward to our Sunday meetups and catching up. The sea air renewed a bright light within her. I had never seen her this way before and it made me glad to share this place.

But there are no more pasta cheat days, only a dream to pursue. I had to remain laser-focused on making it onto a professional team. Earlier this week, I slipped up, feeling pitiful for myself, going to that party in the city, but I'm done. I can't, *I won't* let anything distract me from reaching my goal.

"Shane?" Kira gently nudged. "They called us. We have a table."

"Oh, um, I was reading the specials, deciding what to eat."

"I noticed," sarcasm laced her response.

We headed to the table where Sarah and Brody sat. Sarah shot me a disgusted look, and I knew immediately the rest of the night would be a shitshow. Regular Sarah was barely tolerable. But moody Sarah? I think I'd rather be on death row than here right now.

How did I get myself into this mess?

Kira

I regretted my snap decision to ask Shane Whitmore out on a date, especially on Valentine's Day. I didn't know what I was thinking. I panicked when he asked why I had run out of school. All that popped into my head was Sarah telling me to ask him out. Initially, I thought it was the worst decision, but seeing him standing at my door tonight, vulnerable and nervous? That was too cute.

But now? It was apparent he did *not* want to be here. Shane hasn't said more than a few dozen words since we left my house. Then add sassy Sarah to the mix, and this evening was turning into what I knew it would be. A nightmare. At this point, I'd rather be on death row than here right now.

"Kira!" Sarah yelled loudly, making the tables near us look over.

How embarrassing. "Yes, what?"

"Geez. Can the two of you pretend you want to be here? We're at this beautiful restaurant, but you both look like you're on death row or something."

Shane and I burst out laughing, then looked at each other in surprise. I had no idea what he had found funny, but Sarah had unknowingly read my mind. Leave it to Sarah to bring levity with one of her unintentional zingers.

"What? What did I say?" Sarah asked, confused.

***

The evening went better after Sarah's little mind-reading trick. Shane and I shared another laugh once we figured out why Sarah's comment was so funny. That we were both miserable being here, but not because of each other. Our conversations flowed better, and once Sarah finished pouting, dinner went surprisingly well. And the food was incredible.

Shane had grilled chicken over a bed of vegetables, and I chose the seafood pasta. I swore I heard him groan when they placed the meal in front of me. Then, throughout the meal, a server would stop by our table sporadically with a gift for Sarah from Brody. Flowers. Gift cards. Chocolates. Then the coup de grace was a gold heart charm for her bracelet. Sarah was over the moon to be doted on all evening. Brody really was the perfect boyfriend for Sarah. Dramatic presentation and extravagant spoiling.

Shane squirmed in his seat as if he sat on top of an ant hill. He leaned closer to me while Brody helped Sarah put on her charm. "I'm sorry. I don't have anything for you. I didn't realize... I thought it was only dinner." He said.

"It's okay. I don't have anything for you either. I thought the same." To be honest, I never even gave it a thought about getting a gift. I guess I should have, since it was Valentine's Day. I shook my head for being so naïve.

"Kira, look. Isn't it beautiful? It's gold too. And did you see the chocolates and the great flowers? I'm so lucky," Sarah gushed.

"Yeah. Really lucky," I answered reflexively, listening to Brody berate Shane in a hushed tone "...*not even a flower bro? It's Valentine's Day.*"

Shane wiped his brow and tugged at his collar. His leg bounced, knocking his napkin onto the floor. He made a scoffing sound as he reached down to retrieve it. A crimson hue rushed to his neck as he wiped his brow again. Out of the blue, before I could stop the words tumbling out of my mouth, I ended up putting my foot there instead.

"Actually, I meant to tell you both. Shane asked me to prom in the car on the way here. Since tonight was about two rejected friends, we decided to continue our commiserating at the most annoying couple event of the year." Sarah's mouth almost hit the floor. Shane mirrored her expression.

"He. Asked. You. To. Prom?" Sarah shrieked, "Brody hasn't even asked me yet!" The smile on Brody's face immediately fell as he began digging a hole.

"Come on, babe. I assumed we'd go together, so I didn't think I needed to."

"Didn't think you needed to ask me to prom? Are you being for real!?" Sarah pushed her chair back hastily, stomping toward the bathroom.

Brody jumped up to chase her, "Babe. Come back! I'm sorry." You could hear his pleas even after they disappeared around the corner.

Biting my nail, I slowly turned back toward Shane, who was still in shock. "Shane, forgive me. It just slipped. Brody was grilling you about not getting me anything, and you looked so uncomfortable, and then Sarah was rubbing in all the gifts that she got, and it just came out."

Shane closed his mouth.

I continued pleading, "I'm not even sure where the idea came from or why I said it. Please say something."

Shane was silent. Clearly, I had made the whole situation and date even worse. His face may have been expressionless, but it spoke volumes. I didn't know how to fix this or how to make it right.

How did I get myself into this mess?

CHAPTER 7

...seizing joy.

Shane

SHE CAUGHT ME totally off guard. Unsure how to respond, my mind raced as words struggled to form. I looked into her pleading eyes as her long lashes fluttered and her soft-looking lips quivered.

"Shane, I'm sorry. When they come back to the table, I'll tell them I made it all up. I'll make it right. I promise."

Then, as suddenly as her declaration about us going to prom, I made a snap decision of my own. "Don't."

"Don't what?"

"Don't tell them you made it up because it won't be true."

"What are you talking about? None of that happened."

I searched through Sarah's flowers and pulled an enormous pink Gerbera daisy out of the bouquet. Gerbera daisies were my mom's favorite. She'd put pots of them on the front porch in the spring to liven up the dull facade every year. They were bright and colorful when we remembered to water them.

Turning toward Kira, I held the flower out in front of me. "Kira Sky Bowman. Will you go to prom with me?"

Her eyes widened with an expression of bewilderment. I nudged her hand with the flower, encouraging her to take it. She reached for it cautiously, like I was a snake ready to strike. "Are you being serious?"

"As a heart attack."

"Why are you doing this?"

"Do you have a date for prom yet?"

"No."

"Neither do I. And to be honest, I never gave it a thought until now, but why the hell not?"

"You do not have to do this. I *will* tell them the truth."

"You already told them the truth. I asked you to prom," I shot her a sly grin.

She shook her head, a small sigh escaping her lips as Kira admired her gift. "It's a beautiful flower."

"I know. I picked it out myself. From this bouquet... that Brody bought for someone else." She grinned, making the crook of her lip pull up toward one side. It was cute.

"Thank you, Shane. I didn't mean to make everything awkward. I was trying to help with the whole Brody gift thing... but honestly, my brain wasn't even involved. I promise not to put you in a tight spot again."

"Hey, lean closer." My eyes skimmed up from the flower to meet hers.

"Why?"

"Just do it." Kira leaned closer, and my mouth gently brushed the skin on her cheek. She pulled back, surprised.

"What was that—" she started, quickly realizing that Brody and Sarah had returned to the table. Sarah loudly cleared her throat as she sat down.

"Everything alright?" I asked. "I didn't mean to hit a nerve."

"Everything is *fine*. Now," Sarah answered through gritted teeth. "I showed Brody the error of his ways, and he'll be surprising me with the promposal of my dreams. Very soon."

I looked over at Brody and mouthed, *"I'm sorry."* He waved me off. I felt bad that Kira's attempt to help me put Brody in the doghouse instead. He really loves that fiery redhead for unknown reasons.

Kira's voice caught my attention. "You're right, Sarah. I should have told you before announcing it like that. she apologized, her jaw clenched. She was placating Sarah, something we'd all done at some point, but the urge to defend her from Sarah's obvious narcissism was strong.

Kira was always kind. Almost to a fault. Even after the whole Kyle-Wren debacle, she had come to the hospital with flowers for Wren. We bumped into her in the lobby, surprised by the gesture. The two of us spoke briefly, but only in obligatory pleasantries. I wanted to talk more, but she rushed off. I'm not sure what I wanted to say, but I always felt better after our chats.

I can remember our conversations when she was still with Kyle; the four of us out somewhere together. They didn't seem forced or difficult. The ease we had surprised me, but now I believe it's because we had so much in common. Kira was driven and knew exactly what she wanted. That attitude mirrored mine. Whenever she spoke about her dreams, it was exciting. Her face lit up anytime she mentioned the ranch, her horse, or Montana. Her goals resonated with me, and I felt seen in a way I hadn't before. With anyone.

A gentle warmth unfurled in my chest as I glanced over at Kira finishing the last bite of her pasta. She caught me staring as a few noodles flopped off her fork, hanging from her mouth. Her cheeks flushed as she desperately tried to slurp it back up. I chuckled, prompting her to push the last little bit into her mouth. The reddish hue of her lips was in stark contrast to the creamy remnants of sauce dotted down her chin. I handed over my napkin, which she hastily took to wipe her face.

"That was embarrassing," she quipped.

"It was adorable," I answered, the words slipping out unintentionally.

The server cleared our plates, allowing me to pull myself from my trance. I cleared my throat, shifting uncomfortably in my seat. Peripherally, I saw my date do the same. I thought about taking back my comment. Making up a lame excuse for why I said it. But I didn't want to. She did look adorable, and I left those words dangling between us.

After leaving the restaurant, Brody whisked Sarah away to one more surprise adventure of the evening, leaving Kira and me on our own. An awkward moment of silence passed before I blurted out another apology.

"Sorry, I didn't make plans for us after dinner, like Brody. I'm a little date-rusty, I guess." I admitted.

"No, I asked you out, so it falls on me. The problem is we only have an hour till curfew." She rolled her eyes for dramatic effect.

"Hm, we could go to the river overlook. It's free, close, and beautiful. What do you think, Kira?"

"I think I like having you in the driver's seat." Her eyes widened the moment the words tumbled out. My face burned as soon as her words hit my ears.

We pulled into the parking lot near the overlook; I was shocked to find it packed with cars on a bitterly frosty night. I'm not sure why that surprised me, especially since it is Valentine's Day at a romantic location. I started second-guessing bringing Kira here. What if she felt pressured by unspoken expectations? Before I could say anything, she opened the door.

As we strolled toward the lights, I noticed the icy walkway. This time, Kira took my arm to steady herself. A small smile crossed my lips. It felt nice to be needed. To be wanted. Even if only to keep her from falling.

We edged through the crowd of couples to reach the railing. The lights danced slowly to the beat of a gentle love song, blending in harmony with the sounds. Some couples filmed their evening, while others huddled close and slowly danced. We let the ambiance wash over us, quietly taking everything in.

However, my mind became the opposite of this serene view. It screamed. I had accepted Kira's invitation so quickly that I never had a chance to think about what this date meant. I'm her ex-boyfriend's brother, which is murky territory by high school drama standards. Max said I was overthinking, and I should take this opportunity to get myself out there. But was I ready? It had only been two months since that terrible night.

I looked down at Kira, wind blowing strands of her hair against the side of her face. I reached over and pushed her hair aside. She turned to gaze at me. Her eyes glistened from the reflection of the lights, and a puff of cold air escaped her full lips when she breathed out.

Before I knew what was happening, I leaned down and kissed her. It was slow, gentle but then she opened her mouth slightly, allowing my tongue to trace hers. I pulled her closer, her warmth reflecting my own as we melted into each other. Kira shifted her hands, clutching my jacket in her fists.

My body was alive, and I clung to her like a drowning man. All the stress and pain that I had carefully tucked deep inside floated away in a moment of pleasure. I knew my happiness wouldn't last long. It never does.

But for now, I'm seizing joy.

Kira

My mind melted into mush; the desperation of his lips consumed me. I clutched his jacket tighter until my frigid knuckles were white, feverishly responding to his touch. Shane's arms were muscular and held me tightly, so passionately that it made my knees weak. The light dancing off the river water sparkled around us, almost looking like fireworks. At least I thought it was the lights, but maybe our kiss had summoned actual fireworks.

Our connection happened fast, but it felt right. Much like this date. Sudden, but unexpectedly nice. When he called me Kira Sky earlier while asking me to prom, it surprised me. We had only talked about my middle name once, back in New York City on Black Friday. Wren and Kyle had left us to talk. We discussed our futures, and I mentioned my namesake was after the Montana sky. A highly revered spiritual element in my dad's Crow culture.

With significant effort, I pulled away from him. I looked up into his blue eyes, still feeling unsteady. He held me upright, staring back. Like a deer caught in headlights, I couldn't move. The light that shone from deep within his soul seemed to reach inside me and pierce mine. I shuddered.

"I'm sorry," Shane's voice shocked me back to life.

Shakily, I found my footing and released his jacket from my iron grip. Still dazed, I asked, "For what?"

"For kissing you. I should have asked you first. I blame it on the power of Valentine's Day."

My mind still foggy, I joked, "Damn Cupid."

This entire night was a whirlwind. Going out on a date with Shane on Valentine's Day. Saying yes to prom. And now kissing him? It all sounded absurd. Suddenly, my stomach dropped. What would Wren and Kyle think of this? Sarah? Oh, Mylanta! When she finds out, all hell will break loose.

No. *Stop it, Kira. You always do this.* They don't get any say about what happened tonight. We didn't get any say about what Kyle and Wren did to us, yet we were the ones who had to deal with the fallout. The pain. We deserve some happiness.

Shane interrupted my inner monologue. "Are you ready? We need to get you home by ten sharp."

"He was just messing with you."

"Maybe, but I'm not losing any points the first time I take you on a date."

The first time? Would there be more? "Then yes. I'm ready."

He held out his hand, and I wove my fingers around his fingers. "Whoa. You're freezing. Why didn't you tell me you were so cold?"

"Because I wasn't." I tilted my head up and cast a coy smile. He flashed his gorgeous grin, my legs turning to jelly.

We approached the car, my hand finally toasty warm. As he opened the car door, he suddenly turned toward me.

His blue eyes glistened in the evening light. "I'm going to do things properly this time. Kira Sky, could I kiss you goodnight?"

"Now?"

"Yes, now. I don't think your dad would like it if I kissed you on your porch while he watched us from the front window."

"Right. Good call..."

"I thought so," he smirked sexily, bending down to kiss me gently. His lips warmed me down to my toes.

On the drive home, a million thoughts swirled. *This was not how I thought things would turn out.* I knew it would be an awkward mess, and then we would go our separate ways. I had appeased Sarah, and Shane had appeased Max. Never did I think we would kiss, or that we had a possibility for another date.

I internally chuckled. Dating Shane would definitely frost Sarah's cookies.

My dad says I shouldn't put the needs of others before my own. That it's okay to be a little selfish and not overthink things. He also tells me to be thankful for what I have and not for what I've lost. Tonight, may not have been what I expected or what I needed.

But for now, I'm seizing joy.

CHAPTER 8

I needed to...

Shane

AS I SLOWLY woke, my lips curved upwards. I almost didn't recognize the expression. It had been a long time since I had a desire to smile. Last night was unexpected. I hadn't yet processed what had happened between Kira and me. The river, the lights, the whole date was the right combination to allow myself to feel something other than pain.

I flipped the covers, hopping out of bed to see Kyle still asleep. Tiptoeing to the white plastic laundry basket next to my dresser, I fished out some clean clothes but paused. My tattered brown desk chair held the dress clothes from the night before. I lifted the shirt to my nose. The slightest hint of Kira's perfume lingered, and my heart thrummed. It was hard not to replay our kiss and how warm and inviting her mouth felt.

I practically skipped into the hall toward the bathroom; a huge grin plastered, when Wren stepped out of her room. My smile immediately fell.

"Sorry," Wren said quietly.

"For what?"

"For ruining your good mood."

My teeth clenched. "You didn't ruin it."

She arched her brow. "Right."

With silence building, we both suddenly spoke. *"How was your night?"*

"You first," she offered.

"No. You first," I insisted.

"It was good. Kyle took me to dinner and a movie." She kept her answer short and simple. "You?"

"Kira and I went to dinner and then to the overlook."

"Oh my gosh, it's so beautiful there. Remember last year when we—" She clamped her mouth shut, but the damage was done.

"Yeah. I remember." My words burned as we tried to avoid eye contact.

Wren cleared her throat. "Go ahead." She motioned toward the bathroom. "I forgot something." Wren turned on her heels, slipping back into her room.

I slunk into the bathroom, my mood deflated. The connection I thought I had made with Kira was only my subconscious evoking old emotions. Until now, I had forgotten that I had gone with Wren. It felt like a lifetime ago.

I stood in front of the mirror, studying a version of myself I barely recognized since my senior year started. A face that reflected sadness as any brief whisper of happiness drifted away. The furrowed lines of my eyebrows cut deep into my skin; my image distorted. I clawed at my racing heart as if I could reach in and slow the beating.

In the shower, the panic didn't subside. I let the heat pound heavily on my skull, water dripping down my face. As steam filled the room, obscuring my vision, flashes of memories began. The glint of the gun, a crushing pain on my temple, the blood dripping from my face—I stumbled, knocking the metal shower pole with a loud crash.

There was a bang on the door. "Shane?" Kyle yelled. "Are you okay?"

"Yeah. I'm fine." I answered, turning off the tepid water. "Be right out." I quickly reset the pole, tossing the items back onto its shelves before getting dressed. Both Kyle and Mom waited outside as I exited, but I pushed my way through them toward my room. They followed.

"I'm fine. I just knocked into something."

"I thought you fell or hurt your knee. I was worried," said Mom.

"Don't be."

"It's my job to worry. I can't help it."

"Mom, it's not a big deal. Please stop hovering."

"I wanted to make sure you were—"

"I need space! You're suffocating me! What are you going to do when I leave for Europe? You can't follow me like you did last summer."

"I didn't *follow* you there."

"Yes, you did. The second you heard I accepted the camp invitation to Portugal you were on the phone with HR to transfer to Lisbon."

"I thought you liked having me there..." Mom sounded as dejected as she looked, her voice trailing off.

A lump formed in my throat. "Mom—"

"I'm going to make some breakfast."

"Mom." But it was no use. She had already hustled down the stairs before I could say anything else. *Crap.*

Frustrated, I raked my fingers through my wet hair, glancing over at Kyle, who silently judged.

"What?" I snipped.

"Nothing," he threw his hands up, sulking toward Wren's room.

A scream of frustration rose through my chest, trying to erupt, but it also felt suffocating. I needed air and grabbed my running sneakers. But just as quickly, fatigue burrowed into my bones.

I abandoned the idea of a run and climbed into bed. My head throbbed, ears ringing as my skin felt overwhelmingly prickly. I pulled the blankets over me, blocking the weight of the world.

I needed to escape.

Kira

Instant regret churned my stomach the second I woke up. *What have I done?* Not only did I kiss Shane Whitmore last night, but I kissed him twice. I must be going insane! It was the only logical conclusion. The evidence of my descent into madness? First, I asked him out on a date. On Valentine's Day. Second, I agreed to go to prom with him. And lastly? Cupid made me kiss him.

I snatched my phone off my nightstand and bolted upright. Seeing over a dozen missed messages, my heart fell, worried they were from Shane. That he had come to his senses about our kiss last night. Instead, they were all from Sarah. I wasn't sure why she had blown up my phone, but I knew better than to ignore her. There were no days off from Sarah.

"So? I need all the deets." Sarah immediately questioned.

I hate lying so much. "Deets? There aren't any."

"I don't believe you."

"You never do."

"I wonder why that is," Sarah quipped snidely.

"Sarah, I don't have it in me to fight with you this morning."

"Oh, honey, you haven't seen me fight."

I exhaled loudly in defeat. My fault for returning her call. I needed to pivot. "Where did Brody take you after the restaurant?"

"Well, first he took me to the new cookie place. He set up a decorating station for us, and we decorated a big heart cookie together."

I was a little shocked at how romantic Brody could be. He had layers that I never noticed went that deep. "Wow. That's so… sweet! See what I did there, Sarah? Cookies. Sweet. Get it?"

"Oh, I got it," her tone laced with sarcasm.

Frustrated, I snapped back. "I can't play these games, Sarah. Just tell me what's on your mind."

"The cookie store isn't the only *p-l-a-c-e* we went last night," Sarah said.

I swallowed hard, realizing exactly where they went after decorating sweets. "The river overlook."

"Ding, ding, ding. We have a winner."

"If you already knew, why toy with me?"

"Because I'm good at it."

"Goodbye, Sarah." I hung up.

She is infuriating! Why do I put up with her? Why do any of us? Sarah loved drama, and I walked right into it. I should have known she already knew. I could hear her gloating from the second she picked up the phone.

This meant the entire school would know by Monday morning. She'll make up some annoying catchphrases like *The Whitmore Twin Switcharoo* or *The Twin Flip and Flop* when the gossiping starts. I giggled at my cleverness, but dread replaced the feeling just as quickly.

Sarah caught me in another lie. Being truthful was the one thing I was proud of when things happened with Kyle and Wren. But since then, lying is all I've been doing. I couldn't seem to stop. My body groaned at my hypocrisy, and I crawled back under the covers.

A headache slowly built alongside the churning of my stomach. I squeezed my eyes shut, curling into a tight little ball. I pulled the blankets over me, blocking the weight of the world.

I needed to escape.

CHAPTER 9

It's time to find...

Shane

THE MUSCLES IN my leg tightened and released, making my knee jitter restlessly up and down against the floor. I had to be here, but I felt like I failed having to resort to therapy again. It was only Thursday, but this week had been awful. The rumor mill was out of control, and I may have been semi-consciously avoiding Kira. Neither one of us had talked or texted since our date. I couldn't eat, couldn't focus. The only silver lining was that tomorrow was finally Friday.

As I looked around the waiting room, I was surprised to see that I was the youngest person there. The urge to run overwhelmed me. I almost conceded to my thoughts when I heard my name. My eyes snapped toward the receptionist who motioned for me to come up to her desk.

"Dr. Collier is ready to see you now."

"Okay. Thank you." I used my best formal voice. The woman pressed a button, activating a loud buzzer that opened the hallway behind her. Wandering past a few open doors, I found Dr. Collier. I knocked, and she looked up from the edge of her teacup.

"Shane, how nice to see you. This is a pleasant surprise. It's been a couple of weeks." She set the cup down on her pristine and perfectly organized desk. Crossing the room to shut the door, she gestured for me to sit. "Would you like some tea? Coffee? Water?"

"I'm good. Thanks."

"So, how have you been?" she asked, settling into a soft, powder-blue, fabric-covered chair.

"Okay, I guess," I answered, sitting opposite her.

"Can I assume something is weighing on your mind?"

"You assumed right."

"Tell me what happened," she reached for her tablet beside her.

"I went on a date. A double date. On Valentine's Day."

"And how did that go?"

"Surprisingly, great."

"Well, that's good news. Isn't it?"

My body bristled. "Not really."

"Can you share why?"

"Umm… it was with my brother's ex, Kira."

"I see. So, you had a surprisingly good time, but because of past circumstances, you're conflicted about it?"

"Basically." *Apparently, Dr. Collier could read minds.* "It's just… everything happened so fast. She asked me out, and then I asked her to prom, and then kissed her. Twice…" I rambled, wondering why I couldn't stop talking. "I mean, Kira's great. She knows what I'm going through with the whole breakup thing because it happened to her too. I don't have to explain it, and I don't have to talk about it; she just gets it. But…"

"But she's your brother's ex."

"Exactly. It's already weird that my ex is dating my brother. But then to consciously date my brother's ex?" I mocked. "Just saying it out loud makes it seem even more outlandish."

"Outlandish, or is it something else?"

"What else could it be?"

"Do you think that you're subconsciously trying to get back at your brother for hurting you?"

"No," I answered abruptly. *That was the truth. I really do like Kira.*

"But you said it was weird that your brother was dating your ex."

"He's in love. He's completely happy with Wren," I rebutted, oddly defending their relationship.

"So, your brother has moved on and is content."

I knew where she was going with her questions. "But we're the laughingstock at school. We're already being called the *Swinger Twins,* and Kira and I only went out once."

"Were you happy?"

"Yes."

"Was she happy?" My kiss with Kira flashed across my mind, unknowingly making the side of my mouth twitch upward.

"I think so."

"Then that's all that matters, Shane. Why shouldn't you have happiness in your life? And as for all the naysayers at school chiming in about your relationship with Kira? Tell them to, pardon my French, 'fudge' off."

I walked out of Dr. Collier's office pondering her questions. Why shouldn't I be happy? I deserve it. And if Kira is the reason, then why am I holding back? Screw the rumor mill and screw Sarah for feeding it. Kyle and Wren moved on, and it's time I did too.

It's time to find my happy.

Kira

I've picked up a bad habit: lying, even to my mother. I told her I'd eaten with friends just to avoid family dinner, but really, I came home and hid in bed. All week, I couldn't eat, sleep, or focus. Neither of us talked nor texted each other since our last date.

I hauled myself out of bed and sat at my small white vanity that doubled as my desk. The chipped paint highlighted the nicks and scratches. It looked worn down and sad, reflecting how exhausted I felt from another day of ignoring gossip. The dark circles under my eyes were pronounced, and no amount of makeup could cover them.

The only silver lining: tomorrow was Friday, I mused. Sarah was still pissed at me for lying, and the rumors were in overdrive. They called the four of us *Brother Swappers.* This new moniker was worse than anything I could have imagined. Maybe I should call off the whole prom idea. Let him off the hook since it's clear he regretted asking me. It would be the right thing to do; I basically forced him to ask. I could go on my own. Or not. It wouldn't be the end of the world. I still had another year of high school.

With the decision made, I rushed downstairs to the kitchen to find my dad. He had set up for the evening at our rickety kitchen table, reading the paper after dinner. *He's so old school*, I thought, rolling my eyes.

"Dad," I breathed heavily, "can I borrow the car?"

"It's dark and a school night. Where are you going?"

I hesitated. "To see Shane."

"Is that a good idea? I've heard the rumors, and I don't like them."

Even my dad knows? How? "It's not what you think. I'm telling him I want to end things and that we can't go to prom together."

"Prom? You had one date!"

"I'll explain everything later. Can I borrow the car?" I asked, feeling rushed to get things over with.

"You can't just call him?"

"Dad," I said, perturbed, "Please?"

"Okay, fine. If it's really to break up with him."

"It is. I promise."

He tossed me the keys, and I pecked him quickly on the cheek, making him smile. I ran to the closet by the front door, throwing on my coat, hopping on one foot and then the other as I slipped on my boots.

I threw open the door and crashed right into Shane. Again.

"Oof!" A loud grunt escaped my chest from the thud of my body into his. "Shane? What the hell?" *How was this happening a second time?*

"You're the one who ran into me!"

"What are you doing here?" I asked, confused.

"I came to see you."

"Why?"

"Because I wanted to."

"I meant, why now? You avoided me like the plague all week."

"That was wrong of me. I'm not… used to being mocked. I'm sorry, Kira."

"You're sorry a lot."

"That's why I'm here. To change that."

"Well, I have something to say to you too. That's why I was running out of the house. I was on my way to see you."

"You first," he said sweetly.

"No, you first," I said, firmer than I intended.

We both hesitated a beat, then before I could chicken out, I blurted, "I don't think we should go to prom."

But at the same time, Shane replied, "I really want us to go to prom."

"Wait. What?" He sounded shocked. "You don't want to go?"

"Well, um… it's not that… I… uh," I kept stuttering, losing my nerve.

"Why, Kira?" his voice cracked.

"You heard the rumors. The terrible names they're calling us."

"I have, but I don't care. And neither should you. We're doing nothing wrong. If we want to go together, then we're going together."

"It's not that simple, Shane. You have upcoming training and scouting opportunities. You don't need the extra stress of gossip. I *won't* be a distraction from your goals."

"You're not. You've brought happiness back into my life. And I was recently reminded that I need more of that." He flashed his gorgeous smile, instantly melting my resolve to break things off. I exhaled a sigh of relief.

"I started thinking that you regretted our date."

"I don't regret it all. I want to date you, Kira Sky," his gaze sultry.

He brushed my hair back, his fingers grazing my cheek. Lifting my chin, our eyes met. His gaze flitted down to my lips before leaning in. I stretched up to meet him when I heard my dad clear his throat behind me. We quickly broke apart, and I spun around with a scowl on my face. "Dad!" I hissed.

"You promised," he stated simply.

My heart sank, realizing that I had lied to my father too. "I'm sorry," I mumbled. My dad leaned back into the house, shutting the door behind him.

"What was that about?" Shane asked.

"Nothing," I deflected. "Can we get back to making each other happy?"

"We can." He pulled me close, his arms sliding around my waist inside my open jacket. Shane held me against his chest, radiating warmth—just like taking that first sip of hot cocoa. Being in his arms felt like home.

His lips brushed against mine; a fuzzy tingling shot to where I stood on my tippy toes. The heady musk of his cologne swirled around me and I pressed closer to absorb it all. Our lips moved gently, sweetly, and way too briefly. He kissed the tip of my nose, flashing his signature sexy smile before jogging down the porch to his car. The scent of him lingered near, and I wrapped my arms around myself, trying to capture it. He gave a final wave before driving away.

The light snow made the rectangular outline of his car stand out in the exact spot Kyle had parked when he broke my heart. Now, ironically, it's where his brother was making it whole again. Shane's right. Who cares what anyone thinks about the two of us together?

It's time to find my happy.

CHAPTER 10

why...

Shane

IT WAS OFFICIALLY June. The last four months were a blur. I've been busier than ever with school training, and scout interviews. My coach from Portugal came over to the States in early April to help facilitate my strict diet and skill-training regimen. We worked hard all spring, preparing for a slew of interested scouts who wanted to sign me. I secured two solid offers from Spain and Portugal, but it was never really a choice. Portugal had my heart. It was a big deal in our little town, and back into the newspaper headlines I went.

The one person who kept me sane was my Kira Sky. She's my touchstone, keeping me grounded while my dreams soar. She's my happy. After we started officially dating in February, we immediately went all-in, never looking back. However, it wasn't always easy.

First came carving out time to see each other with my soccer commitments and a chaotic training schedule. But she never missed a scrimmage. The second obstacle? Our parents. Each had multiple reservations and opinions about the two of us together. Kira's dad still enforced an early curfew, ignoring her protests. Luckily, I made sure we were never late.

Tonight was an oddly warm, clear night. The two of us finally had a rare moment to breathe after my hectic spring. Prom was in two weeks, and before the onslaught of everything prom-related, Kira and I planned to go to the lake for one of her famous "star walks." Her vast knowledge of constellations and the universe astounded me.

"Remember, curfew is at ten!" Mr. Bowman bellowed as we headed out.

"Dad!" Kira objected, like always.

"Ten sharp. Got it," I answered. My date rolled her eyes dramatically, then gave her father a quick peck on the cheek.

"And Shane, remember fishing tomorrow morning starts…"

"…at the butt crack of dawn. I remember." I responded, making her dad smile. A small break in his steely exterior.

In the car, Kira beamed widely at me. "Why are you grinning?" I asked.

"Did you see his smile? My dad *smiled.* At you! I knew those Sunday bonding brunches would work," she answered giddily.

"Hold up, Kira Sky. Don't read too much into it."

"Oh, I'm totally reading too much into that smile." Her eyes crinkled at the edges, face lighting up the night.

I loved her giggling. I loved her smile.

I loved… her.

***

It was finally prom day. My liberation day. The beautiful end of a year fraught with betrayal, lies, and pain. My dreams were becoming reality, and Kira Sky was by my side for all of it. The last two weeks felt different because I was different. On the night of our star walk, I told Kira I loved her, and she said it back without hesitation. We made a promise and planned to be together in a long-distance relationship until she could join me in Portugal after graduating.

I rose early to run before everyone woke up. It was eerily quiet except for my feet thumping against the hard, dry pavement. This was part of my training regimen, but it had always been part of my routine before it became my job. It was a chance for me to think and reflect—a form of meditation that helped center me. Keep my head clear. Except today I ran into Wren in the driveway when I got back and promptly made our conversation awkward. I took another lap around the block to clear my head and shift my focus back to prom. To Kira. I entered the house, greeted by the powerful aroma of hazelnut. I darted into the kitchen, endorphins still coursing through my veins, and found my mother sitting at the table.

"Good morning, Mom," I greeted.

"Good morning, sweetie. How was your run?" She asked, pouring herself a cup of coffee.

"Much needed." Thoughts of being with Kira later sprung into my head. "I'm excited about tonight."

"I wanted to talk to you regarding that..." Mom sounded ominous, clinking the spoon against the side of the cup as she stirred.

My mood deflated again. "About what?"

"Are you sure this whole 'going to prom with Kyle and Wren' thing is a good idea?" She quickly took a sip, peering at me over the edge.

"It's a little late to be asking me this today, don't you think?" It felt impossible to hide my annoyance.

"I just meant... since you're... taking your brother's ex." She fiddled with the placemat on the table.

"And Kyle is taking my ex. What's your point?" I countered.

"My point is... that the event might be awkward for everyone."

"Seriously, Mom? I live with my ex. Prom is the least of our problems." My head suddenly throbbed. "Please don't be weird around her or her parents tonight. I beg you."

I couldn't escape fast enough, heading upstairs to shower. I stomped into my room and surprised both Kyle and Wren. They jerked out of their embrace, as if they were caught cheating on me again. My stomach twisted in a familiar knot that I thought had long untangled.

"I'll come back," I blurted.

"We were just saying good morning," Kyle sputtered out.

Silence filled the room. I tried to decide whether to speak or flee when Kyle spoke first.

"I didn't get a chance to congratulate you. It's so cool you'll be playing professional soccer after graduation. It's what you've always wanted." Kyle gave me a quick hug. As he stepped back, Wren approached and surprised me with a hug as well.

My mind muddled, body reacting involuntarily. I wrapped my arms around her and held her tight. Just this once, I allowed myself to melt into her. How familiar and unexpectedly warm. I snapped back into myself, glancing at my brother as I pulled out of the embrace. I couldn't describe the exact expression on his face, but it wasn't approval.

"Thank you both." I decided it was best not to stick around and rushed to the bathroom, shutting the door behind me.

As it locked, an old familiar sound bombarded my ears. Unsure of the odd noise at first, I swiftly realized it was my breathing, coming faster. It's been six months, and I was doing so well. Confusion washed over me as I wondered where I had failed. I leaned forward, trying to slow my breaths, my thoughts repeating the words: *In. Out. In. Out.* Alongside one nagging question.

Why now?

Kira

I sat up in bed and stretched my arms high into the air. It was finally prom day, and I was going with Shane Whitmore. Never in my wildest dreams did I see any of this coming, especially when last Fall my world as I knew it blew up.

I glanced dreamily toward the gorgeous dress hanging on the back of my bedroom door. The fabric was a deep coral with hot pink tulle layered over the skirt and around the waist. The pink stretched up into the V-neck bodice that twisted with the coral material, like a toga, as the straps covered my shoulders. It reminded me of a Montana sunset; it was stunning.

Sarah and I had gone dress shopping right after her great, big, wonderful promposal that Brody may or may not have planned entirely on his own at the end of February. Her gown was slinky and alluring, a lavender sequined material with a long slit down her left side to the floor. It had a sailor-cut bodice and spaghetti straps. All the sparkles reflected her bright personality and made her fiery locks sizzle.

I heard a quiet knock. "Are you up?" my dad asked through the door.

"Yes, come in."

"Can I finally see the dress?"

"I hung it up last night."

My dad stepped in, turning past the frame to admire it. "Wow, Kira. It's spectacular. Looks just like the sunsets on the ranch."

"I know, right? I thought the same." My grin mirrored my dad's.

It was the first thing we had agreed on in a long time. The whole dating situation made my dad a nervous wreck, leading to a lot of arguments over the previous few months, and I get it. He didn't want to see me get hurt again, and honestly, that's what I wanted too. I slowly realized I may be more like my father than I wanted to admit.

"What time do we head to the Whitmore's?" Dad asked.

"We need to be there at four-thirty. And *you* need to be on your best behavior. I mean it," I chided.

"Me? Not on my best behavior?"

"Dad," I said exasperated, "I'm being serious. Best behavior, or you can't come with us. Mom will send you all the pictures while you sit at h—"

"I'll be good. I promise," he smiled slyly.

"You better be." I sighed, shaking my head.

***

With one final warning, my parents and I walked up the front porch of the Whitmore's house and rang the bell. My stomach twisted into knots while we waited for someone to answer. The anticipation of who would get there first made me shudder as I fixed a practiced smile onto my face. My mind reviewed the abundance of small talking points I had prepared earlier.

I physically jumped as the door opened. Standing there with his gorgeous smile and blue eyes was Shane. My legs threatened to wobble as I grabbed hold of the frame. He hugged me, allowing structure to return to my weak legs, before he strode over to welcome my parents.

I stepped inside, making eye contact with Shane's mom. "Oh, my goodness, Kira. You look beautiful," she gushed.

"Thank you so much."

"Those colors look amazing on you! I have a shade of lipstick that would match your dress perfectly. I can go grab it if you'd like?"

"That would be great, thank you."

"Be right back," she said excitedly, running up the stairs.

My eyes inadvertently followed her as Kyle descended. Butterflies flooded my stomach; their fluttering wings encased my heart. I tried to push aside the memories of last homecoming.

Shane snuck behind me, causing me to jolt for the second time tonight. He whispered into my ear as he embraced me, "Well hello there, Kira Sky. Sorry I didn't welcome you properly." I diverted my attention to him.

"That's okay. Did you earn a few more points with my dad?"

"One or two, I think," he smirked.

"Well done." I reached up and placed the palm of my hand on his cheek. He didn't hesitate to lean into my touch.

A moment later, his eyes flashed away from mine, his smile vanishing. I spun around, already knowing the reason. At the bottom of the stairs stood Wren in her jaw-dropping two-piece prom grown. It was a sparkly cotton-candy-pink T-shirt style top, with only a hint of her midriff showing. Her skirt was the same color, in shimmering silk, that pooled slightly onto the floor. She literally glowed as if she were an actual ethereal being.

The room hushed, and everyone gawked in her direction. Including Shane. The quiet emphasized the despair taking over me at his response. Alongside one nagging question.

Why now?

CHAPTER 11

was this...

Shane

I FELT FROZEN to the floor. My gaze followed Wren as she greeted Kira's parents. Seeing Mr. Bowman thawed me enough to snap my attention back toward my girlfriend. Kira had pulled her hand from my cheek, walking away.

"Kira," I begged, but she ignored my plea. Instead, she greeted Sarah, who busily chatted up Mateo by the fireplace. *I'm such an asshole.* I slipped into the kitchen, avoiding Wren at all costs, and pulled out my phone to text Max. His sage advice was to "avoid and distract." So, that was the plan, and I knew the perfect person for the job.

"Hey, Sarah," I greeted as I tapped her on the shoulder.

"Hey there, handsome," she pulled me into an enormous bear hug. I tentatively reciprocated, keeping my focus trained on Kira's demeanor.

"Um… we should start pictures soon so we're not late to prom." That tiny nudge worked like a charm.

Everyone took their turn engaging in obligatory couples and group pictures our parents expected. It bought me enough time to work on an apology, although Kira's indifference unnerved me.

After exchanging corsages and boutonnieres, Sarah herded us out to the two cars in the driveway. Kyle and Wren took one, while we rode with Sarah and Brody. Thankfully, we made these arrangements prior to tonight.

Kira hugged her mom and pecked her dad on the cheek before hopping into the back seat of Sarah's car. I reached out to shake her dad's hand, which he firmly took. But as I went to pull away, Mr. Bowman squeezed harder.

My posture stiffened when I looked to see his steely expression and flared nostrils. He released me after a tense beat of silence; no words exchanged between us. I understood his message loud and clear. I shook out the tingling, hopping into the backseat.

Mom gave a little wave as we backed out. I watched Mateo wrap his arm around her as she casually laid her head on his shoulder. A twinge of jealousy coursed through me. The love between them seemed comfortable, easy, and perfect. They didn't have to work on their relationship; it came naturally.

I shifted my attention to my girlfriend. who sat as far as possible from me, looking out her window. Any further, and she would have fallen out of the car. I winced, knowing it was because of my stupid involuntary reaction to seeing Wren. Hurting Kira was never my intention, but that's what happened.

I glanced at Brody in the front passenger seat as Sarah drove. She was blabbering about something, and he listened intently, stars in his eyes. They always struck me as complete opposites, yet they worked. I just don't get it. Love is weird. It just chooses you sometimes.

Guilt tugged at my chest, compelling me to pull out my phone and text Kira. A last-ditch effort to get an apology out before we got to prom since she wouldn't look my way.

Im sorry

She glanced at her phone, slowly tapping out a message.

You always are

I deserved that

Why now after all this time

I don't know
Read 5:01PM

Please don't prove my father right

She looked at me, tears threatening to pour from her eyes. The tightness in my chest felt like a snake wrapping around its prey. I reached for her, only for her to turn away, resuming her staring out the window. I dropped my head toward my chin, inhaling the tainted air between us, slowly and steadily.

Fear overtook my remorse. Fear that I might have undone everything we had together in one instant. It didn't help that I knew her pain too well. Old twinges, burns of betrayal, snuck up and invaded my being without even a whisper of it previously lurking.

Now that it had a foothold, I wasn't sure I could stop it. Kira's final message weighed on me like a pile of bricks for the rest of the car ride.

Was this always inevitable?

Kira

I reeled through a spectrum of emotions I didn't even know how to name. The way Shane had looked at Wren was something I had seen while dating his brother. But this cut deeper. My relationship with Shane was different. We made plans after our respective graduations for our future together. But his face when he saw her walk down the stairs? It was a sharp knife I didn't notice at first. Not until I saw the metaphorical blood.

Parking at the hotel was the only thing that brought relief. Like I had been drowning, and only just managed to breathe. I leapt from the car into the hazy twilight, filling my lungs with the fading day.

"You okay?" Brody asked sweetly, holding my shoulder.

"Yeah," but my thoughts screamed the opposite.

Shane came around, offering his arm. I took it, deciding it was the easiest way to pretend that everything was fine. We headed inside the hotel's Grand Banquet Hall, decorated to the hilt with ornate spotlights and beautiful white twinkling strings. They reminded me of stars falling toward Earth. A part of me yearned to make a wish on them; for this night to be better than how it started.

The glow of the hall danced off Sarah's lavender sequins, reflecting little beams of light. It was magnificent, as if Sarah were the shining sun. I chuckled, knowing she would love this analogy.

Suddenly, my date stiffened, almost forgetting to breathe. Turning around, I wasn't surprised to see Kyle and Wren heading straight toward us. My own body felt immobile as I gripped his arm tightly, bracing for the impending awkward interaction, when I heard Max call over.

"Hey, wait up!" he yelled, quickly closing the distance. He greeted Shane with a bro-hug that seemed suspiciously overzealous.

Then, he turned his attention to me. "Wow, Kira. You look amazing!" He picked me up, spinning me around. Something was definitely up.

I watched the rest of the group head into the venue. "Where's your date?"

"I think it's you," he laughed boldly.

I blinked, then pointed to myself hesitantly. "Me?"

"They bailed at the last minute," Shane interjected. "I told him he could be our third wheel. I hope that's okay."

"Um… sure. Of course," I sputtered. "Do I know them?"

"You've never met 'em. It's someone I've been seeing from the city." There was something off about his tone.

"Well, it's their loss."

"No worries. I'd rather go with you guys anyway!"

Shane patted him on the shoulder. "Well then, should we head in?"

"Yup. The coast is clear now…" Max trailed off.

"Clear of what?" I asked.

"Nothing. I just meant, uh… that the um… crowd is gone," Max stuttered, suspiciously, rubbing at his nose.

Max didn't seem himself with his weird glances toward Shane, I couldn't help but feel on edge. As we handed over our tickets, I hoped my tingling senses were wrong, but doubt kept pestering my brain. Did Shane really invite Max because he had no date or was there another reason?

***

Loud music echoed through the hall as hordes of teenagers milled about the ballroom. The appetizer buffet had a large charcuterie board with every finger food known to man, and I was so here for it. I hadn't eaten yet and was starving. Plus, there were some nerves related to finding our table, so I could always come back to fill a plate.

Making our way, we went under the glass dome ceiling above the ballroom. The night sky framed the floor, creating the illusion that we were outside. It almost felt as if Shane and I were on one of our star walks, a bittersweet thought. The wooden dance area, centered beneath the dome, seemed large enough for the entire school to be on it at once.

Sarah waved her arm, signaling that she had found our seats. As we sat, I noticed two unoccupied chairs. Nervously, I scanned the room for Kyle and Wren, finding them at a different table. An audible sigh escaped me.

Finally, able to grab a heaping plate full of charcuterie meats, cheeses, dried fruits, and crackers, I settled down to enjoy my food. Unfortunately, we were celebrating prom on Sarah's time. Before I could eat more than a cheese cube, she had arranged for us to take our formal pictures. We followed her blindly since it was easier to placate.

Shane and I went through the motions of pictures, both of us not fully present. However, anytime he was close, or we touched, my skin prickled. It was hard not to react to him in his classic black tuxedo; he was a real-life daydream. But it wasn't difficult to remind myself that I was mad.

Dancing opened after dinner, but the two of us remained at the table, picking aimlessly at our desserts. The ebb and flow of teenagers on the dance floor increased as the night wore on. Unfortunately, so did my irritation. Every time I glanced out, my brain would focus on her. The cotton-candy color of her dress was a magnet for my eyes. I couldn't look away.

"Would you like to dance?" Shane's question caught me off guard.

"Would you?" I asked reflexively.

"If you do, then yeah. You've been watching the dance floor for a while."

"Um, sure."

He took my hand as we moved into the crowd, spinning me in a circle around his body before pulling me close. His arm settled at my waist, holding my hand to his chest with the other. His body against mine felt right. But just as quickly, the feeling disappeared when the music stopped. The chasm between us split deeper. It didn't help that Max kept "checking on me" and then seemed to collude with Shane anytime we weren't together. My imagination ran wild.

Sweaty from dancing all evening, Sarah sat and took a sip of her punch. I followed suit, ready for a heaping dose of her sass to distract me from my intrusive thoughts.

"Hey, Sarah. You looked amazing out there."

"I know, right?! The total opposite of you and handsome."

"What do you mean?" I feigned confusion at her obvious observation.

"What do I mean?" her voice shrill, "I mean the fact that the two of you were total strangers out there."

"Oh, you noticed?"

"The whole school noticed. Well, Max noticed. Fishy, if you ask me. How many times is he going to 'check' on you?" Sarah made air quotes as she spoke.

"What is that supposed to mean?"

"Whatever you want it to. Either Max is making a play for you, or he's running interference."

My heart sank. That's exactly what I was worried about earlier tonight. Suddenly, the charcuterie board betrayed me, my stomach turning queasy. The enormous lump that formed in my throat made it hard to swallow. "You're wrong. Max had a date for tonight, but they bailed on him at the last minute."

"No, he didn't. He called me an hour before prom, begging for a ticket. Obviously, being the head of the prom committee, I hooked him up. Who told you he did?"

Blood drained from my face. "Both Max and Shane," I answered with a slight tremor in my voice. Sarah looked at me like I was the most naïve girl to ever exist. I recoiled, not knowing what to believe. *How could they lie to me?* Searching out the pair amongst the promgoers, the two were as thick as thieves. Sarah had faults but lying wasn't one of them.

Blood boiling, I surprised them. "HEY!" I yelled louder than I expected. "Which one of you is going to tell me the truth?"

"Kira—"

"Don't Kira me, Shane. I'm not sure I can accept any more of your half-assed apologies. Call this what it is. I'm the placeholder."

"That's not true."

"Really? Because I saw how you looked at her tonight! I fought for you, Shane. Against my better judgment. Against my dad's better judgment. I defended you over and over again. I told my dad you were different! That you wouldn't hurt me because you've been there. That you understood because it happened to you too. But here we are!"

I drew a crowd with my lack of control, but I couldn't stop. I didn't want to stop. Flashes of Whitmore brothers swirled in my head. My body trembled as anger boiled to the surface, exploding from my mouth.

"You never wanted me. It's always been her! I was only helping you pass the time until she changed her mind. And don't even try to deny it! Robbie, *AAGGHH*— Wren, has you under her spell. She has everyone under her spell! I don't know if it was the whole damsel in distress thing or what, but her power over you... actually, over both of you brothers is infuriating!" My breath came in loud, uneven waves.

Shane groveled, "I never meant to hurt you. Please believe me, you're my person! You understand me like no one else. That's the truth!"

"I don't believe you. Not anymore. And frankly, I'm done." Seeing only red, I stormed away.

He shouted after me, "Wait, please. Don't do this. I need you, Wren!"

I froze. The collective gasp in the ballroom was deafening. My cheeks burned, tears stinging my eyes. I slowly turned around, facing him head-on. He stood like a statue, his eyes wide and jaw slack.

"And that's my proof," I spat. I rushed to leave but almost crashed right into Principal Harper who came to see what all the yelling was about. "I want to go home. Please! I need to go home," I pleaded, sobbing into the principal's lapel.

"I can take her home," Brody offered immediately. He threw a look at Sarah's direction, and she tossed her car keys to him without a second thought. He ushered me out of the ballroom into the cool night, away from the spectacle that had just occurred.

Brody drove me home just like the night I ran into Shane back in February. I sobbed uncontrollably, attempting to text my dad through the haze of my tears. He waited for me as we pulled up. Thanking Brody, I hopped out and ran into my dad's open arms. He held me tight as I wept.

My sobbing eventually slowed enough to look up at my father. He wiped the tears from my cheeks with his warm thumbs. I choked out, "You can say it now, Dad. You were right."

"Diiawachisshik, Kira," Dad said tenderly.

"I love you too, Dad." I hugged him as if my life depended on it.

When I got to my room, I tugged off my prom gown, leaving it in a heap on the floor where my heart lay battered and bruised. I flopped onto my bed, exhausted from tonight's freak-out in front of everyone.

I half expected to see my phone blown up with a hundred missed calls or texts, but there were none. Not even from Sarah. What hurt even more was that there weren't any messages from Shane either. I thought I knew him well, but I guess I didn't.

Was this always inevitable?

CHAPTER 12

I had to...

Shane

LAST NIGHT I did exactly what she asked me not to do: prove her father right. The hush that swept over the ballroom was like a tangible vice squeezing the breath from my lungs, and the look on her face was my final gasp.

After the shitstorm, I couldn't stay there, and I couldn't go home. It had taken every ounce of my willpower to subsist after Kyle and Wren before, but now my will was completely shattered.

Max let me crash at his place, despite my significant Freudian slip. His fondness for Kira almost swayed him to walk out on me too, but he relented. I told my mom where I'd stay, having learned my lesson after not doing so the day of my kidnapping. Luckily, Max had seen everything and sent help, or the outcome would have been worse.

Lying on my back in Max's room, I replayed every moment of prom, haunted by the memory of countless eyes fixed on me as Principal Harper took charge as Brody quietly led Kira out. The dance resumed, but my heaviness lingered. I had caught sight of Kyle and Wren, their faces exhibiting unexpected sympathy. Knowing they'd relay everything to Mom and Mateo spared me from having to return home immediately.

Max's snores filled the small room, an oddly comforting background noise. The blow-up mattress I'd claimed was hardly better than sleeping directly on the hardwood, but comfort was beside the point. I wouldn't have slept well anywhere. My mind wouldn't let me. As the early morning dragged on, restless and endless, every creak of his room was a reminder that I was far from home in more ways than one.

Maybe it's for the best. I was leaving for Europe after graduation, and our silly plans for a long-distance relationship weren't realistic. Look at how well my relationship with Wren had worked out, and I had only been gone for the summer. This time, I intended to make this move permanent.

"Hey, did you sleep at all?" Max asked groggily, rubbing his eyes.

"Nope."

"Did Kira text you back yet?"

"I didn't text her." I admitted, cracking my knuckles.

"What?" Max shot up in bed. "Why the hell not?"

"It wouldn't change anything. Plus, I'm leaving for Portugal soon. Clean break and all."

"Idiot." Max kicked off his covers.

"Why? I'm being practical."

"No, you're being an idiot. Hasn't that poor girl been through enough with you Whitmore brothers?"

"So, you're on her side now?" I asked, irritated.

"C'mon, man. I'm always on your side. That's why I can call you an idiot when you're being an idiot." Max checked his phone.

Exasperated, I stuttered, "Wh... what would I even say?"

Max shot a death glare. "Start with an apology, for one thing. Then maybe claim insanity?"

"Not helpful."

"You gotta talk to her, Shane. You can't leave her thinking you both chose Wren over her when that's not how you feel."

"I want Kira. That's why I don't understand how Wren's name came out instead." My voice wobbled. "Did you see the look on her face when I said it? She'll never forgive me, let alone talk to me."

"At least try."

I flopped onto the half-inflated mattress with a sigh. Max was right. I needed to talk to Kira. But I didn't know how to explain why it had happened. I'd accepted that Wren had chosen Kyle. I even came to terms with the fact that she lied to me, about so many things. I shut my eyes tight. Maybe I wasn't quite over the betrayal as much as I led myself to believe.

Being with Kira was effortless. We connected through the shared experience of getting dumped in the worst possible ways without even needing to talk about or even deal with it. But perhaps that was the problem. Maybe we were doomed from the start. Everything happened so fast, and then it was a freight train out of control. You couldn't stop it, and you couldn't jump. So, was my slip of the tongue a way to jump?

My eyes snapped open. "Max, lend me your keys," I demanded.

I jumped to my feet as Max threw them over. "That's my boy. Go get the girl. But first, put on some pants. I beg you," he joked, scavenging through his dresser for clothes and some sneakers since I only had my tuxedo.

Phone in hand, I rushed out before I lost my nerve. There was a lot to tell her and so much to apologize for. Not just about yesterday, but for not being the person she believed in. I fell short of her expectations.

Despite genuinely loving Kira, she deserved someone without baggage. Someone who could make her their top priority. Even if it was subconscious, I had put soccer first. My inadvertent name slip was a wake-up call. Although my mind was in direct conflict with my heart, I needed to do the right thing.

I had to let her go.

Kira

I must have cried myself to sleep as my cheeks felt stiff with dried tears. Why do I trust so easily? It was my greatest weakness. Not only had I fallen for one Whitmore brother, but I fell for both. Just like Wren.

I blamed her for somehow mesmerizing the brothers, when honestly it may have been the other way around. The brothers' close age gap of twelve months made their bond a twin-like dynamic. Their deep connection almost seemed metaphysical. Their life force summoned an energy that drew people to them like an invisible tractor beam, impossible to break free.

I rolled over, screaming loudly into my pillow. I despised defending Wren, especially when I was nothing like her. But deep down, a nagging feeling gnawed at my insides that I was. Regardless, he needed to know he hurt me and that I am worthy of better.

My phone buzzed, slicing through my thoughts. Scared to look, I lifted it cautiously, conflicted between hope and dread that the text was from Shane. Especially knowing what had to happen next.

Can we talk? im out front
Read 10:34AM

I practically leapt out of bed and ran to my window, eagerness and fear tangled together. Of course, Max's car was parked in the same damn spot—Shane's text déjà vu. I physically gagged, realizing it was happening again.

A small knock at my door made my heart stop. "Kira?" my dad asked softly. Relief loosened my chest.

"You can come in."

"How are you feeling this morning?" he asked innocently. I pointed out the window. "I can tell him to leave. Just say the word."

"No, I need to do this. As you always say, *'One has to face fear or forever run from it.'*"

"I can't take full credit since it's an old Crow proverb, but I will take credit for teaching it to you." I groaned. "Hey, I need the dad points." he winked, wrapping his arms around me in a hug.

Dad always knew what to say to make everything okay. My resolve set, I shot off a text to Shane that I was coming down. I slipped on some shoes when dad interjected.

"If you need me—"

"I know. Thanks, Dad." I pecked him on the cheek and hurried off.

On the porch, I took a cleansing breath. Stepping into the warm brightness of a new day juxtaposed sharply with my current mood. I plodded down the front path, my stomach twisting from the echoes of the past. Before I lost my nerve, I jumped into the passenger seat.

Being here again, in a car with a Whitmore brother ready to break my heart, destabilized me. With clenched fists, heat rose from my core despite the air conditioner blowing cool air. I didn't plan on sitting idly while listening to his excuses. Not this time.

"Kira Sky—"

Hearing him say my name like that? "No. You don't get to talk. It's my turn."

His voice cracked. "Okay." Pain filled his beautiful blue eyes, and I wavered.

"Let's call our relationship what it was: a rebound. We were delusional to think this could go anywhere, that our baggage didn't matter. And the way we pretended it wasn't an issue? It's a travesty. Even if I weren't a placeholder girlfriend, yesterday was inevitable. We had fun, but it's time to face reality. You're graduating, and I'm not. You're leaving, and I'm not. And that's okay. We'll be okay."

"Ki—"

"I'm not finished," I curtly interjected. Shane quickly closed his mouth.

"Both you and Kyle have been the best and worst part of my life. I can't regret it because it's made me who I am now. But I deserve better. I would have put my dreams on hold to follow yours, but not anymore. I'm making myself a priority for once. Go to Portugal, Shane. Follow your dreams and be great."

His puppy-dog eyes almost broke me, and I nearly recanted everything. I fought a fierce urge to wrap my arms around him, kissing his trembling lips. I longed to tell him I loved him and would disregard everything to follow him anywhere. Still.

But I didn't. On the verge of losing it, I ended us. "I wish you the best, Shane. I do. I know you'll do amazing things with your life. But I don't want to see you again. Please respect that. The Whitmore brother drama is over." His shell-shocked look made me want to leave as fast as possible. "Goodbye, Shane."

Sobs surged as the dam of emotions burst and I rushed into the house. I immediately went to the front curtain, peeking out at his unmoving car.

"Everything okay?" I startled, at my dad's voice behind me.

"Yeah," I said, stifling my sobs. "Why is he just sitting there?"

"Do you want me to tell him to go?"

"No!" I answered abruptly.

My father threw his arms up in surrender. "Did he at least apologize?"

"Actually, he never spoke. I did the talking."

"And…"

"And… it's over."

"Is that what you want?" He asked the only question I couldn't answer.

I went upstairs to my room, looking out the window toward the street where his car sat, glued in place. Reaching for my phone, I contemplated my next move as he finally pulled away.

I really thought having control this time would make the breakup less painful. But it was worse. To be hurt by someone is terrible but intentionally hurting a person you love is agonizing. Although my mind was in direct conflict with my heart, I needed to do the right thing.

I had to let him go.

Chapter 13

Shane

I FELT THE August summer breeze rolling off the Atlantic Ocean; the sun warming my skin. The waves lapping at my feet bring me peace. Sitting on the heated sand, I effortlessly took in the salty air. This was my happy place.

This past year was a whirlwind of pressure both physically and emotionally. I left my old life the moment I graduated high school, escaping to Portugal and never looking back. Soccer training was intense, but it made the perfect distraction from everything else. I thought it would be hard to leave home, move to a new country, and start a new life. But it wasn't.

In fact, it was the opposite; it was cleansing. Rejuvenating. Freeing. Back in New York, there were so many times I would have to check I was breathing to make sure I was still alive. But I don't have to do that anymore. I'm grateful to live the dream I chased my entire life. It's not lost on me that not everyone gets to have that. But I do.

I was startled when my watch alarm blared. I had to get to the airport. Mom and Mateo were flying in for a visit. They said they were here for Mateo's family, but I knew they were here to check up on me. Mom lamented repeatedly about how long it had been since we saw each other. I wanted to be excited to see her but could already feel the crushing weight of my past.

I closed my eyes, taking a last deep cleansing breath, psyching myself up to see Mom again. I could do this. I could invite my past to meet my future and survive. I think.

I saw her face bobbing up and down through the crowd, hunting for me in the airport terminal. When she finally caught my gaze, she grinned from ear to ear. She flew toward me, and I scooped her up, swinging her around. Her familiar scent tugged at my heart as I let it soak into my memories of home. My mom held me so tight, my body shuddered. I wasn't sure if that was a good thing or a bad thing.

"My baby! I'm so happy to see you," she said, sobbing into my shoulder.

"I'm glad to see you too, Mom," she squeezed tighter, "…Mom."

"I've missed you so much. It's been over a year, Shane! Can't a mother be excited to see her son?"

My mouth armed itself with a sarcastic retort, but I decided against it. I set her down and turned my attention to Mateo.

"Olá, Shane."

"E aí, Mateo."

"It's good to see you. You've really grown," he said, looking up.

"Yeah. I guess so," I replied awkwardly, quickly changing the subject. "Oh, congratulations on the engagement. I'm happy for you both."

"Thank you, sweetheart. That means a lot. But back to you. Are they treating you well?" Mom asked.

"Yes, Mom. You worry too much. Everything is fine." I answered, a bit annoyed. Mom either ignored my tone or didn't notice.

"I watched every game I could, but I'm so excited to see you play in person. You're amazing!"

"Thanks," I said, my heart thudding.

"I was telling the gals at work—"

"Are you ready to head to the hotel?" I curtly interrupted.

"Um… sure. I guess we can catch up later. It would be nice to freshen up before dinner; I had forgotten that long plane ride was killer."

The thought of dinner made my stomach twist as we walked to my car. I suddenly felt unsure if I was ready to hear the latest news from home, especially with how everything ended last June.

After prom, the final two weeks of school were fraught with whispers and gossip... again. The demise of my relationship with Kira eclipsed any other news happening in our senior year. Thankfully, finals, training, and graduation prep kept me busy.

Max was my only refuge from the noise. He didn't agree with me giving up on Kira, but he didn't hold it against me either. Not like Kira's Dad. My Mom had run into Kira's mom, Leah, at the store right after prom and received an earful. Leah said that Levi wanted to come over and *'give me a stern talking to and then some'*. Thankfully, Leah was the voice of reason. I had seen her in action a few times at their home during Sunday morning brunch. Levi and Leah were yin and yang. Opposite yet perfectly balanced.

Then there was Sarah...

"Did you make reservations?" My mom's voice cut through the memories.

"Oops. I didn't even think about it." Which was the total truth. My roommate Paulo and I cooked our own meals to eat cleanly, but I wasn't against the promise of a cheat day.

"No worries, I'll make a call," Mateo said.

At dinner, I steered the conversation toward their proposal and subsequent wedding plans. I could still remember the day Mateo called me to ask for my mother's hand in marriage. Kyle was home for winter break while I was present on the speakerphone, and we gave him our blessing. I deeply appreciated the thought and respect Mateo gave by asking to marry our mom. He really was one of the good guys. He makes her happy, and she more than deserves a good relationship at this point. *She sure as hell didn't find this kind of happiness with my deadbeat dad.*

Melancholy encroached on my thoughts about such a perfect relationship. I couldn't help but wonder if Kira was happy. Max gave sporadic updates, but since summer started, we haven't really talked. He had taken a gap year to work and save money. Ironically, he worked for Levi at the Bowmans' car dealership. Levi and Kira weren't thrilled, especially with Kira helping out after school a few days a week, but Mrs. Bowman intervened. As a result, Kira and Max became close this past year. A sharp green pang stung inside my chest.

I rubbed my temples, trying to soothe my splitting headache. Seeing Mom had dredged up too many memories. Before anything could break through the surface, I needed to push them down and keep my focus. On soccer. My dream. Because the old me was gone. That chapter of my story was over.

So, why does it feel like it's just beginning?

Kira

I felt the August summer breeze rolling off the Montana range; the sun warming my skin. Horses galloped freely on the ranch property, bringing me peace. I sat on the split-rail fence, taking in the earthy mountain air. This was my happy place.

Last year had been a whirlwind. I tried to keep Shane out of my mind but found it painful when the whole school constantly yapped about him. It didn't help that his face was splashed across the local media too. "Small Town Kid Scoring Big in Portugal," or "From Prisoner to Portugal," or my favorite, "Shooting to Stardom: Senior Survives Shooting, Then Shoots to Soccer Stardom." I mean, come on. Who writes this stuff?

Wren moved to New York City and was living with her cop friend last I heard. She's majoring in forensics or something at John Jay College for criminology. It made sense after her major contribution toward taking down a dirty NYC cop and taking a bullet. Lauded as a hero, the college offered her a full-ride, or whatever. I rolled my eyes.

Sarah also moved to NYC to attend the Fashion Institute of Technology (FIT). That decision was so Sarah. This past spring, she had her first runway sample included in a prestigious show for a famous designer named Rachel something. It was a big deal, and she made sure all of us knew. Which again, is so Sarah.

Then there were the rest of us—me, Brody, and… Kyle. We were finally seniors, but it didn't feel like the exciting finish we'd been promised. With one-third of the *Hero Trio* still in town, it was enough to keep the rumor mill happy and the media's obsession with *Shane the Soccer Phenom* placated. The perfect storm of annoyance, chaos, and noise drowning out the best year of my life. I couldn't graduate fast enough to move to my Uncle Nash's ranch in Montana.

A slow smile formed as I thought about the only shining light. Max. He had been my rock, oddly enough. Our friendship didn't blossom straightaway. I had reservations about his close ties to Shane. But whenever thrown together at work, he wore me down. It's strange how life surprises you. I couldn't imagine surviving my senior year without him.

"KIRA!" Clay shouted, startling me out of my reverie.

"What? You scared me to death," I snapped back.

"I called your name like a hundred times."

"A hundred times?" I mocked.

"Yes. A hundred. I counted."

I rolled my eyes. "What do you want?"

"Not me. Your Uncle Nash. He said you were going to meet him at the main stable at noon?"

"Oh, shit. What time is it?"

"Quarter after."

"Shit. Shit. Shit," I muttered, hauling ass as fast as my boots could carry me over the dry, rocky ground. As I rounded the corner, I saw my uncle with a small group of clients. It looked like he was entertaining them with his vast knowledge of the program due to my tardiness. As I slowed to a jog, I could hear my uncle promoting the therapy.

"I started this program for my dear wife. Rest her soul. She deeply believed in the healing power of horses, and it's true. Horses have a rare ability to calm not only the mind and body, but your spirit too.

Research has shown that they can reduce stress, improve emotional regulation, and relax the nervous system. Our well-trained horses here on Spirit Ranch not only help people build trust, empathy, and confidence, they build relationships to foster communication and social skills.

During your specially guided riding therapy some of the physical benefits are balance, core strengthening, and relief from muscle stiffness. This program has a proven record for treating a myriad of social-emotional and physical traumas.

I'm excited for you to learn more. Once my niece arrives, she'll take you on a tour of the facilities and horses. I hope you'll consider utilizing and supporting our unique therapy approach." Uncle Nash's pitch was spot on, and his speech always warmed my heart.

"Ah, there she is now. My talented and skillful equine coach in training." Uncle Nash gushed, raising an eyebrow.

Breathlessly, I welcomed them. "Hi everyone! I'm Kira."

"This is my niece from New York City. She's been working here for many summers; now officially part of our staff." He patted me hard on the shoulder. "Kira is in the mentoring program, working toward her license as an equine therapist. But today, she'll be your knowledgeable tour guide." He turned to me. "Everything ready?" My uncle asked me with wide *'I better say yes'* eyes.

"Yes, sir. Everything is set." I tried to catch my breath before addressing the clients. "Everyone, please follow along." My uncle stalked beside me; his brows furrowed deep. "I'm super sorry I'm late. It won't happen again," I whispered.

"This program is new to the ranch, Kira. I really want it to be successful. That means dedicating your full attention to it."

"I know. And I will. I was busy grooming, and time slipped by."

His voice softened. "Kira, if you need more time, Clay can lead until—"

"No, I'm ready. I promise. And you don't have to coddle me because I'm your niece and my dad told you to." Uncle Nash shot a crooked smile.

To be honest, I did feel unsteady, but I couldn't tell him that. A social media post from Kirstie Whitmore had thrown me for a loop. She had traveled to Portugal to see Shane play, fawning over his accomplishments. Mateo, her now fiancé, went with her to spend time with his family and celebrate their recent engagement. The post hurtled me back into the past again.

Since coming to the ranch nearly two months ago, I had put everything behind me, mostly. Except for Max. He called every week since I got here, and I missed him. What I didn't miss was thinking of Shane. *I am never late for ranch tours*. Heat clawed up my neck, blooming across my face.

I wouldn't let Shane take up space in my head again. My uncle needed all of my energy into the ranch and equine program. I wanted him to fully trust me and show him my focus. On horse therapy. My dream. Because the old me was gone. That chapter of my story was over.

So, why does it feel like it's just beginning?

Chapter 14

To protect...

Shane

I WAS AN absolute wreck, and on the verge of losing the few contents of my stomach. For the last few days, I haven't been able to eat, but it couldn't have been nerves. I was never nervous before a match. If anything, my adrenaline went into hyper drive. *What is wrong with me*? It had to be the heat or intense training. The only other difference was my mom and Mateo coming to see me play a professional match in person for the first time. Besides that, nothing else had changed.

"Whitmore," my teammate Paulo called out to me.

"Yeah?"

"Your mom is outside and wants to see you."

My stomach lurched, and I sprinted to the bathroom. After I came out of the stall, I washed my face and rinsed my mouth.

"Você está bem?" Paulo asked.

"Yeah, I'm okay." He patted my back, following along as I went to meet her.

Mateo and Mom were dressed in my team's colors from head to toe. They looked like a walking advertisement for Sporting CP (Sporting Clube de Portugal). Their fit screamed foreigners visiting the country. I chuckled, watching Mateo, obviously trying hard to impress my mom. Although, I didn't understand why. He had already put a ring on it.

"Oh. My. Gosh. Look at you! You look like a professional soccer player in your jersey," Mom gushed.

"I am a professional soccer player, Mom," I sharply inhaled through clenched teeth.

"You know what I mean. You're so… sporty!" I couldn't help but roll my eyes at her attempted compliment. "I saw that."

"I meant for you to."

"Okay, okay. I get the hint. I'll shut up now," she playfully waved me off.

"Just trying to keep my game face on—"

"And I'm ruining your mojo. I got it. We'll go to our seats. See you after the game. Good luck!" She gave me a quick peck on the cheek.

As they walked away, my teammate Francisco ran up to me. "Is that your mamá? Oohh… Belíssima!"

"Don't even think about hitting on her. She's taken."

"Me? Hit on a pretty woman?" Francisco asked in a sultry tone, wagging his eyebrows. I playfully nudged his shoulder before he could run off. Watching him bust out laughing as he shouldered open the locker room door.

***

Paulo angled his kick, sending a precise pass to me. Receiving the ball, I dribbled fast down the field. My heart throbbed in my throat, breath huffing each time I tapped the ball between my feet as I thundered toward the goal. I scanned, assessing the defenders and looking for a pass. I sharply pivoted, but Paulo was covered. I had no choice but to continue across the pitch when Francisco appeared, clearing a path. I sprinted hard toward the endline, and the goalie squared up.

I faked left, setting up the pass to my winger when I abruptly tumbled to the ground. A defender pulled up on my flank, and I rolled off the pitch, hissing at my blatant mistake. Stunned, Francisco held out his hand to help me to my feet.

I furiously raked my hand through my sweat drenched hair. Paulo rushed over, patting me on the back.

"Shake it off, mano," he said, trying to reassure me. But as I jogged back into position, I saw the opposing team score.

Overall, the game was great. My playing, however? Yeah, it sucked. Everything felt off since I woke up today and I couldn't put my finger on why. Fortunately, my teammates picked up the slack, and we came out on top. To celebrate, Mom wanted to go to the coastal restaurant we frequented when we lived here before my senior year.

That summer was the last time I truly felt myself. The last time my life was on track. Living out a dream of traveling and playing soccer, all the while knowing I would return to my final year of high school to the enigmatic girl I was dating. Or so I thought.

When I finally started seeing Dr. Collier in earnest, she encouraged me to reconcile my feelings surrounding that summer by taking the perspective of Wren and Kyle. Not to condone their behavior, but to try to understand the trauma they experienced together. I resisted anything related to the two of them and my relationship with the pair suffered as a result.

Then Kira entered my life. It was sudden and unexpected in the best possible way. Even from the beginning my relationship with Kira felt different from what I had with Wren. Different from any of my relationships. Her drive and her focus were intoxicating. I never knew where I stood with Wren because of the walls she built, but Kira wore her heart on her sleeve. Then I ruined everything and moved across the world, almost like I did it on purpose. I wondered if she'd ever forgiven me, but I didn't have the courage to ask Max when he called.

An uncomfortable churning inflaming my stomach as a distant memory invaded my headspace. A nugget of information my therapist shared that hadn't impacted me until now. She said that many people, when faced with fear or a traumatic experience, will mask their true feelings. This response could be voluntary or involuntary. Of course, Dr. Collier was referring to Wren keeping us in the dark about her past. But maybe it applied to me, too.

I grabbed my bag, leaving the locker room. I had always regarded the prom incident as an involuntary slip of the tongue. But what if it was my mind trying to protect me that night?

To protect my heart?

Kira

Dust flew around me as I rode my horse Honey around the paddock, my hair bouncing the cowboy hat right off my head. Out of the corner of my eye, I saw Clay run across to grab it before scaling the fence on the other side. I galloped past, and he hooted and hollered in encouragement. I smiled, squeezing the reins tight and pulling them to the left while I whizzed around the paddock. My horse was amazing. Honey was sharp and crisp in her movements, needing little guidance from me.

It was nice to cut loose for a bit and ride hard, at a different pace than therapy horses. Their training was gentle, steady, and slow to build trust with their riders and allow for security. It became a relationship and friendship. It was a fulfilling job and very effective.

Last summer, I personally benefited from my bond with the therapy horses, especially Honey. She helped me move past some pain I still held onto. After multiple venting sessions with Clay, I thought I would be ready for my senior year. Until I got home, bombarded by reality again.

Ugh. I promised myself I wouldn't think of the past, but it had a way of creeping into the corners of my mind. I slid off the saddle, slowly walking Honey into the stable when I felt my phone buzz in the back pocket of my jeans. It was Max; his timing was uncanny.

"Max, hi, how are you?" I asked, casually walking Honey into her stall.

"Hey there, cowgirl. It's sooo good to hear your voice."

"Uh-oh. What's wrong?" I tilted my hat back so I could tuck the phone closer to my ear.

"Nothing. Can't I call my favorite girl?"

I shook my head. "Now I know there's a problem. Spill."

"There's nothing to spill. I was just thinking of you."

"Mhm," I replied skeptically.

"It's true."

"Is it my dad's getting on your nerves thinking of me or thinking of me because you were thinking of me?" I asked, lazily finger combing Honey's mane.

"The second one?" He didn't sound convincing.

I shook my head, grinning. Max had a way of pulling me out of my funk.

"So, are we going to talk about it?" I questioned.

"Talk about what?"

"Kirstie's Facebook post." I tapped my foot on the straw-covered floor.

"You saw?"

"Yup. And good for her. She deserves love in her life."

"I meant the part that she's going to Portugal to see—"

"Why would that bother me?"

"She'll be posting about it. With pictures. Involving you-know-who."

"So?" I replied, placing my hand on my hip.

"So... I was checking on you."

"Max, that was a lifetime ago. He moved on. I moved on. I'm good." My heart pounded in my throat. "I'm in the middle of work, gotta go."

"Okay. I'll call you in a few days. I miss you. It's not the same without you."

"I miss you too," I echoed, and then quickly hung up.

Why does Max know me so well? I thought. It's annoying, actually. He had realized without me saying a word that Kristie's Facebook post would affect me. I still wasn't sure why it even did. I hadn't seen Shane in over a year.

I know I had explicitly told him not to contact me, but I didn't think he'd follow through. Max said he was trying to be a good guy and abide by my wishes, but seeing Shane move on without giving me another thought hurt.

Kira! Snap out of it. I scolded myself. *You wanted him out of your life, and he is.* I should be happy it was a clean break. From him, from school, from our little town. How infuriating that a single post could undo me so easily.

Our relationship was a rebound. It wasn't real. He all but admitted he had been thinking of Wren the entire time. I was right to demand that he not contact me again. That we go our separate ways. I made it crystal clear that night in the car that I wanted nothing to do with him. Ever.

My mind was made up that night, and I chose correctly. So, why was I wavering now? Because of a Facebook post? What if my mind was trying to protect me the night we broke up?

To protect my heart?

Chapter 15

And that starts with...

Shane

THAT COULD HAVE gone better. My less-than-stellar performance in today's game was an absolute embarrassment. Not to mention that I missed a penalty kick that anyone on the team would have considered a freebie. I couldn't get my head in the game or out of this funk. I tried not to sulk at dinner, focusing on the time with my family. Having exhausted every topic under the sun to avoid the elephant in the room, I finished my last bite and took the initiative.

"How's Kyle and Wren?" I asked abruptly.

"Um... uh... they're good," Mom tripped on her words. I glanced to my side, watching Mateo wipe his already clean face with a napkin.

"And Wren's first year at John Jay?"

She cleared her throat, setting her fork down to pick up her glass of wine. "Very well, she's at the top of her class."

"I wouldn't expect anything less. When she sets her mind on something, she's unstoppable." Mom held a nervous smile. "And Kyle? Is he excited for his first semester this Fall?"

"Yes, he is. He declared his major as computer science a few weeks ago and wants to parlay that into forensics or intelligence analysis."

"The FBI's new dynamic duo," I tried not to sound mocking.

Mom released a tense giggle as if I had crushed any eggshells she carefully avoided. When Kyle enrolled at the City College of New York last spring, I offered to pay his tuition. Mom immediately refused, but I insisted. My salary through my Fútbol Club was more than enough to cover my living expenses and his education. But I made her swear never to tell my brother. It had always been my plan to support our family when I went pro. A rocky relationship wouldn't change that promise.

I felt ecstatic that I had made it through another day of tricky dinner conversations. But I shouldn't have indulged in the thought. Immediately jinxing myself, Mom threw out one more zinger.

"Shane, I wanted to invite you home for the holidays. I know you spent the previous winter with Paulo, but you haven't been back for over a year now. I miss you. Everyone misses you."

I consciously closed my mouth, unprepared for this. I wasn't even sure why I had gotten surprised. This was the same woman who asked me to think about visiting at the end of every phone call.

Now it was my turn to stumble. "Um…uh…we'll see how the rest of the season shakes out. Winter in Brazil is still conducive to outdoor practice. New York isn't. And after how I played today? I clearly need it."

She dropped the topic, but the question dangled precariously like a melting icicle, ready to dislodge at any moment. My unbuttoned polo shirt felt like lead on my shoulders, and I hastily said my goodbyes.

Returning to my apartment, I sat on the corner of my bed with my face in my hands. It was one thing to talk about Kyle and Wren, but to go back to sharing a space? If the end of my senior year was any indicator, it would be a complete shitshow. I wasn't sure I could handle it. In fact, I knew I couldn't. The stress I've felt since Mom and Mateo arrived was more than enough.

I clutched my chest, heart pounding. My body shook as sweat beaded over my brow. *Am I having a heart attack?* Fearful, I pulled out my phone to call for help. As I started to tap out a message, an overwhelming feeling of nausea and dizziness consumed me. I wobbled just enough to throw off my balance, losing control. I tumbled off my bed, landing with a thud. I pushed up from my hands to stand, but the room went black.

***

"Shane? Wake up," Paulo aggressively shook my shoulders. I slowly came to, finding myself sprawled out on my bedroom carpet. My teammate helped me sit against my bed frame.

Groggily, I blinked slowly. "Where am I?"

"How much did you drink tonight, amigo?"

"Nothing? Just water."

"Sure. Sure, mano." He helped me sit on the bed. "I thought you were dead when I came in. After getting sick this morning, I wondered if food poisoning had gotten to your weak stomach or something." Not the guy teasing me for my spice tolerance when I was already down.

"I must have fallen, that's all. I'm fine."

"If you say so. But I'd check in with the doc tomorrow, just in case."

"I said I'm fine," I snapped, partially angry that he was harping at me, but mostly embarrassed.

"Okay, okay!" He gritted his teeth. "I'm only trying to help."

"I don't need your help," I barked. He needed to get off my case. Paulo lifted his hands in surrender, muttering in Portuguese as he left my room.

Shit. I held my throbbing head. I must have knocked it when I passed out. *Passed out? What the hell was wrong with me today?*

***

Morning came seemingly the moment after I closed my eyes. I felt like a herd of bulls ran me down and stomped my body to a bloody pulp. My brain took the brunt of the attack. I don't think I had more than ten minutes of continuous sleep, fitful dream after fitful dream. All of them of home.

Home. I don't remember the feeling of it anymore. I only knew it was something to avoid at all costs. The three of us living together didn't go well last time. Even though I'd only be visiting, I wasn't ready to confront any memories.

One reflection that still haunted me was from the day of senior prom. In retrospect, I see how this single conversation with Wren sabotaged my relationship with Kira. Consciously or not, it had repercussions. While it happened over a year ago, it played through my mind as if it was yesterday.

Finishing a long morning run, I spotted Wren heading up the driveway, a bag across her shoulder. There wasn't time to deploy my normal avoidance strategies, so I braced myself for impact.

"Hey," she greeted innocently enough.

"Hey, back." I tried to seem upbeat. "Ready for prom?"

"Yeah, Sarah just dropped me off. We got manicures." She flashed her freshly done pink set.

"They look good."

"Thanks. I've never got them painted at a salon before, but Sarah insiste and well, you know Sarah."

"I do, and good call. Don't want to poke the bear on prom day." An amused chuckle floated between us.

"By the way, congratulations on getting a professional roster spot. How exciting! Your dream is finally coming true."

"Thanks." My lame response had me cracking my knuckles repeatedly. With silence lingering between us, I spoke the first thing that popped into my mind. "Congrats on getting into John Jay."

"Thanks, I wasn't sure I would."

Taken aback by her lack of confidence, I answered far too honestly. "I was. You're smart, cunning, and brave. Plus, your real-life experience gives you an edge. They'll be lucky to have you." I couldn't stop laying on compliments, rambling to fill the space. "And I heard you'll be staying with Tanya in the city.

That's cool of her. It'll help to have her as a resource..." Please shut up, Shane. "...especially with your studies and stuff."

"I appreciate that," she laughed. "Tanya's been great. Having her support and the letter of recommendation was generous. I owe her a lot. Obviously."

Nervous to word-vomit again, I held back. This was the longest conversation we had in a super long time. I didn't know what to make of that, but it shook me out of my fog. But I pushed my luck. "Wren, do you ever wonder what would have happened if I had stayed last summer?"

"Shane, don't do that. We can't play the would've, should've game."

"That's not what I meant to ask. If last summer was different and there were no, you and Kyle, where would you be right now? Because I know... I know I wouldn't have been enough of a reason for you to stay like you did for Kyle." Immediate regret seized my entire existence.

"Shane..." My name fell off her lips in a whisper. I turned my head away, unable to meet her gaze.

"Forget it. My therapist has messed me up, working on feelings and all that crap. What I want to say is, I'm happy you stayed." After a quick pause, "Anyway, I'm gonna take another quick lap before I head in. See you inside." I took off, needing to escape.

Moving forward was my only option. I pushed harder than I had in months. My footfalls slammed against the pavement. I'm so done with this therapy shit. It only stressed me out and made me over-share the quiet parts out loud. I couldn't cohabitate with old memories and heartache anymore.

Home still haunted me despite being an ocean away. It would break my mother's heart, but I can't return to New York for Christmas. For my own sanity, I had to find the strength to tell her this was where I belonged now. I wanted to move forward. I needed to move forward.

And that starts with not going back.

Kira

I was in my element, giving tours to potential clients and sponsors all week. Uncle Nash's therapy program would change lives and bolster the area's recently slowed economy. It was easy to show enthusiasm for it after seeing the benefits myself. These majestic creatures could bring powerful healing; a wonder to behold. I was genuinely proud to be a part of it.

I took the last tour group of the day through the stables, gently reminding everyone to watch their step. As we passed Honey's stall, she whinnied and lowered her head so I could reach. I stroked her ears and down her beautiful face. She gave an exaggerated, approving snort—her way of saying she liked the attention. The group chattered in amazement at the sweet interaction. That was Honey; her sweetness healed the body, mind, and soul.

After the successful tour, several clients met with Uncle Nash to become program sponsors. He was so proud of me, I practically skipped back to the stables to see my special girl. I grabbed a handful of carrots that Honey gladly munched on as I pulled over the hose to refill her water trough. I happily hummed to the tack room as I gathered grooming supplies.

"You're in a good mood." Clay surprised me as he leaned against the door frame, looking confident and smug, all rolled into one.

"Had a good day, that's all."

"Well, it looks nice on you." He waggled his eyebrows, but I only rolled my eyes. Typical Clay. So full of himself. He's always flirty but has amped it up since I moved to the ranch permanently.

Clay grew up on the reservation, but his family had known mine for years. He started working for my Uncle Nash as a pimply-faced middle schooler and never left. When he graduated from high school two years ago, he began working here full time. Clay was one of his best ranch hands Uncle Nash has ever had. By the time he's thirty, he'll be running the ranch's day-to-day affairs.

The guy was also a hard worker and built like a Native American Hercules. Meaning, he was strong, ridiculously handsome, and annoyingly very aware of that fact. He drew a ton of attention anywhere we went.

Clay picked a stray string off his leather glove. "Before Honey's grooming session, how about we go on a quick trail ride? It's a beautiful day, and you—"

"Yes."

"Wow, that was fast. Who are you? Usually, I gotta coax you into doing anything fun on the clock."

"I guess it's the new me."

"Well, I like this new you." He smirked, his dimples appearing. I quickly glanced away, getting too focused on whatever was stuck in this brush. *Geez, he really is good-looking.*

We saddled the horses and started up the trail at the ranch's backside. The sun was blistering, but I welcomed how the warmth felt on my skin. On my soul. I had to give credit to Clay for riding beside me silently, allowing this trip to be what it was. A time to be one with our horses and the earth. The only sounds were hooves against the ground and the occasional soaring hawk.

Suddenly, Clay whooped loudly, and his horse, Raven, took off. He glanced back with the toothiest grin and an unspoken challenge. I accepted as I signaled Honey to gallop. She took off down the trail, following the kicked-up dust from Raven. I smiled too widely and dirt peppered my mouth. I closed my lips, leaning forward onto the saddle horn to help my momentum.

I grasped the reins tighter, encouraging Honey to close the gap. Knowing her? She easily could. Clay kept looking back, trying to gauge our distance and keep his comfortable lead. He was howling with excitement, and it made me giggle at his boyish charm. I liked this side of Clay.

The fresh air, nature, and my horse brought me so much joy, I realized. I was made for ranch life. It's where I wanted to be for the foreseeable future, and I'm ready for that now. No more distractions from the past. I wanted to move forward. I needed to move forward.

And that starts with not going back.

Chapter 16

...further from the truth.

Shane

THE DAYS THAT followed were a double-edged sword. After my poor performance, it was nice to recover between games. Unfortunately, Mom insisted on visiting a million tourist traps we'd never experienced previously. She filled our time with visiting the Belém Tower, São Jorge Castle, Jerónimos Monastery, and the Lisbon Cathedral. We even squeezed in the Oceanário de Lisboa aquarium and the National Tile Museum. *As if I had ANY interest in the history of ceramic tiles.*

Then every night, Mateo had a new restaurant to share from his childhood. His, what seemed like a never-ending stream, of family members joined us at dinner each night to celebrate the happy couple. It was exhausting spending this much time with my mother, Mateo, and a bunch of strangers. Plus, the invisible pressure of answering her question to come home to visit.

When game day hit, it granted an easy enough excuse to bow out of another tourist site. I woke up early to practice drills and complete my daily meditative run. Beginning at a steady pace, I tried to clear any trepidation about breaking my mother's heart. They were leaving tomorrow, so I couldn't put off telling her I wasn't coming home this winter. Actually, I wasn't coming home ever.

With the decision made, why was I filled with so much dread? *This was a good thing, right? I get to stay here and live my dreams.* I shook the disquieting thoughts from my brain and pushed harder. My Steven knee, yes, I called it that now, screamed, but I nudged past the pain.

Finally returning to my apartment, the need to ice my joints became intense. I flopped onto the couch, glad that Paulo wasn't there to see me in this state of pain, worry, and shame. I was still embarrassed that he witnessed me passed out from a panic attack. *I'm such a fucking wuss.* I'm just glad he thought I had gotten drunk.

Later, right before the game, Mom and Mateo visited the locker room to wish me luck. I bounced left to right, psyching myself for the match but really filled with nervous energy—about the talk with my mom later.

"All set to go, sweetie?" Mom asked, decked out in my team colors again.

"Uh… yes," I forced myself to believe my own words.

"I'm so excited that we can see you play again before we head home. Good luck, honey. We'll meet you back here after!" The skin wrinkled in the creases of her eyes from her wide, excited grin. It crushed me.

"Thanks, Mom," I whispered, hugging her tightly and jogging back into the locker room. *How was I supposed to tell her?*

***

I had the best game of my career. My dribbling and passing were on point, and I finally got some points for my team. Despite pulling a yellow card after my drive for taunting, I finally felt like I had my groove back. It also put the team one goal ahead of our opponent at the halftime whistle.

"Boa, amigo!" Francisco said, slapping me on the back.

Paulo bear-hugged me from behind, lifting me off the ground. "Mano, he's right. You're on fire!"

Feeling euphoric from excitement, their praise re-energized me. I was born to play soccer, and now it has made my decision to stay in Lisbon so much easier. I had my purpose. Worry dissipated as I emerged for the second half, basking in the admiration of our cheering fans.

When the whistle blew, we executed an attack play that our coach had been drilling into us since I joined. The American in their back pocket. I waited on the right side of the field for Paulo to drive the ball forward, passing it to me as I sprinted for the end line.

I rushed toward the goal, keeping an eye on my flank this time for the Sport Lisboa e Benfica, (SL Benfica) defenseman. When suddenly, one appeared on my left. I hopped the ball up with my shin, quickly pivoting to avoid crashing into the defender behind me, and the goalkeeper who had rushed forward from the box. What hadn't I seen? Was the second defenseman. The same one that I had been yellow carded for earlier.

A sudden snap was deafening even with the cheering fans packed into the arena. As I lay on the pitch, the words *career-ending injury* rang through my head before anyone reached my broken body. I screamed bloody murder during their assessment and attempts to reassure me that everything would be alright. But I knew.

The fact that I no longer felt my *Steven knee* spoke volumes. I could feel that damn knee even when I was asleep. I didn't have to look at my femur to know it was bad. The gasps and quiet murmuring of the crowd were solidifying proof.

Despair seized my fragile spirit. This was the last time I would touch the pitch, hear the cheers, or smell the grassy field. The last time I would see the ball teeter at my toes as I ran toward the goal line, edging out opponents as I went. The last time I'd feel adrenaline surge my entire frame, with the desperate high I craved and never wanted to quit. It's over now.

What had even happened? I remembered the momentum paired with a quick pivot; I couldn't stop. The bastard defenseman had gone to slide tackle and intercept the ball but hit my shin instead. I felt the ligaments and tendons tear from the large bone protruding out of my thigh as I fell to the grassy field. The hammering in my body echoed throughout my head as it took the secondary brunt of the collision. I saw the red card held up by the referee for the defenseman's tackle, but it was of no solace to me now.

My eyelids were difficult to keep open, but before they closed completely, I recalled a story about a fellow player with a similar gruesome injury. He never returned to the game. In just one instant, I lost it all. An awkward twist of my *Steven knee* and the snap of my bone had ended my dreams. Right when my life had just begun.

The medics worked on stabilizing my leg and head as carefully as they could for what seemed like hours. As I went in and out of consciousness, my coach crouched next to me mumbling prayers as dozens of voices jumbled together from the crowd. Again, not a good sign. The medics finally got me onto a gurney, the movement making me writhe in pain.

That's when I heard her. My mother. She was screaming hysterically in the distance. As her screams grew louder, Paulo yelled to security guards to let her through the crowd. Mateo feverishly translated the information from the medic to my mother about my condition.

Mom was allowed to ride with me to the hospital, a slight comfort. She grasped my hand, bringing it to her mouth, and gently kissed my knuckles. "Is he awake? Shane? Honey?"

"I'm awake," I grunted.

"Oh, my baby." I hated that I made her worry. I groaned through my oxygen mask as the pain medication took hold. No words formed from my numb mouth, but my eyes slipped shut. Before succumbing to the dark, I heard her say, "Everything's going to be okay, Shane. You're going to be okay."

But that couldn't be further from the truth.

Kira

Today was a monumental day for me; the next step toward becoming a Therapeutic Riding Instructor involved working with a mentor. They would teach, observe, and sign off any required hours, including equine handling skills. Recently, I completed my CPR training and First Aid requirements, a major part of the curriculum.

"Uh oh, someone's nervous." Clay appeared out of nowhere.

"Why do you say that?" I retorted sharply.

"It's the *'butt crack of dawn'* as you always say, and you're already fussing over Honey."

"I want to make a good impression." I brushed Honey's already smooth mane almost maniacally.

"You mean you wanna be the teacher's pet."

"No, I want Honey fresh for whatever we're doing today." I jumped up to refill water and grabbed her a snack.

"You realize your mentor will probably just go over expectations and paperwork. You'll never get near a horse."

"Well then, I'll be ready for anything."

"Okay, teacher's pet," he taunted. I flipped him off as he sauntered out of the stable. *Ugh! Who the hell even looks that good rolling out of bed at five in the morning?* I scoffed, knowing I looked like the crypt keeper.

Since moving to the ranch, my temporary summer bedroom in my uncle's house had become permanent. The building was an old farmhouse with a modern addition on the back. The original front half had a typical den on the right-side entrance hallway and a stairwell leading to three bedrooms upstairs. One of the three, of course, being mine.

At the end of the hallway, there was a full bathroom on the left. The newest section of the house sat straight ahead. Back there was a large great room with sliding doors to the deck. It held the dining area, kitchen, and a sizeable living room. On the far side stood a massive rock fireplace from floor to ceiling as a focal piece. It was crafted from material found on the land. My aunt had painstakingly collected all the rocks during the renovation.

According to her, the old farmhouse kitchen was too basic and tiny. She envisioned a chef's kitchen in the space where you lived on one side and ate on the other side. She always said this addition would be the heart of the home, and she was right.

Finally presentable after my shower, I rushed downstairs to grab some food before my mentor session. In doing so, I unfortunately smacked directly into Clay. *How did I keep crashing into people?*

"Aagghh! I can't get rid of you this morning," I grumbled, nudging past him.

"You're welcome," he chuckled; I rolled my eyes.

"Why are you here?" I asked half-heartedly. Clay had a small room in the barracks, but you wouldn't know it with all the time he spent in the main house.

"I enjoy bothering you. It's fun," he laughed, which turned into a snort. I burst out laughing at him myself. "Oh yeah, yuck it up, teacher's pet." He teased, tickling me.

"Stoppp… Clayyy!" I breathlessly gasped as he continued, "I give!"

Clay immediately let go as I collapsed in his arms. His intense stare made me pause. He steadied me upright before snatching my cowboy hat off the floor. He placed it back on my head, tucking a strand of hair behind my ear. His unabashed gaze held me in place. My eyes darted down to his lips for merely a second when he flashed a cocky little smirk.

It was enough to break my trance and push him away. Reality had slapped me in the very red hue of my cheeks. I bolted, grabbing a muffin before bursting through the hand-carved wooden screen door.

My feet carried me so quickly that it felt like I was floating on a moving conveyor belt. I couldn't help but relive my embarrassment as the image of his smirk flashed across my brain. *What was happening?* I've never looked at him like that. *UGH! I didn't need this distraction today.*

"There she is. Kira! Come meet your mentor," Uncle Nash called me over as I entered the stables.

I wiped my sweaty brow, suddenly feeling little mushy clumps across my forehead. That's when I realized I was still holding a muffin that I had subsequently rubbed onto my skin.

"Dammit, Clay," I muttered under my breath. I threw it to the ground and tried my best to wipe the muffin off my face with the hem of my shirt.

"Uh, hello," I sputtered. "I'm Kira Bowman." I stuck my hand out to shake, but felt our palms stick together when she took mine. "Oh my gosh, I'm so sorry." I snatched my hand away to rub it on my jeans.

"No problem, Miss Bowman. My name is Misty Olson. I'm looking forward to working with you," she stated formally.

"I look forward to it too. Can I show you around the stables?" I asked.

"I would love that," Mrs. Olson answered before turning to my uncle. "Your ranch is beautiful, Nash."

"Thank you. I take great pride in this ranch's legacy, which was handed down by my ancestors. My beautiful wife was an incredible steward of our land for decades, rest her soul." He placed a hand on his chest.

"Well, it certainly shows."

Uncle Nash smiled. "Lead away, Kira," he gestured for me to guide us. On the way, we passed Clay, who was loading the truck full of fence-mending tools. The veins in his arms protruded as he flexed, his body glistening with sweat from the sun's heat. It made his skin shine a glossy bronze. My heart raced. *Get a grip, Kira. You're not interested in him.*

But that couldn't be further from the truth.

Chapter 17

But that's not...

Shane

THE RIDE TO the hospital felt endless. Every time I faded back into consciousness, Mom put on a brave face. But the unsteadiness of her voice gave her away. Once there, they quickly whisked me to the back of the emergency room.

As two doctors assessed the damage, a nurse immediately drew blood and started an IV with a bunch of fluids. While I've learned a fair share of Portuguese while living here, I couldn't make out any of the names. I flinched from the needle puncturing my skin, internally mocking myself. The absurdity of flinching from a tiny needle but not at the sight of my mangled leg?

The pain finally became distant, my eyelids drooping shut. Forced to rely on my hearing, once again, to help me gather my bearings. Chatter bounced throughout the room, obnoxious beeps drummed off the machines, and a voice boomed from the loudspeaker. Yet, it was my mother's heartbroken gasp that willed me awake.

I peeled my eyes open. Mom stood near the foot of my bed with the doctor and Mateo. I heard the words "broken," "blood," and "surgery" as Mateo quickly translated for my mom. He drew her close, gently rubbing her arm. My lips turned upward slightly, glad he was here and to support her. Mom only had

Kyle and me for all these years. It was nice to know she had someone reliable and kind who deserved her.

"Shane, honey. They said you'll need surgery immediately to fix your leg. These are the papers you need to sign for it," Mom gently shared. I felt like I should be anxious about this, but the pain meds felt like a heavy blanket over me. As if I were watching this happen at the back of a movie theater, my life playing on the big screen.

A nurse loomed over the bed with a clipboard. This time, Mateo informed me further, "I read the form. It gives your consent for the surgery. You just need to write your name here." He pointed to a line. I nodded, and the nurse held the clipboard closer, pen in hand. Carefully reaching so as not to tangle my tubing, I signed.

Mom kissed my forehead, her warmth surrounding me with a moment of comfort, like when she would kiss my injuries as a child. An odd melancholy drifted through me, longing for those easier, carefree days. The tears flowing down her cheeks grew steadier. I squeezed her hand, in reassurance, before they shuffled her aside.

When they wheeled me out of the room, I gave her a thumbs up. My last attempt at easing her distress. Mateo held her tightly as she weakly waved goodbye before dissolving into a puddle of anguish. I could still hear her forlorn cries as we continued down the corridor.

A shiver rippled through my frame while lying in the cold and sterile operating room. Glad for whatever narcotic running in my veins, as it did its job well. Although the initial injury brought the worst pain I had ever experienced, the realization that it ended my career was torture.

My expectations for the surgery were bleak, but I tried to cling to hope. I was a hard worker, and possibly after a year or two of rehab, I may play again. My *Steven knee* had never been the same since that day. So hopefully, this surgery could correct that too.

Bastard! Of course, it all ties back to him. How that knee failed me during a normal pivot during a driving play. Feeling the... ligaments and tendons...

snapping… making me lose control… crashing into the other players… sealing my fate. The grogginess grew heavier. It was too hard to think. *I wish… I wish I had… never met… Rob… Wren.*

I awoke with sweat dripping down my face. I reached up to wipe the salty stream from my brow, hand impeded by the forgotten tubing attached, giving me copious amounts of pain medication. My dream, now a nightmare, continued echoing through my mind, a wave of nausea overwhelming me. A retching spasm threatened to break free, overtaking the monotonous beeping of machines observing my vitals. The harder I tried to hold back the bile rising from my stomach, the quicker the sounds increased. Then, my desperate gasping finally matched the device's rhythm.

Rushing over, a nurse barked out orders in Portuguese to several other staff behind her. As one activated my bed to rise, another placed an oxygen mask over my nose and mouth. Almost involuntarily, I felt myself sucking in huge breaths, unable to slow it down. With wild eyes, I caught a nurse injecting some sort of viscous solution into my line that looked like the Karo syrup my mom would use to make pecan pie at Thanksgiving.

Suddenly gasping louder, a memory filled my head of that fateful Thanksgiving almost two years ago—my senior year in high school. The signs I overlooked for months about Kyle and Wren were all there. Finding them in a compromising position after Thanksgiving dinner never sat well with me, but I let it go. Then the next day, in NYC, they disappeared, leaving Kira and me alone together again. It became a habit of theirs. But I chose to believe their lies because it was easier than the truth.

Last year during Thanksgiving, I was here in Lisbon, granting me the perfect excuse not to come home. I extended that hiatus through the winter holidays following Paulo to Brazil. I think that's why Mom was pushing me to return home this winter, since I haven't been home since high school. But I guess that's a moot point. My heart pounded deep in my chest, knowing that returning to the States was now inevitable.

Living with my brother and my ex was difficult the first time around. Adjusting to Robin's new name took a lot of time itself. I was still unsure how to address her since Wren still felt unnatural on my tongue. Others seemed to use her two names interchangeably, and she answered to both. It made the situation more stressful and confusing. Dr. Collier had advised I offer myself grace with all the changes. But that was easier said than done.

Kira had been my touchstone as I navigated that new normal. She had been affected too, and we clicked—a natural bond between us. Finding our way through the dark and back into the light together. That shared experience may have hastened our relationship as a couple, but my feelings were genuine.

But her calling it a rebound? Those were her words, not mine. It's true that I left her abruptly when she broke up with me, but I thought it was the right thing to do. I agreed with her that she deserved better. So, when Kira told me to never see her again? That's what I did. I moved to Portugal after graduation and respected her wishes.

My breathing slowed. Merely thinking of the woman that I was still in love with starved off my panic. Through the oxygen mask, I watched the urgency among the staff disappear. With calm washing over me, the medication finally kicked in and weighed down my body. I could barely move my limbs.

Blinking slowly, I glanced down at my frame. I caught a glimpse of my broken and useless appendage, wrapped up tightly with a tube draining a gross, thick pink fluid. My eyes shut tight, trying to block the offending image from my brain. I became overwhelmed at how quickly my life changed. I thought the worst part of my life was behind me and that I could pursue my dreams. And for a while, I did.

But that's not my reality now.

Kira

The way Clay fixated his eyes on me in the kitchen was palpable. I never thought of him that way, but had I stayed one second longer, I think he would have kissed me. Though the real question was, *did I want him to?* My mind endlessly cycled through the image of Clay's muscles as he loaded the truck. It had my insides knotted every which kind of way.

It's not like I swore off men forever. I just swore off some men—the Whitmore Brothers, to be exact. Last I heard, Kyle and Wren were happy together, and Shane enjoyed his life in Portugal. I snickered, being able to see him actually married to his sport. Till death do they part.

To be honest, his drive and determination allured me. To set a goal, and achieve it, deserves recognition. Not many of us get to fulfill our dreams in one short lifetime, but he did. I admired him for that and hoped he—

"Kira?" Uncle Nash called out, startling me out of my reverie as I mucked out horse stalls.

"In here, Uncle Nash," I hollered back.

"Sorry to interrupt chores, but Clay called. Copper slipped out of the broken fence on the southwest corner. Can you ride out to corral him so Clay can finish mending the fence?"

"Sure, I'll finish up the stall and get Honey saddled right away."

"Thanks, Kira. That's a big help. All my other ranch hands are busy."

"Will do." I took any excuse to ride, especially during sunset when the Montana sky showed off its glorious colors.

Uncle Nash's ranch was like a living organism, steeped in Crow tradition and culture. Customs, stories, and kinship were tenets that my aunt felt strongly about. She was adamant our heritage be spread throughout the ranch, infusing floral and geometric designs that were sacred to our culture.

My aunt treated the staff as an extension of her own family and earned their unwavering loyalty. Most were day workers, with a couple of them being my distant cousins. But there were a few who lived in the barracks on the property, such as the Barn Manager and a Wrangler. These were no ordinary barracks, as they had private rooms with a shared bath/shower at the end of the building.

Clay was the only ranch hand who currently lived in the barracks. My aunt was very fond of Clay; he practically grew up here while his dad was our farrier until he passed away suddenly.

I finished cleaning the stall and grabbed Honey's saddle. She whinnied with excitement, knowing exactly what that meant. Once we were past the last outbuilding, I clicked my teeth, and Honey took off running. She galloped smoothly despite the rough and rocky terrain. My girl followed the pull of the reins without hesitation, whinnying with joy. A smile spread across my face; her mood was infectious.

The sun hung low on the horizon, washing the land in rich jewel tones of rose, carnelian, gold, and amethyst. My breath hitched at the sky's beauty; unable to believe this was my life now. It was so far from where I came from that I often worried it wouldn't happen. But here I was.

I caught Clay working in the distance near his truck. He gave me a little wave, and my heart skipped a beat. That moment felt like I was riding toward my future, finally leaving my past behind.

"Whoa, girl," I whispered as we approached. He flashed a huge grin. "What?" I questioned.

"Something's different. With you, I mean."

"I think you have a heatstroke. I'm just here to save your butt and to wrangle Copper."

"Save *my* butt? So, you've been thinking about my butt, then?"

Warmth filled my cheeks. "You wish."

"I do wish," he mumbled quietly. I hesitated a moment after that admission, trotting off quickly with a cloud of dust behind me. I scanned the property's open plains for Copper.

I needed a minute to gather my thoughts. *What are you so afraid of Kira? Clay's a good guy, and he's clearly interested.* Then again, he was arrogant and flirty with everyone. I made that mistake once before. Fell for the confident guy who turned everyone's head, only to be burned. I'm not sure I'm ready to jump into that kind of fire again.

Finding Copper, I slowed our approach to a casual stride so as to not spook him. Putting my lasso skills to use, I spun it low by my side, outside his line of sight. The loop circled Copper's head on the first try, and I pulled it tight as he resisted. I latched the rope to the saddle horn, and he unwillingly fell into line behind Honey.

We slowly trotted back to the fenced area where Clay had resumed working. I kept Honey and Copper tied together as I dismounted and looped the reins onto the truck's hitch. After adjusting my cowboy hat, I ambled over. The sun touched the horizon, daylight fading fast.

I picked up the fencing and stretched it as Clay followed up and attached it to the posts he had already reset. We worked in silence, but my mind battled over my next move. We finished the fence with the efficiency of a well-oiled team. Working together came naturally and effortlessly for us. The sun had dipped below the horizon by the time we stowed the tools back onto the truck. Clay drove cautiously with his headlights on while the horses and I followed.

At the ranch, we returned the horses to the stable. Clay hopped off Copper in a flash, rushing over to me as I was ready to dismount. He raised his toned arms up toward me, and I took his cue. I placed my hands firmly on his shoulders, swinging my leg over the saddle. He easily held me as my body slowly slid down the entirety of his until my boots touched the ground.

I gazed up at his handsome, tanned face, my hands still firmly planted on his shoulders. His grip slid to my hips and gently guided me toward him. The humming energy between us was intense, he leaned toward me. *This is it, Kira. Take a chance on your future,* I demanded.

My phone vibrated, deflating the steaming air between us. As I retreated without a second thought, his face was contorted in disappointment. I pulled out my phone, checking the screen. My heart immediately sank when I saw the contact's name. Kyle.

Blood drained from my face, Clay raising a brow. He knew me well enough to understand that this was important. A lump formed in my throat. Here I was, trying so hard to seize my future and leave the past behind.

But that's not my reality now.

Chapter 18

...them both.

Shane

MOM SLOWLY SHIFTED, floating between a conscious and unconscious state. She had been slumped in an uncomfortable wooden chair next to my bed with her neck crooked at an odd angle. I knew she'd pay for it later. Her resting face carried the burden of the day as she grimaced and twitched. Guilt rushed though me. Another tragic event to add to the ever-growing list. And now, I've let everyone down. My success professionally was our ticket to a better life. It meant Kyle could go to the college of his choice. It meant mom could finally travel. If only I had—

The beginning of my spiral quieted as I watched her stir. Even while I blamed myself, she still found a way to smile at me. "You're awake. How's the pain?" Mom asked.

"I'm okay, very little. Must be good drugs." *A big, fat lie.*

"Oh, that's such a relief. The surgery was longer than they had anticipated. I was worried about you. I'm glad the meds are helping."

"Yeah. I'm doing well." *More lies.*

Her phone buzzed. "Hold on a sec. I need to take this."

She hurried to the door, whispering into her cell. I assumed it was Mateo until I heard her say, "Mateo will pick you both up at the airport." *They're coming?* I heard a machine's beeping sound quicken and immediately took a deep breath. A nurse hurried to my bedside.

"In pain?" she asked in a thick Portuguese accent.

"Uh, maybe a little." I couldn't think of how to answer.

I heard Mom continue talking in the background. "Look, I've gotta go. See you soon." I inwardly groaned. First, I didn't want to see Wren and Kyle. Secondly, we didn't have the money to fly everyone to Europe. And third, why?

The nurse injected something into my IV and changed the bag holding the hideous pink fluid. Mom returned to my bedside, adjusted my blankets and held my hand. I didn't need it, but I knew she did. The nurse elevated the bed a little and slid the tray table over with a full glass of water.

"You drink water. Then food later. Okay?" she stated.

I nodded, and the second she left the room, I grilled Mom. "Why are they coming?" I could feel my eyelid involuntarily twitching.

"They're concerned."

"I don't want to see Kyle and Wren."

"Wren's not coming. It's just Kyle and Max." I wasn't sure what to think of that. Did she not want to see me, or did Mom ask her not to?

"Kyle's going to miss his freshman orientation."

"That's in two weeks. He'll make it back in time. Don't worry."

"Why are we wasting money having him fly out here? I'll be flying home in a few days." The word *home* caused a lump form in my throat.

Mom squeezed my hand tighter. "Shane. They're not discharging you in a few days. They're keeping you here at least two weeks to monitor your healing. This was a very serious injury. Your leg could swell or form blood clots if you fly too soon. And it also depends on…" she stopped talking abruptly.

"Depends on what?" My eyes widened as I jerked my hand from hers.

"There was a lot of damage, Shane. They've stabilized you for now, but they are unsure if it will be enough."

"Enough?" My world spun out of control. *Stabilized for now… So much damage… Unsure if it's enough. What did that even mean?*

"You have a lot of healing to do and… the hope is that someday… you'll be able to… walk again," she squeaked out, tears slipping from her bloodshot eyes.

I stopped breathing. I knew I had fucked up my knee badly enough to end my career, but to jeopardize my ability to walk? To run? That's all I know how to do. And now it was gone?

Unable to catch my breath this time, Mom yelled over for help. The nurse dashed over and secured an oxygen mask on my face. Furiously, I sucked in air as she injected another liquid into my tubing at my hand. My lids deadened rapidly, and I welcomed the dark escape from my reality.

Dreams and reality. It was a fine line and a delicate balance.

And I hated them both.

Kira

My hands trembled. I knew the only reason Kyle would ever call me was if it was something terrible. I could barely swipe to accept the call.

"Hello?" I answered, my voice shaking.

"Hi, Kira." Kyle's voice mirrored mine, forcing my thoughts to run wild.

"What's going on?"

"It's Shane."

"What about Shane?" I uttered, terrified to hear his answer.

"There was an accident and—"

"Is he alive?" Clay steadied me, placing his palm on my back. Honey nibbled on my shoulder, hearing the concern in my tone.

"Yes, but he needed surgery. It was bad. Like really bad. They're not sure if... he'll need a lot of time to learn to walk again. He has to stay in Lisbon for a couple of weeks before he can fly back to the States."

"Oh, my gosh," my voice whimpered.

"Max and I are flying to Lisbon tomorrow to be with my mom."

"Your poor mom," I said desperately. "She must be absolutely distraught."

"She is. But she's trying to be strong for Shane. I'm thankful Mateo is there with her too."

"How did it happen?" I bit my bottom lip. Do I really want to know?

"On the field. I guess he was making a play, and several players crashed into each other, and he went down. When the melee settled, it was clear he was losing a lot of blood. Mom saw it all. She's traumatized."

"I am so, so sorry, Kyle." I truly meant that from the bottom of my heart.

"I wasn't even sure if I should call you. I know you swore off any involvement with us Whitmore's but I—"

"No, I'm glad you called."

"I didn't think it was right for you to find out through social media or the news. You deserved to hear about it first."

"Thank you. I really do appreciate that." I was impressed with his maturity. His forethought to reach out to me despite our bumpy past was pretty self-aware. It showed a growth in empathy and responsibility that neither of us had when we dated. "Will you tell Shane, if he's willing to hear it, that I'm thinking of him and hoping for a fast recovery?"

"I will."

"And Kyle? Would you mind keeping me posted?"

"No, of course not. I'll text you when I get any news." Then after a notable pause, "Well, take care. Goodbye, Kira."

"Goodbye, Kyle."

I stood there, frozen in time. Tears slipped down my cheeks, and a sob finally broke free. Clay pulled me into a hug and held me tightly and silently.

Every time I was ready to let go of my past and move forward, the Whitmore brothers had a way of yanking me back in again. I knew this time it was out of their control, but that didn't lessen the anguish and heartache bubbling to the surface. I was on the other side of the country from Kyle, and half a world apart from Shane. Yet I couldn't seem to escape their pull. This news made me doubt all the hard work I'd done to carve out a future for myself. A future I deserved without interference from the past.

Dreams and reality. It was a fine line and a delicate balance.

And I hated them both.

Chapter 19

This was not how I...

Shane

I AWOKE FEELING like I had just done ten rounds in a boxing ring. My head throbbed, as if a hundred knives pierced my gray matter repeatedly. But my leg? My leg was worse. Painful muscle spasms in my thigh amplified the tightness of my swollen tissue, leading to an extreme stabbing sensation making any movement excruciating. I pushed the call button. Her entrance woke Mateo, who I hadn't realized was sitting in the chair next to my bed. I was glad Mom decided to rest at the hotel. She hadn't left my side for two days.

"In pain?" The nurse questioned.

"Yes. A lot. Like a lot, a lot." I didn't hold back since my mom wasn't in the room. I always tried to shield her from how much pain I was in. Well, the physical pain at least.

The nurse added medication that I hoped would allow for any type of relief. She mentioned the doctor would stop by soon as she hurried out of the room.

"Can I get you anything?" Mateo offered.

"Maybe some fresh, cold water. With ice. I'm dehydrated as hell."

"Sure. On it." When Mateo returned, he had someone with him. "Look who I found wandering the halls." Mateo handed me the water. I noticed a figure behind him as I took a large gulp.

"Hey, mano. Looking good," Paulo mocked, fist bumping my hand.

"Yeah. Feeling good too." I scoffed, my sarcasm thick. "How are the boys?"

"They all say *fique bem*, get well. But the hospital will only let one of us come see you right now." He rubbed the back of his neck, eyes scanning across the medical equipment. It felt good to see Paulo despite everything in that moment. I wondered if we had won that game. I'd have to grill him for details when life didn't suck.

"Well, thanks for coming. I appreciate it."

"When do you get out?" Paulo asked.

"In a couple of weeks, but I won't be able to walk for a long time." The words stung my tongue.

"Oh, amigo." I could hear his heart break in real time.

"Yeah. I'm fucked," I lamented.

"It will be okay. You are strong," Paulo encouraged.

"What have you been up to?" I asked.

He launched into a story about how Francisco got in some hot water the other night. "Not sure if you heard, but we won both our matches this week. The one… um, the game you had your, uh… and the next one." Paulo awkwardly cleared his throat, clearly unsure how to navigate the situation. "To celebrate we went to Spot Lisboa and Francisco had a few pints. He decided it was a good idea to leave our table to go flirt with a gal at the bar."

I knew he was trying to distract me from my situation, but I wasn't really listening. Mom had just entered the room.

"He found out that not only was she married, but she was married to the owner. Hah! Who did not take kindly to Francisco's attention towards his wife. They had words and well, long story short, he almost got us all banned for life!"

I watched Mom make a beeline for Mateo, talking to him and gesturing animatedly. She always talked with her hands when stressed.

"We finally convinced the man not to ban us once we told him we played for Sporting. Leave it to Francisco to pick the one girl that was totally off limits. But you know how he is when he sees a pretty girl…"

I tried to eavesdrop on Mom, catching only a few words. *Transfer, Lisbon office, airport*. That's all I needed to hear. She was transferring her work to the Lisbon office, meaning I would be here longer than she was willing to divulge. I cursed internally at my predicament. The fact that I turned everyone's lives upside down caused me to wince. I should have known once I heard that Kyle and Max were flying to Portugal. My anxiety swelled.

"You okay?" Paulo interrupted my sulking. I forgot that he had been talking. As I tried to respond, nothing came out except loud gasps.

"Shane?" my mom asked, alarmed. She rushed over to my bed, feeling my forehead. "He's burning up. Get a nurse," Mom hollered at Mateo, desperately slamming the call buttons. Mom secured the oxygen mask over my face as we waited for assistance. When the nurse finally appeared she immediately took my vitals and temperature. She stated that it was 104 degrees.

"What does that mean?" My mom fearfully probed.

"I'll get the doctor," the nurse answered.

"Hurry!" she bellowed, turning to Mateo in a panic. "I don't understand. I only left for a few hours. He was fine!"

Mateo rushed to her side. "It'll be okay, Kirstie."

I focused on my breathing, trying not to panic. Mateo spoke in Portuguese to Paulo, and I watched him hesitantly leave as the doctor charged in.

"He's having trouble breathing. High fever," Mom quickly explained, holding her fiancé's hand in a death grip.

Mateo took over. "He also mentioned that his knee was in severe pain, even with meds." I gawked at him, betrayed. First, sharing that information at all. And second, in front of my anxious mother.

I grasped the sheets on either side of my body, grimacing through my mask as the doctor assessed my leg, and the gross yellow tinged fluid that flowed freely from the incisions. He conferred with the nurse, the woman typing copious notes into her tablet. She removed the water by my side as Mateo placed his hand on my mom's shoulder.

"What? What's going on!?" Mom demanded, looking between Mateo and the doctor for answers.

"He has a severe infection. We need to operate right away otherwise it could turn into sepsis. That would be…" he paused, trying to find the right words in English, settling with a common description, "very bad."

"My poor baby," Mom cried, tears falling from her eyes.

"It'll be okay. He's strong and in expert hands," Mateo reassured.

Pulling the mask off my face, the shock halted my labored breathing. "Don't cry, Mom. Mateo's right. I'll be okay."

Though being honest, I wasn't sure I believed my words either. Just a couple of hours ago, my only problem was learning how to walk again. Now, that was the least of my worries. At this rate, I'd be lucky if I survived this horrible injury.

This was not how I thought my day would start.

Kira

I awoke, feeling like I had just done ten rounds in a boxing ring. My head throbbed, my entire body ached as if I had finished an intense workout. It all stemmed from the news about Shane. I stared at the dark ceiling, letting the light breeze flutter through my window to cool my rising stress. The last thing I wanted to do was start my daily chores, let alone leave bed. I was spent, both physically and emotionally.

My thoughts bounced from Shane to Clay, who was exactly what I needed last night. His quiet strength and support offered a new perspective on his personality. For all his bravado and ego, he was reassuring and sympathetic when he wanted to be.

I finally lugged myself from my room, using up almost every ounce of strength I had. I took a quick shower, opting not to wash my hair. No one would see it, I'd be tucking it under my hat, anyway. It was the middle of August, and the forecast predicted it to be hotter than Hades today.

It was still pre-dawn when I jogged downstairs to the kitchen, expecting to see Clay. He always raided our fridge, claiming that he was starving all the time. But he wasn't there. Deflated, I nibbled on my muffin and drank my orange juice at the kitchen table, waiting for Clay to pop in at any moment. He didn't.

I hoisted on my dusty boots and grabbed my cowboy hat. The ranch was still quiet and peaceful this time of day. The way I liked it. I made my way to the stable, pausing when I noticed a light on in Honey's stall. *Did I forget to turn that off last night?*

I quickened my pace to check on my girl and found Clay at her side, grooming her. He had his earbuds in, bouncing to the beat of his music. A small smile crept onto my face. I stood at the door watching him dance before Honey gave me away with a loud snort. Clay lifted his head and grinned his mischievous little cocky grin.

"Good morning," he chirped warmly, pulling his earbuds out.

"Morning, didn't have enough chores of your own?"

"Just being a nice guy."

"You? Secretly a nice guy? Who knew." I teased. His grin widened, making his dimples more pronounced.

Before I could stop myself, I strode over and kissed him. Clay pulled away swiftly, gauging my actions. Without any words, his eyes darkened, and he drew me to him. I tilted my head upward, my hat falling off my unwashed hair. Reaching up my arms to pull down his tall frame, Clay obliged my silent request and lifted me off my feet.

Our lips crashed into each other like waves breaking onto the shoreline. It was wave after wave of need. His tongue slipped into my mouth, and I accepted it willingly. His hands crawled over me, exploring with the ferocity of someone starving. My knees threatened to buckle. Had he not held me inches off the ground, I would have crumbled into a heap.

After a few moments of our passion, he slid me down his body until my feet touched the floor, never breaking that sacred kiss. I sensed his cravings grow with every moan, butterflies flitting wildly in my stomach. He walked me backwards until my back pressed against the stall wall. When he pulled his lips away, I raised my head above water to catch my breath. His mouth lingered down the side of my neck, sparing desperate kisses on my skin. A fight to savor the moment instead of burning through it.

Completely absorbed in each other, I mustered the audacity to reach my hands down to the back pockets of his jeans. He released a low, guttural groan, rushing to return his mouth to mine and playfully biting my bottom lip. He kissed me harder, and a moan of his name escaped my throat.

Frantic hands roamed my body; the kiss frenzied and passionate. He tangled his fingers in my hair, positioning my head how he wanted, while his other hand pulled in my waist. The intensity between us all-consuming.

A loud thud near the stable's entrance made me push Clay away. With two hands set firmly on his chest, we stood motionlessly, minds spinning about what came next. Honey whinnied through our tension, disrupting our inert state. The two of us hastily broke free from each other.

Clay picked up Honey's long-forgotten brush on the ground, returning to her groom. I threw my hat back on, tucking my hair under the brim as Uncle Nash entered the stall.

"Oh, hey you two. Just checking why there was a light on," Uncle Nash said.

"Good morning," Clay and I responded simultaneously, giving each other an awkward, frazzled expression. So much for playing it cool.

"We were… uh… just talking." I lied, not having an excuse as to why we were both in the stall together.

Clay interjected, "I was helping Kira with chores since she got up late."

"Whoa, whoa, whoa, wait a minute. What happened to your 'being a nice guy' and all?" I ribbed. He shot a cocky smirk at me.

Uncle Nash narrowed his eyes. "Well, I need your 'nice guy' fence-mending skills at the paddock right away. I want all the posts stabilized and checked. We have a large tour coming today, and everything needs to look its best."

"I'm on it, boss."

"Kira, remember I need you to do the therapy tour again, right at noon. So please, don't be late this time."

Warmth flushed my cheeks. "I won't. I promise." I assured my uncle as he walked out.

"Yeah, don't be late, Kira," Clay mocked.

"Shut up," I joked back.

With that smoldering side-grin of his, he strutted past me. "I'll see you later, teacher's pet." He whipped his face toward me enough to throw a little wink in my direction. What a cheeseball. I felt a grin creep across my face as I rolled my eyes. Clay sauntered out of Honey's stall and I exhaled deeply, filled to the brim with exhilaration and bliss.

This was not how I thought my day would start.

Chapter 20

Promises were...

Shane

MY EYELIDS REFUSED to open, anesthesia still wearing off. I wasn't sure if this was all a bad dream. With the unmistakable beeping of medical equipment and the smell of antiseptic and infection permeating the air, it slowly became obvious that I was awake. Blinking slowly, my vision adjusted, objects and people coming into focus. The tubing in my hand impeded my ability to rub the crust from my eyes, nausea suddenly rolling in waves. I let out a loud, woeful sigh. This was indeed reality.

"There you are, sweetie," Mom greeted, sitting in the chair next to my bed. "I'm so glad you're awake. How are you feeling?"

I tried to speak, but my voice felt gravelly from surgery. "Tired. Other than that, okay, I guess."

"Are you in any pain?"

"Oddly, no." I lifted my head to catch a glimpse of my leg when Mom grasped the side of my face.

"Kyle and Max are here. They got here during your... surgery and were here when the doctor talked to us after the... when everything was done. Can I bring them in to see you?" I furrowed my brow. Something was up.

"Uh, sure." Mateo opened the door and ushered them in. My interpretation of their pitiful expressions stiffened me.

"Hey there, bro," Kyle spoke first.

"Hey, bud," Max said next.

"Good to see you guys. It's been a… while."

"Yeah, you really know how to get our attention," Max joked.

"You know me. I love the limelight," I said, rolling my eyes. "But you guys didn't need to come. They said I could go home in a couple of weeks once my leg was stable enough."

Both Kyle and Max looked nervously toward Mom.

"What?" I asked, looking suspiciously between them. Silence hung in the air a few moments too long. Mom picked up my hand and squeezed it tightly. I hadn't noticed how pale she was or how sullen her eyes were until this very moment. "What's going on, Mom?" I repeated my question.

"The infection in your leg was worse than they thought. They cleaned out as much as possible in the first surgery and put you in an induced coma to heal for a couple of days. But it didn't work. The infection spread," her voice cracked. "They had to do another surgery and… and they had to amputate to save your life. I am so sorry, honey," she whimpered, tears flowing freely.

Bolting upright, adrenaline and horror coursed through me. I pulled the covers back to reveal my worst nightmare. My right leg was missing just above my *Steven knee.*

"My life is over," I groaned. I couldn't stop staring at the bandaged stump, my hands unknowingly shaking.

"Don't say that," Mom squeaked out, trying again to hold my hand, but I couldn't process the comfort.

"It's not over Shane," Kyle echoed. "They said you'll make a full recovery."

"RECOVERY? Recovery from what? Soccer was my life. Everything I worked so hard for is gone!" I screamed, making my mother recoil.

Kyle reached for me, but I batted him away. "Get the hell away from me! All of you, get away from me!"

A sharp pain in my chest made me gasp. Unable to catch my breath, I flailed about in the bed trying to somehow escape this nightmare. A nurse heard the commotion from the hallway, appearing before the group and injecting my IV with a syringe. My hands instinctively went to pull my tubing out, but I was stopped by a very muscular hospital attendant who had walked in with the nurse. He strapped my wrists to the bed, and I released an anguished scream. The nurse secured an oxygen mask on my face.

I tried breaking free with all my might, but it was no use. I hated the feeling of being helpless again, my body not wanting to give up against a different type of captor. I glanced over at my family with disdain for the position they put me in. All they could do was stand frozen, their mouths agape. Mom wept openly as Mateo held her close.

I thrashed, desperately trying to yell through my mask, but they ignored my pleas. I fought to keep my eyelids open, but they drew heavy. Mom leaned over me, splotchy from crying, and kissed my forehead. I gave her a loathsome stare.

"It's only to help you calm down. You'll be okay. I promise."

Drowsiness seeped into my entire being. My breathing regulated while the corners of my vision faded. Everything I dreamed of, worked so hard to accomplish in my life, was gone after one single mistake. I didn't want her empty promises.

Promises were a sham.

Kira

Clay and I did the *"will they or won't they"* dance all week. Which was sweet, but annoying at the same time. He gave me space, which I appreciated, since I was fraught with worry over Shane. But it still made me wonder if the boy was toying with me since the brothers had infiltrated my life again.

When Kyle called the second time, I had hoped for a good update. That Shane looked better than he expected and would come home to the States soon. Instead, Kyle brought the worst news imaginable. Shane's leg was amputated. *The word felt wrong on my tongue.* Shane's whole future depended on his legs and now… well, this result was something that never even crossed my mind. And my heart broke for him.

Kyle mentioned that when his mom broke the news, Shane didn't take it well. Understandably. Poor Kirstie. I had such sympathy for the whole family, if I'm honest. Much more than I thought I was capable of, despite the water under all our bridges. I cared for them deeply once, and I guess I realized that I still do. Despite everything.

Clay knew the Whitmore boys were a sore subject since last summer and gave me the space and time I needed to grieve. I didn't know he had this side of him, and I liked it.

"Hey there, teacher's pet," Clay called out, jogging over to me.

"Hi," I said cautiously.

"Did you call Shane yet?"

"No. Why would I?" I asked, taken aback.

Clay threw a pointed stare. "Because he still has a hold on you."

Does he? I thought. Clay always spoke his mind. "Is that why you haven't tried to k…" I abruptly dropped that line of questioning.

"Is that why I haven't what?"

"Never mind," I said shyly with a huff.

"No. I want to know," he questioned. Frustrated, I strode away. "Kira, hold up." Clay chased after me, catching my arm to stop me.

"It's embarrassing, stop!" I begged, trying to pull away.

He gently tugged me to him. "I haven't tried to kiss you because I was giving you space. I was waiting."

"Waiting?"

"I've always been waiting for you."

Breathlessly, I whispered his name, "Clay…"

He leaned down, pressing his lips to mine. Gentle but firm. He held me to his body, and instantly, we were like magnets, attracted to each other. I grasped his arms, his muscles flexing involuntarily under my touch. A longing rose through my gut, and I was thankful to feel it again. I haven't had that feeling in such a long time. Not since… Shane.

I suddenly pulled away. *Maybe Clay was right that Shane has a hold on me.* Clay looked at me with yearning. Panicked at this possible reality, I made an excuse to bolt. "I have to meet my mentor in a few minutes. I can't be late."

"Right." His tone sharp.

"Hey, I'll see you later?" I asked.

"Sure. Later." And he sulked away.

With a heavy heart, I lumbered to the main stable. I had hurt Clay, and it didn't feel good. I was being just like the Whitmore brothers; indecisiveness pulled me apart at the seams. I hated that feeling, and I had done the same thing to Clay.

In high school, I had everything planned for my future. Moving to Montana, working on my uncle's ranch, becoming an equine therapy instructor. Then the Whitmore brothers almost derailed my life. I liken the brothers to a harrowing roller coaster ride of highs and lows that I needed to get off. Moving to the ranch a couple of months ago, I thought I had left them behind. But they continued to mess everything up.

I needed to shake off their hold. I had promised myself I'd pursue the life I deserved, and maybe that included Clay. Unfortunately, I couldn't force my heart to follow promises my head deemed best.

Promises were a sham.

Chapter 21

I need...

Shane

I COULDN'T BELIEVE I caved. Mom badgered me for weeks to return to therapy since getting home around mid-November. I'd spent over two months in Portugal between the hospital and rehab until fully healed. The amputation alone precluded me from flying due to the risks of blood clots, and then further complications arose after that. I needed yet another surgery to repair the tissue covering my stump, further extending my time overseas.

During recovery, my compulsory sports insurance kicked in with my career-ending injury. While it made it possible for Kyle to continue college, I still felt like a massive burden. Both Mom and Mateo had rearranged their entire lives for me. They both temporarily transferred to the Lisbon office, allowing one of them to always be with me as a caretaker. It was suffocating.

Being back in the States had its own challenges. Our house wasn't designed for a wheelchair, and part of the living room became my daytime bedroom. Then at night, Mateo would help me upstairs to the room I once shared with my brother. It was humiliating to be dependent on others.

Soon, Wren and Kyle would be home for winter break. Another component of my growing stress level. I'm sure they meant well, but their constant offers to help at Thanksgiving made everything worse. They tiptoed around my injury when really, I just wanted to be treated normally. But I wasn't the same Shane. Not anymore.

Gnawing on my cuticles, I trained my eyes on the familiar wall clock in my therapist's office. Willing the seconds to tick by at warp speed, I sat in my wheelchair across from Dr. Collier. The powder-blue chair I usually occupied sat empty at my side. I wondered if the blue fabric was intentional. I had heard once that it was supposed to be a calming color. But as my heart thumped, waiting for my therapist's short yet loaded questions, I could confidently say that it wasn't.

"It's good to see you, Shane," Dr. Collier warmly greeted.

"Dr. Collier," I responded formally.

"I think the last time we saw each other was—"

"...when I had two legs?" I quipped.

She paused but then smiled warmly. "That's right. When you still had two legs. I remember now." My blood boiled. She was a coward for not taking the bait. I could hear the air leaving my lungs.

"Would you like some water, Shane?"

"No."

"How about some sour candy?" she asked, holding out a bowl of packaged Sour Patch Kids.

Perplexed by her offering, I answered sharply, "No!"

"Alright, let me know if you change—"

"Nothing? You're not going to address this? Ask me how I'm feeling about losing a leg? My career? My life?"

"Is that what you'd like me to ask you?"

"Fuck this. I don't have time for games. I knew I shouldn't have come here." I tried to unlock my wheels, hand slipping in my haste.

Sweat formed on my brow as I finally wheeled myself to the door. Reaching out for the handle, I discovered it opened inward. I cursed, maneuvering my wheelchair to sit parallel. But when I tried to open the door, I knocked it into the chair, not having enough space. My teeth clenched, continuing to try unsuccessfully as a prickling warmth flooded my body. With disdain, I furiously glanced at Dr. Collier, who hadn't moved. She infuriatingly took a sip of her tea.

"You're just going to sit there!?" I shouted.

"Do you want my help, Shane?"

"Aarrggh!" I roared; my chest heaved as a familiar gasping started. My anxiety attacks were commonplace now.

"Count with me, Shane. 1-2-3-4. 1-2-3-4. 1-2-3-4." Dr. Collier repeated in time with some symphony orchestra song that was now playing in the background. She called it box breathing, or some shit.

Fuming, I struggled to protest her directive, but only exasperated noises escaped my lungs. Abruptly, a cold pack was placed on my neck as Dr. Collier continued. "Shane, count with me. 1-2-3-4. 1-2-3-4."

Abandoning my objections, I counted through shaky breaths. It felt impossible at first to find the rhythm, but soon my voice matched Dr. Collier's. Ultimately, my breathing normalized, and Dr. Collier guided me back toward the blue chairs, handing me a bottle of water. I gulped it down as if I had returned from a desert isle.

She crouched next to my wheelchair, speaking softly. "I'm here for you, Shane. This is a safe place, and you don't have to hold back."

And that was it. The floodgates of tears immediately flowed. She had turned on a faucet that I couldn't turn off. Relief washed over me for the first time since my accident. "I'm so tired."

"I know." Dr. Collier handed me a tissue, gently squeezing my shoulder. Returning to her chair, she took another long sip of her drink. "While you're here in this office, nothing is off limits. You can talk about and share anything you want. Our time is non-judgmental and confidential." I nodded in acknowledgement. "All I ask is that you buy into therapy and the techniques you learn here. Practice them at home when feelings get big and see me once a week. Are you willing to try, Shane?"

Fighting my flight response, I quickly agreed to her conditions with a nod. I couldn't look up from staring at the water bottle in my hands. Every fiber of my being felt like it was screaming. Screaming one thing.

I need help.

Kira

It had been six months since I had moved to the ranch, and my family was visiting for the holidays. I pulled into the airport parking lot, excited to see my mom, dad, and brother. I wasn't homesick, but I was family-sick. Uncle Nash was family, and the ranch-hands were great, but it wasn't the same.

After our back-and-forth, Clay and I had finally made our relationship official. Uncle Nash wasn't keen at first, but he warmed up to us being a couple. Dad, on the other hand, would be a different story.

"Kira! My little sweetie!" Mom squealed, rushing out the security gate. She practically plowed over my little brother trying to see me.

"Hey, Mom. I missed you," I gasped as if she had lassoed a loose mare.

When she finally released me from her clutches, my brother gave me a quick and unenthusiastic hug. "Sup," he muttered.

"Hey, E."

"Don't call me that! I'm not a kid anymore," he griped.

"Sorry, Zachariah." I tried to correct my inadvertent blunder using his first name instead, but this only made him huff louder. He put his earbuds in, essentially ending our reunion.

"He goes by Zach now since starting high school. His middle name isn't cool anymore," Dad explained, pulling me into his warm embrace. "Kahée, my Kira."

"Hi, Dad. I really missed you and your hugs."

"I missed you, too. More than you know." I looked up at him, exchanging a warm smile when suddenly his demeanor changed. "Let's get on the road. I have a boy to interrogate at the ranch."

"Dad!" I hissed. But he ignored me, heading toward the baggage claim.

***

Turning Uncle Nash's truck onto the long drive toward the ranch, snowflakes fell on the windshield, partially obscuring my view. I twisted the knob to activate the wipers. As they swished, I realized that the only sounds in the truck cab were the heater and wheels crunching the finely packed driveway stone.

Had we been riding in silence this whole time? I wondered. I had been driving on autopilot, so worried about the grilling my father would give Clay that I hadn't noticed that no one was speaking. The awkward silence felt heavy, and I blurted a question that was meant to be asked in my head alone.

"Have you seen Shane around town since he got home from Portugal?" *Why did I ask that? I was thinking about Clay, so how did a question about Shane come out instead?*

My dad hesitated. "Um… not really. I heard he was back in town, but I haven't personally seen him."

Mom interjected, "It's such a shame what happened. Not only did he lose his leg, but he lost his career too. Poor boy." I winced. Shane would be furious if he knew he was being pitied.

Zach eagerly exclaimed, "I heard he never leaves the house, and Max's brother said he saw his stump and it's super gnarly and looks like a gross—"

"That's enough, Zach. You know better," Dad admonished.

Zach pouted in the back seat while my stomach curdled from his description of Shane's injury. Hesitantly, Dad asked, "Have you spoken with him?" My mother looked up, waiting for my answer.

"No, but I've been getting updates from Max and… Kyle."

"You're talking to Kyle?" he questioned.

"Not really. Well, sometimes."

"I see."

"What does that mean?" I asked defensively.

"Only acknowledging," Dad simply stated. *Ugh, how does he do that? Grate my nerves with two little words.*

We pulled up to the main house as my uncle burst through the front door. Dad hopped out of the truck as I pulled the seat forward for Mom and Zach. I glanced around the ranch for Clay, breathing an enormous sigh of relief when he was nowhere to be found.

"Hey there, old man," Dad teased Uncle Nash as they embraced.

"Yeah. Yeah. Yeah. You're not that far behind me, little brother," Uncle Nash quipped back. He sharply turned his attention to Mom. "Hello, Leah. You get more beautiful every time I see you," he greeted and hugged Mom tightly.

"You haven't changed a bit. Still a charmer," she gushed.

Uncle Nash pulled away, pecking Mom on the cheek when Zach caught his eye. "There he is. Earth, Wind, & Fire."

Zach rolled his eyes but held out his hand for Uncle Nash to shake. He knew better than to refuse, especially after the exchange with Dad in the truck.

"He goes by Zach now. The name Earth is too 'hippie' for him," Dad mocked, making air quotes.

"It's my middle name. Nobody calls Kira by her middle name. So, I don't want to either. It's weird." Zach grumbled.

Uncle Nash and my father exchanged a look I couldn't pin. "Well, it's good to see you again, Zach," Uncle Nash re-greeted my brother. Changing the subject, he motioned toward the house. "I'm sure it was a long trip. You'll want to get cleaned up. Supper is ready."

"First things first," Dad stated firmly. "Where's the boy?"

My heart sank through the ground. Like a burr on a blanket, Dad wouldn't let it go. He wasn't easy on either Kyle or Shane, so I worried about Clay. Plus, I'd been living in this nice little parent-free bubble while here on the ranch. Now, it was about to burst.

My neck itched, but clawing at it didn't quell my stress. Excitement about their visit quickly turned apprehensive. My family's mere presence was affecting me more than I thought it would, and now every fiber of my being was screaming. Screaming one thing.

I need help.

Chapter 22

...that simple.

Shane

MOM PICKED ME up from Dr. Collier's office. She drove me to my appointments and therapy sessions now. It's humiliating, but I couldn't do anything about it. Not that I had any interest in going anywhere. I'd rather curl up and disappear. The only reason I went today was to appease Mom. Despite Dr. Collier asking me to give it a try, I knew nothing would change.

"How was therapy?" Mom inquired.

"You can't ask me that."

"I don't mean for you to tell me what you talked about. I just meant, do you think it's helpful? Are you going back?"

"Yes, Mom. I'm going back." I sighed loudly.

"Because you want to or because I want you to?"

"I said I'll keep going. Isn't that enough?" I unintentionally barked. Her body jerked toward the steering wheel.

She was quiet as we slowed at a red traffic light. "Yes. It's enough."

Mom sniffled during the remaining ride home. The sound pierced my heart. *I made her cry... again.*

"I'm sorry, Mom. I didn't mean to snap at you."

"It's okay."

"It's not okay. I'll do better." She gave me a weary smile, then returned her focus to the road.

I meant it when I said I'd try, but I knew deep down that I wouldn't change. The phantom pain in my leg was nothing compared to what clawed at my heart. It's an ache that was always there, even when I forced a smile on my face.

As we pulled into the driveway, a pit formed in my stomach. Kyle's car sat by the curb, meaning he and Wren were home for winter break. A whole month crammed into our little house. I could feel a migraine starting already, pressure building at my temples.

I glanced over to see Mom wiping the remnants of her tears in the visor mirror. Mateo would be irritated with me for making her sad again, and she would cover for me like always. *I'm the worst son in the world.*

I reached for the door handle when it opened. "Hey, bro!" Kyle exclaimed.

"My wheelchair is in the trunk," I acquiesced. He jogged to the rear of the car on his two functioning and well-conditioned legs. A pang stabbed my heart. I haphazardly transferred into my chair, and Kyle offered to push me up the ramp. I accepted the help only because Dr. Collier's session had completely drained me.

Mateo greeted Mom warmly, pulling her into a loving hug. She returned the gesture, tucking her face into the crook of his neck as he held her tight. Seeing how happy he made her, it warmed my soul. I'm thankful they found each other, even if it made me envious. Mateo stayed over most nights and was a good buffer since returning home. The transition hadn't been easy on Mom. I hadn't been easy on Mom.

My eyes scanned the living room as we entered the house. They landed on Wren standing in the kitchen doorway. I chewed the inside of my cheek. When she was home last month for Thanksgiving, I wasn't very nice to her. Thanksgiving conjured up too many terrible memories, and the weight of my new normal made me lash out. I had nothing to be thankful for and made it well known. Truth be told, I was terrible to everyone.

But like Kyle, Wren welcomed me with a warm smile. "Hi, Shane."

"Hey," was all I could muster. Emotionally spent, I had nothing more to give and just wanted to wallow in my bed for the night. I couldn't fathom finding the energy to entertain family. I managed to squeeze out one question to cut through the awkward air between us. "How's Tanya?"

"She's been great. Busier than ever since the… well, since her private contracting business took off. She wanted me to tell you, 'Hi.'"

"Well, good for her. Glad the kidnapping and shooting incident worked out in her favor." I flinched as my sarcasm snuck out without thinking.

Mom interjected quickly, "Did you both get everything up to your rooms? Is there more in the car?"

"Got it all, Mom. We're good," Kyle answered.

"Perfect. So, how is everyone? Should I order food? What does everyone want?" Mom asked, ending my conversation with Wren.

***

After dinner, fatigue set in firmly. My bed called for my presence and usurped every thought. It took all my willpower to stay focused on conversations about college, work, and old high school friends. I sat numb in my chair, listening to the banter and stories. Everyone had a lot to share. Me, on the other hand, I had nothing. I was either here or at an appointment. The end.

As the night wore on, I continued to keep my eyes open and my mouth shut. I had promised Mom I'd do better, and this was it. Not mocking their stories and sitting here quietly. The migraine from earlier raged on, spreading between my temples. Squinting and blinking didn't assuage, and my irritation intensified.

Wren stood up from the couch, nodding for me to follow her to the kitchen. With little energy to protest, she guided me to the kitchen sink, where she then soaked a towel in hot water.

"Tilt your head back," she directed. I did as I was told, and she laid the towel on my forehead.

"Whoa!" I yelped, partially shaking it off. Wren readjusted the cloth, holding it in place for me.

"It'll cool quickly. Give it a sec." She was right. With the heat now tolerable, she explained her reason for the towel. "Keep your eyes closed while taking slow breaths. This will help your headache."

"How did you—"

"I get them too. Now and then. I know the signs, and you looked like you were in pain." *Boy, she hit the nail on the head.*

"Thank you," I said, closing my eyes to take a slow, deep breath.

"Of course. When the cloth cools, leave it on. The heat relaxes your muscles, and the cooling can reduce the pain. Then voilà! Headache gone."

You've got to love her enthusiasm. Hot then cold, and the pain will go. If only that strategy worked for all my pain. Heat and cold couldn't reach that deep.

But I wish it were that simple.

Kira

My face and ears burned ablaze. I knew my dad would grill Clay mercilessly if he managed to find him. Especially after the Whitmore brothers' debacle. Scratching my neck furiously caught my mother's eye just as Zach spoke, tugging on my dad's sleeve.

"Daaddd, I'm starving," Zach said, exasperated.

"You're always starving," Dad mocked.

Mom jumped in. "Levi, there will be plenty of time to harass Clay later. It's been a very long day. Zach's hungry. I'm hungry. Let's get settled and have something to eat," she reasoned.

"It won't take me lo—"

"Levi 'Gray Wolf' Bowman! It was not a suggestion." My brother and I flinched at her tone.

"Yes, dear," he acquiesced, following Uncle Nash into the house.

Mom gave me a little wink as she started up the front porch steps. Mom to the rescue. I let out a sigh of relief, hanging back to text Clay immediately. My head snapped behind me when I heard his phone ping in that direction. I watched as Clay hopped up into the back of the truck, shooting me a sly grin.

"What are you doing?" I asked, my smile stretching from ear to ear.

"Earning points," he said confidently, grabbing my family's luggage out of the truck bed. Huh. Shane used to say that. I clenched my jaw, not wanting myself to always immediately think of Shane. He just never seemed too far from my thoughts in any situation.

"How's it going with your family?" Clay asked as he approached. I showed him the claw marks on my skin. "That good, huh?"

"Yeah. That good." I sighed, shaking my head as I tucked my arms around myself. Clay strode past me with the bags and went right up the porch stairs. I followed him, quickly grabbing his arm. "Where are you going?"

"To dinner."

"Oh no, you're not." I grabbed his sleeve to stop him.

"Face fear or forever—"

"Seriously? You sound like my dad." I dramatically rolled my eyes.

"I'm not the little hellion he remembers running around the ranch all those years ago. I need to show him I'm all grown up and dating his daughter."

I slapped my hand to my forehead. "Well, I'm not ready."

"It'll be okay. I've got this." He pecked the tip of my nose and nodded toward the door. I reluctantly opened it for him as Clay carried their bags into the house. Heart pounding, I took one last deep breath and crossed the threshold after him.

***

Dinner was the epitome of ease and comfort. I had to shut my mouth a few times from the amazement at how well my dad and Clay got along. It was like they were long-lost buddies, talking in Crow, and joking with each other. I looked over at Mom several times in complete and utter disbelief. All she could do was shrug.

Then there was Zach. He ate dinner as if he was on death row, and this was his last meal. I've never seen someone consume that much food. The entire dinner felt like I was surrounded by a new family that I just met tonight. I knew Dad and Clay had interacted before today. Clay worked on the ranch every summer after school ended, but my dad hadn't seen him since his tween years.

Blood rushed to my cheeks thinking of how much he'd matured since I even met him. The sweat that glossed his skin as he worked, and the sexy little dimples of his smile. Don't even get me started on how he could fill a pair of jeans... I shook off my wandering, lustful thoughts—darting my eyes down to my plate before my boyfriend caught my gaze.

Even when Uncle Nash shared that Clay worked *and* lived full time on the ranch, the information didn't sway my father. The dad of my past would have made his opinions well known, especially when it came to who I dated. Kyle and

Shane were perfect examples of his preconceived judgment. But tonight? He was a father that I didn't recognize.

Could he have turned over a new leaf where he's willing to give Clay a chance? Or did he finally see me as a grown woman who could make her own choices without his interference? Nonetheless, deep down I had a sinking feeling that this version of Dad was all for show.

But I wish it were that simple.

Chapter 23

And there's nothing...

Shane

THE HOLIDAYS BLURRED past. For that, I was thankful. Mom kept trying to guilt me into joining family dinner, and I felt like I couldn't refuse. She had placed her life on hold to support me. Mom and Mateo both went part-time at work and declined any holiday festivities. It was nice to see him put my mom first, since I always made her put herself second.

Mindlessly, I scrolled through New Year's Eve coverage on tv while enduring "family time" downstairs. I tried to ignore the hushed conversations between the happy couples. But that was basically impossible when I was the main topic. My left eye twitched when I heard them changing plans so someone could be a caretaker tonight. I pulled out my phone and shot off a text to Max.

Hey max

Hey bud whats up

Got room for one more tonight

Hell yeah I do

But I need you to come get me

Be there in 10
Read 7:23PM

The weight on my chest lifted slightly as my anger cooled. I wheeled into the kitchen, interrupting their chatter. "Nobody has to babysit tonight. I'm going to Max's New Year's Eve party. He'll be here soon to pick me up."

They all sheepishly stared for a beat before Mom spoke up. "Shane, are you sure you're ready? You've barely been out of the house. Wren mentioned there were a lot of guests attending."

"I know. It's perfect. Sink or swim, right?" I joked.

"I guess," she answered hesitantly, unwrapping a leftover piece of Christmas chocolate while she contemplated.

"Stop changing your plans for me. Go out with your fiancé and have fun!"

"He's right, honey. You do deserve some fun," Mateo echoed.

"I don't know," she wavered, biting off a piece of chocolate.

"Kyle and Wren will be there, and of course, Max. Plenty of people watching my every move. I'll be fine."

"But what if—" Mom started.

"I have you on speed dial. Don't worry." She fidgeted with the foil wrapper.

Wren placed her hand on Kirstie's arm. "Kyle and I are picking up Sarah and Brody on the way to the party. So, Shane's right. There'll be plenty of people there if he needs anything."

My eyes flashed toward Wren, thankful for her support. She smiled warmly, taking Kyle's hand and guiding him out of the kitchen to get ready.

There was a loud knock at the front door. "That's Max. Gotta go," I said, wheeling toward the living room. Max strode into the house. After all these years he knew how to let himself in.

"Ready?" he asked, rubbing the cold out of his hands as he grinned widely.

"You have no idea how ready." I replied, grabbing my coat.

"Hi, Kirstie. Hey, Mateo. I'll take good care of him, promise!"

"You call for any reason, Max," Mom hollered pointedly.

"I will!" Max yelled over his shoulder, popping a wheelie with my chair over the threshold. Max always had my back.

We slid down the icy ramp; the biting wind stung my face. It was glorious. I had physically and emotionally checked out these past few weeks, but right now? I felt alive.

***

The party was packed, and I loved it. It felt like high school, where all my dreams were still intact. When my body was still intact. It was a much needed change from my current reality, and I sought to embrace it. Max and I immediately went to the kitchen to have our friendship shot. We had a ritual at the beginning of every party for as long as I could remember, and tonight was no different. Max filled our glasses with Fireball, and we clinked them together before gulping it down. Inevitably sloshing it everywhere. The cinnamon burned all the way, stoking a desire to make the most of this night.

As Max zipped in and out of the kitchen greeting guests, I reacquainted myself with my good friend *Jim Beam*. Feeling a pleasant buzz, I rolled my way to the living room where finally my brother, Brody, and the girls arrived. Wren and Sarah made a beeline for me.

"Hey there, handsome." Sarah flopped her arms around my neck, pressing her mouth to my ear. "Are you having fun?" Warmth spread across my skin from her proximity, but there was an odd shift in wooziness.

"I'd have more fun if I had another drink," I replied.

"Your wish is my command." And the little freckly firecracker skipped toward the kitchen. One redeeming quality about Sarah? She knew how to make a damn good drink. I leaned back, watching her walk away as a smirk slid across my face.

"How's it going?" Wren asked, kneeling next to me so we could talk at eye level. It was cool of her to get Kirstie off my back earlier.

"Good. Better once I get that drink I ordered."

"Make sure you pace yourself. It's been a while since you—"

"You don't have to care about me anymore." My nose scrunched, trying to look her in the eyes, but it was almost like she had a second set. *Is she wearing glasses?* "We're not together, remember?"

"Shane, I just meant—"

"Can't I have some fun without you killing my vibe? Go find your boyfriend and harass him." Wren took the hint and slinked away.

"Where's my damn drink?" I grunted.

Then, right on cue Sarah appeared. "Here you are, sweetie." I grabbed it from her, pounding it down in one go.

"Looks like I need a refill," I barked. Sarah took the glass and bopped back into the kitchen. I caught Wren staring in my direction; an involuntary sneer formed on my lips. She quickly turned. The look on her face? Oh, man. I released a loud, rumbling roar of laughter.

Sarah soon appeared with another drink in hand. "Here you go, honey."

I opened the back of my throat, downing that concoction in a single swig. Some of it spilled down my shirt. Sarah went to wipe it off, but I pulled her onto my lap. "I know you had a crush on me in school," I teased.

"Everyone knew that. E*xcept you, apparently*." She rolled her eyes.

"Do you still have a crush on me?" I asked, swaying in my chair.

"You're drunk."

"And you didn't answer my question." I placed my hand on her leg, fingers playfully sliding across the fabric of her tights.

She recoiled, leaping out of my lap. "Don't make me regret grabbing you that booze. Your chance is long gone and I'm done with you, Mr. Whitmore."

"You're done with me because I only have ONE leg?" I shouted, clutching her wrist to make my point.

"No, I'm done with you because you're being an asshole!" she yelped, pulling her arm away. Seemingly out of nowhere, Brody appeared.

"Lay off her, man. I will punch you, wheelchair or not," he threatened.

I threw my hands up. "Take it easy, bro. She was flirting with me like she always does. I have no idea why you stay with her."

He let out a low growl, balling his fists. Sarah looped her arm through his, tossing a bottle of water onto my lap. "Here, I suggest you drink it."

Sarah shot me a look of disgust, as the two went over toward Wren and Kyle. Wren looked either disappointed or appalled. *Was it something I said?* I thought mockingly.

I tossed the water onto the couch, watching the lovebirds tattle on me. Whatever. I returned to the kitchen to grab another round myself. Not knowing anyone, I drank alone. Another reminder of my stupid new reality.

Later, I tucked a few beers onto my lap before heading back to the living room. Kyle, Wren, Sarah, and Brody were all grabbing their coats to leave early. "Good fucking riddance," I muttered under my breath.

So much for plenty of people here to keep an eye on me, I chuckled. I opened a beer, using a bottle opener to cut into the side and shotgunning it quickly. Now we could get the party started.

"How you doing, man?" Max asked, crouching in front of me.

"Fannntaastic," I responded through a flurry of hiccups. He laughed.

"Okay, buddy." He patted me on the shoulder and went over to another group to check in. Since I didn't recognize anyone, I remained in my wheelchair of despair and popped open another can. *Party of one, please.*

The room spun, and I instinctively grabbed the chair's arm to steady myself. After a couple more beers, my attention was drawn to the countdown on a big flatscreen that everyone crowded around. Max came over to hand me a glass of champagne before filling guests' cups.

The final few ticks of the clock brought the end of this miserable year. Everyone raised their glasses to cheer. Revelers hugged and kissed the special person in their life all around me. As I watched this unfold, I slowly lowered my arm. Realization hit me hard. It was a new year, yet there was no future for me. I had nothing. My life would never be the same. I would never be the same.

And there's nothing I could do about it.

Kira

The holidays blurred past. Having my family here wasn't as bad as I had anticipated, especially when it came to Clay. Dad's support of my relationship certainly eased my anxiety. With that resolved, I could concentrate on my ranch work. Although it was winter, we still had a few clients who used our indoor training arena. I was happy I got to show my parents how essential this program was to helping people of all walks of life.

It was New Year's Eve, and with my family being here, we continued our tradition of playing board games all night. Clay fit right in, and Uncle Nash had plenty of games to choose from. We were halfway through a cutthroat game of Monopoly when our snacks ran low. With two hours left before midnight, Clay and I wandered into the kitchen to grab more.

My phone buzzed in my back pocket, and I couldn't help my grin. I pulled out my cell, knowing it was Max since it was already midnight on the East Coast. I started to shake when a different name appeared on my screen.

Shane Whitemore.

Clay froze mid-potato chip bite when he noticed my panic.

"Shane?" I warbled out after managing to answer. I hadn't spoken a word to him since our breakup. Why was he calling now?

"Hey Kirraa. Appy neeww yeerr," he slurred.

My shoulders dropped, brows furrowing as I leaned against the countertop. "Are... you okay?" I stole a confused look at Clay as he tilted his head.

"Finer. Than-n. Frog-gg hair, baby," he stuttered through hiccups.

"Are you drunk?" I asked next, shaking my head.

"Yup."

"Where are you?"

"Aatt a parrttyy." A party? Looked like Zach's report about him not leaving the house was wrong.

"Are you with someone?" I asked next, but he didn't answer. "Shane? Shane?" As my voice grew louder each time I said his name, I felt Clay's steady hand on my shoulder.

"Sheesh. Chill. Was chugging mmyy derink."

"I think you've had enough."

"OK, Mom. Can't a one-ne legged, washed up, futbolleer have somme fuuun? It's a new-ew year Kir-ra and I'm celebrat-ing that I have noth-wing to lookk forw-ard to." His hiccups were getting worse. *How much did he consume?*

"That's not true. You have friends and family and—"

"I. Havve. Nowthingg. Kirrwa Sky!"

"Stop saying that!" I yelled back, resisting the urge to throw my phone.

"NO! You stowp it! I ha-ve no legg. No fut-baall! It's all oo-ver. My li-fe is fu-cckk-ing oo-ver. I juus-st waant it all..." Then silence.

Alarmed, I shouted his name. "Shane?!"

Faintly he whispered, "Kirraa Skky, I'mm so soorryy. I wisshh... goodbye."

And the line went dead.

Tears streaked down my face as a small sob escaped. Clay rubbed my shoulder, definitely hearing the latter half of our screaming match. "Hey, hey, hey what's going on?"

"Shane called."

Clay let out a low hum of acknowledgement. "I heard that much. But what happened, Kira?"

"He's drunk, but I think he's in trouble." I ran the conversation through my head again.

"Trouble, how?"

"I don't know. He seemed so lost... er, hopeless. Saying that he had nothing left. No future. Nothing. Clay. I've never heard him sound like that before and I'm afraid."

Dad suddenly interjected, "Where is he, Kira?" I looked behind me, not realizing my shouts had been heard by the others in the house.

"I'm not sure. Kyle said he never leaves the house. But Shane mentioned he was at a party."

"You call Kyle, and I'll phone Kirstie."

"You're calling his mom?" *Shane would be furious.*

"Yes. If he's in trouble, then she needs to know. I would want to know if someone was worried about you." I couldn't help but feel like I had betrayed Shane as my dad tapped on his phone. I sighed deeply as I called Shane's brother. Kyle answered almost immediately.

"Kira? Um, Happy New Ye—"

"Are you with Shane?" I interrupted. Something in my gut told me time was of the essence.

"No, why?" Kyle asked.

"I think he might be in trouble."

Kyle grumbled. "What do you mean he's in trouble?"

"He just drunkenly called me and didn't sound good. He was slurring and talking about having nothing left. That his life was over. I've never heard him sound so defeated, Kyle." I tried to stop my voice from trembling, pacing between the kitchen and hallway.

"He's at Max's party still. Wren and I left there a little while ago to watch the fireworks at the overlook. I'll call Max."

"No, I'll call Max. Get back and check on him."

"I'm on it," he said without hesitation as we both hung up.

I tried to steady myself while Clay came over to embrace me. The pressure of his touch was the only thing keeping me out of fight-or-flight. I heard my dad in the background talking calmly to Kirstie, but I knew this was a conversation she dreaded having.

I dialed Max, but when the call went to voicemail, my panic swelled. I called him back immediately.

Max answered out of breath. "Shane's okay. I got him, Kira."

"How did you know I was calling about Shane?"

"I saw him slump over in his chair and drop his phone. When I was helping him sit upright, he kept blabbering about you. That he called you. And talked to you. And that he still… Oh, shit. His mom is calling. Gotta go." And he hung up. I looked over at Dad, who was no longer on the call with Kirstie.

"What did Kirstie say?" I asked, slipping my cell back into my pocket.

"She was upset, of course. It's always hard to see your child struggling. Did you get a hold of Kyle?"

"Yeah, I got ahold of Max too. He's with Shane."

"Good, Kirstie said she was on her way there now. That's all we can do. She'll get him the help he needs. Don't worry," Dad reassured.

Sitting idly by was not how I operated. Not being able to help tugged at every fiber of my being. Plus, I couldn't shake the nagging feeling that this was the tip of the Shane iceberg.

And there's nothing I could do about it.

Chapter 24

But it was only...

Shane

MY NECK WAS stiff, yet my body moved like jelly. I'd lost control of my remaining limbs, helplessly dangling as Max hoisted me upright. He grunted while speaking on the phone. My ears perked up. *Did I hear him say Kira? My Kira?* I tried grabbing it from him, but my arms refused to cooperate.

"Le-et mee twalk to heerr," I demanded.

"Shhh, it's your mom." *My mom? Why was she with Kira?* Fuzziness settled across my vision. I lazily swatted for his phone again, but Max deftly batted me away. Frustrated, I tried a third time, but Max hung up. I wanted to yell at him for hanging up on Kira, but my tongue felt numb. I groaned in defeat.

"Okay, buddy. Let's get you upstairs so you can sleep this off." Max scooped me out of my chair, taking me to his room. I wanted to resist, but the numbing sensation had spread. He laid me on his bed instead of my usual blow-up mattress. The covers restricted any objection, and I succumbed to the dark.

The next morning, I looked over at Max sleeping on the floor, his snoring had stirred me awake. I still felt discombobulated as the jackhammering in my head reverberated through my body.

"Hey!" I shouted, tossing a pillow at his face. "Max!"

"Whaatt?" he responded groggily, pushing the pillow away.

"What the hell, man?" I gestured to his bed. "I don't need to be babied."

"Last night proved otherwise," he countered, voice gravelly.

I watched him rub his eyes. "You're overreacting. I just got a little drunk."

"A little drunk? You had the entire country worried about you."

"That's an exaggeration," I replied through clenched teeth.

"Is it?" Max sat up. "Because last night, Kira called me from the state of Montana. Montana, Shane! Worried sick."

"Kira?" *That was really her on the phone?*

"Yeah. You don't remember drunk dialing her? Telling her you had nothing to live for? She freaked out, dude. Your mom, too. Do you understand how difficult it was for me to convince her to let you stay? I had to swear on my dead halmeoni I'd watch you all night. So, I don't want to hear it, man."

I leaned forward, head in my hands. "I was blowing off steam. That's all."

"Yeah, well, your little pity party almost landed you in the hospital either to get your stomach pumped or placed on an involuntary hold."

I rubbed my temples, trying to conjure any memories of last night. Still unable to remember any of the chaos I unleashed remorse finally settled in. "I'm sorry I freaked everyone out."

"And?" Max prodded.

"And...?" I echoed, unsure of what he wanted.

He motioned to himself, waving a hand across his face. "Thank you, Max, for..." he started with a glare.

"Thank you, Max, for... convincing my mother not to have me committed."

"You owe me big time, Shane." His words lacked their usual playful tone.

"Noted."

***

The next few weeks were rough for everyone. Mom had me on complete lockdown. To be honest, that was fine with me. I barely left my room as it was, let alone the house. And now that Wren and Kyle had returned to school, I had the room to myself. Just the way I liked it.

My phone buzzed on my nightstand. Lifting my hand out from under the covers, I checked to see who had texted me. It was Max again. He didn't know when to give up. I get that he meant well, but I didn't have it in me to go out into the world. I'd tried that already, and it had been a shitshow.

I rolled over, pulling the covers over my head again, when I heard the bedroom door quietly creak open.

"Shane? Are you awake?" Mom whispered. I remained frozen, hoping she would take the hint. "Dr. Collier said she has an opening this afternoon. I can take you if you'd like?"

I rolled my eyes. That was the last thing I wanted to do. I didn't want to talk about my feelings, or losing my leg, or having no future. I didn't want to talk about how I scared everyone on New Year's. I didn't want to talk at all. I lay as still as possible until I heard the bedroom door close.

Finally releasing a breath, I squeezed my eyes shut. I needed to quiet my inner monologue of despair, shame, and guilt. And the fastest way to do that was to sleep. Sleep had become my new best friend. My solace.

But it was only temporary.

Kira

The next few weeks passed in slow motion. My family flew back home a couple of days after New Year's. I wasn't prepared for the deep ache in my chest when they left. I thought it would be a relief to see them go. To be back on my own. Do my own thing. But it was the opposite.

Clay and I silently groomed a few horses before another therapy session later that day, which left me to my thoughts. My sullen mood had been affecting my daily life. My focus, my work, and my relationship with Clay. I felt powerless to stop it. I knew Clay was trying to understand my feelings, but it always led to arguments centered around Shane.

I tried to convey to Clay how the emotional weight of Shane's accident was so much more burdensome than the physical. How Shane's ambition was tightly woven into the fabric of his brain, heart, and soul that losing it became devastating. How his drive made him the person he was as a son, brother, friend, and boyfriend. He lived and loved life like no other. He never gave up and made his dream come true.

But I could never properly find the right words to impart the depth of Shane's character to Clay. It only drove the wedge between us deeper. I had to admit to myself that Shane's drunken call on New Year's Eve had been terrifying. And although Max reassured me that Shane was being monitored, my gut told me that his phone call was a cry for help.

Since working full-time on the ranch, I'd seen therapy change people. I saw it every day in our program. Our clients used the tools learned here to heal and to fight to get their lives back. To find the light again and reclaim their stories...

"Oh my gosh!" I exclaimed out loud.

"What?" Clay asked, popping an earbud out of his ear.

"Shane needs to come here. To Spirit Ranch."

"Kira, you can't be serious..."

"Max said Shane was getting worse. He won't leave his room or see his therapist. And he's completely withdrawn from family and friends."

"If that's true, will being here change anything?"

"I don't know, but we have to do something."

"*WE d*on't have to do anything." He crossed his arms over his chest.

"Clay—"

"Kira, I get that he's your friend and that you care about him. But have you forgotten how he made you feel? Because I haven't. That summer after your junior prom, he hurt you badly. But I held my tongue. I supported you, and I listened. I even let you cry on my shoulder when all I wanted to do was find him in Portugal and pummel him. He's no good to you. And like you always say, you deserve better. Well, I'm that better."

His words gutted me. Everything he said was the truth, and it killed me that my suggestion pained him. The tightness in my throat held, making it nearly impossible to get out what I wanted to say. "I can't explain why, but I need to help." Clay's eyes grew sad, but he nodded in understanding. "Please, I don't want this decision to hurt you," I begged.

"That might be true, but..." He sighed, shaking his head before turning to walk away. I tried to call his name, but only silence formed in my dry mouth.

Standing alone, conflicting thoughts raced through my head. It felt excruciating, but not as agonizing as the bruise that formed on my heart. Any decision I made hurt somebody. But if I didn't try to help and something terrible happened, I couldn't forgive myself.

Despite the look on Clay's face, I already knew my decision. I nudged my forehead into Honey's, letting out a deep sigh. "What do you think, girl?" She nudged me back as I pulled out my phone to call my dad. I was only a few sentences in when the conversation headed downhill.

"I think Clay is right, Kira. This isn't a good idea." My Dad reasoned.

"He's struggling, Dad. Max said—"

"I know Max means well, honey, But Shane has support. He has Kirstie, Mateo, and the rest of his family. Plus, he has therapy—"

"He hasn't been going to ANY of his therapies," I interrupted.

"Kira, this isn't something you can fix. Nor is it your responsibility to try. They will get him the help he needs."

"But I'm the help he needs. I mean, horse therapy can help him, Dad. I've seen the most desperate souls find hope again. Shane can find hope too. Here."

My dad sighed loudly. "Kira, I hear you. I do. You have a kind soul and pure intentions... so, although I think this may be a completely misguided and futile endeavor, I'll speak to Kirstie."

"You will?" Although he couldn't see me, I jumped up and down.

"Yes, but don't hold your breath. I highly doubt she'll let him out of her sight. Don't get your hopes up."

"I won't. Thanks, Dad!"

"I only want what's best for you, Kira. I'm not totally convinced that this idea is the right decision. But I saw the horse therapy in action when I was there. I know you can work miracles. However, all the therapy in the world won't help Shane if he doesn't believe it will."

"I know."

"I'll talk to you soon. I love you, my sweet child."

"I love you too, Dad."

My dad was right. Either this plan would be the best thing for everyone involved, or the worst. But we wouldn't know until we tied. What I did understand was that having Shane at the ranch would put a bigger strain on my relationship with Clay.

But it was only temporary.

Chapter 25

Shane

THE DOORBELL RANG, waking me up from a dreamless sleep. Checking the time, I realized it was almost noon. Of what day? I wasn't sure. Days had been running together for weeks now. I propped myself up on my elbow, expecting to hear Max. Instead, there was the low baritone voice of Levi Bowman. I grabbed my phone, craning my neck to hear better.

Kira's name immediately stood out in the faint conversation Levi had with my mother. Hastily, with muscles burning from their lack of use, I hauled myself into my chair and wheeled to the top of the stairs. I locked the wheels, leaning precariously forward as I focused my hearing on the discussion below.

"I don't know, Levi. It's far away, and he's so fragile right now. We can't even get him to go to therapy here."

"I understand your reservations. I have a million myself."

"I'm surprised you're entertaining Kira's idea after what happened between the two of them."

"I balked at first, but I've seen how horse therapy can transform lives. When I was there a few weeks ago for the holidays, I witnessed firsthand as clients came to the ranch for their sessions. Also, Kira thinks the change of scenery could do him good. Montana is a wonder to behold. Every time I visit, it gets harder to leave."

"It sounds wonderful, but I'm not sure if it would be good for Shane and Kira to be thrown together again."

I couldn't see what they were doing, but I heard Mr. Bowman clear his throat. "Respectfully, I must admit that I tried to talk her out of it since she currently has a boyfriend on the ranch." The news jolted through my entire frame, and I wobbled in my chair. *There's a boyfriend?*

"She's in a relationship? Levi, this sounds all sorts of messy."

"I thought that too, but—"

The deafening ring of my phone startled me out of my melancholy. The volume seemed louder than a sonic boom, and I fumbled rapidly to silence it. In my haste, I knocked it onto the floor. Attempting to escape, I realized the wheels of my chair were still locked. I desperately tried to release them in a flustered panic before Mom discovered my eavesdropping.

"Shane?" Mom called. She entered the stairway and stopped short when her eyes locked with mine.

"Uh, yeah. Hey, Mom."

"Do you need help coming downstairs?" she asked cautiously.

"Uh, no. I was just going to the bathroom."

"The bathroom's behind you." Her eyebrow hitched upwards.

"I know. But I heard someone and was curious."

"Kira's dad, Levi, is here."

"Ah, so that's who that voice is." I exaggerated my nod, as if I didn't know.

"Do you want to come down and talk to him?"

"No, Mom. I haven't showered in days. I look like shit." I rolled my eyes.

"I'm sure he wouldn't mind. I can carry your wheelchair downstairs."

"Seriously? This is so embarrassing." I scoffed.

"Levi has a proposition for you. It was something Kira suggested. I think you should hear him out..." She paused abruptly, her brow furrowing. "Actually, let me rephrase that. Come down here and talk to him. I'm telling. Not asking," she demanded, her face steely.

I knew that look all too well and took heed. Standing slowly, Mom came up to get my chair. I steadied myself with the railing as she lugged it downstairs. My one-legged hop to descend the flight of stairs was still a haphazard mess. At the bottom, my chair was open and ready, but I chose to stand before Kira's dad instead.

"Sir," I greeted respectfully, sticking out my hand.

Levi shook it. "Shane. It's good to see you, son."

After an awkward beat, I remembered to speak. "Mom mentioned you wanted to talk?" Levi glanced at Mom, who nodded at him to proceed.

"As you're aware, Kira is working on my brother's ranch in the Equine Therapy program. She suggested you come out and try their curriculum. It's a multi-faceted approach to address challenges with both the body and the… uh, mind." *Levi delicately stated that last part while facing the one-legged mental case before him*, I thought flippantly.

"In Montana?" I questioned.

"Yes."

"With Kira?" I added, my tone more skeptical.

Levi swallowed hard. "Yes, with Kira. She thought the change of scenery would be a good thing. I can't disagree. The Montana sky alone will change you. I promise you that." I looked at Mom in disbelief, then back at Levi.

"I don't think we can afford something like that right now with my mom working part-time. But thank you for the offer," I said dismissively.

Mom interjected, "Levi said we can check our insurance coverage, and that his brother would discount the cost."

"So, a charity case," I grunted.

"Shane," Mom scolded.

Levi asserted, "Not charity. You'll be working your ass off there. Trust me. It won't be a free ride. My brother will see to that."

"Well, did you inform your brother that there's only seventy-five percent of me left that can still work?" I asked scornfully.

"He's aware. And that changes nothing." *The one time I try to lose points with Levi he ignores the bait.*

Cautiously, Mom spoke, "I think you should go."

"It's not up to you!" I snapped, heat flaring in my chest.

She narrowed her eyes. "No, it's not up to me. But being here isn't helping you either. And to be honest, I'm not sure if I can keep watching you wallow. Your situation sucks. It's not the life you saw for yourself. But what you're doing now isn't a life either. Lying in bed all day. Not seeing your friends. Doing nothing. The old Shane would kick your ass, and you know it."

"Geez, Mom. Thanks for the sympathy."

"Enough!" Her nostrils flared. "All I've ever done is give you sympathy. No more! I've put my life on hold, too. This doesn't just affect you. You've abandoned everyone and I'm done! I'm done coddling you, and I'm done waiting for you to fight. You need to fight Shane! For your family, for your friends and for yourself! Fight, Shane! FIGHT!" Mom puffed, her breath labored. She stormed out of the living room, leaving me with my mouth agape.

I looked over at Levi, whose expression mirrored mine. Then he declared, "I'll let Kira know you're coming to Montana."

With that ultimatum, the decision was made for me. I reeled over the quick turn of the conversation. *What the hell just happened? And how did I agree to go to Montana?* I had a horrible feeling in the pit of my stomach that this would be the worst decision ever.

But what if it wasn't?

Kira

Shock washed over my body in a wave. I hung up the phone with my dad. Shane had agreed to come to Montana. My heart thrashed against my ribs as if it were trying to escape. But was it excitement or trepidation? Honestly, I never expected him to say yes.

I know I had asked, but I didn't think it would actually happen. Inviting my two worlds to collide: Shane from my previous life as an innocuous high school girl and Clay here on the ranch, where I was a completely different woman—a confident equine specialist. It was quite a juxtaposition.

I threw on my heavy jacket to find Uncle Nash. I needed to tell him that Shane would indeed be coming and thank him for his generosity. Almost to the barn, I heard Clay call out my name.

"Kira," his voice seemed strangled. I whipped my head toward him. "Did he say yes?" I froze. The optimistic look on his face fell, and he walked away.

"Clay," I called out to him, but he jumped in the pickup truck and sped off. "Shit." I buried my guilty face in my palms.

"I guess that's my answer," Uncle Nash announced, walking toward me. I looked up at him, my remorse on full display. "Just give him some time. He'll come around. He always does when you're involved." That stung worse than the way Clay had looked at me.

Without thinking, I jogged into the stable and started tacking up Honey. She whinnied with excitement as I got her blanket and saddle securely into place. When I put my foot into the stirrup, she steadied her muscular body as I hoisted myself up. We trotted past the paddock and into the pasture, where I increased her speed to a gallop.

Until that moment, I hadn't noticed the bite of the winter air. I'd been so distracted by the news that all logic had abandoned me. I pulled up my thin paisley bandana to cover my mouth and nose, but it was futile against the wind whipping past. My stinging hands numbed, and I scolded myself for leaving my gloves behind.

I scoured the vast pasture for any sign of the truck, almost giving up my mission to find Clay. As I rounded the property's far side, I finally saw the pickup. I squeezed my legs around Honey's chest, determined to get to him as quickly as possible. As we approached, Honey whinnied loudly, and I tugged her reins sharply to halt our movement.

Clay spun to look when he heard the commotion. "Kira?" He jogged over.

"Clay!" I answered eagerly, dismounting my horse.

"What's wrong?"

"I needed to find you." My breath made small puffs of condensation.

"On your horse? Are you crazy? It's freezing out, Kira. You could've hurt yourself being exposed to this type of cold. And where are your gloves?" he asked, gently rubbing my hands.

"I… forgot them. I had to see you."

"I was coming back after I finished the fencing." He lifted my hands to his mouth, breathing warm air onto our interlaced fingers.

"This couldn't wait," I said breathlessly.

"What couldn't wait?"

I tugged my hands free, flung them around his neck, and brought his face to mine as I kissed him on the mouth. I could feel his hesitation at first, but he surrendered, kissing me fully. He pulled me in, embracing me in a way that left not one speck of space between our bodies. The wind howled, swirling about us, sending a shiver up my spine.

"You're freezing. Get in the truck," he directed. I did as he asked and hopped into the passenger side. He started up the loud, familiar roar and switched the heat on high. I held my red, shivering hands next to the vents.

"So, you rode all the way out here on a horse in near freezing temperatures just to kiss me?" he teased, his mouth quirking upward.

I looked at him with a raised brow. "You can wipe off your grin, Two Irons."

"I can't," he replied, his voice low and lustful. Electricity pulsed between us.

"Um…" my mind stayed flustered as I cleared my throat. "I wanted to say that I hadn't meant to upset you. My decision to bring Shane here for therapy isn't an easy one. But I really think he's in trouble. I'm scared for him, Clay."

"First off, I left because I had work to do. And second, you didn't really think I would be scared off that easily, did you? I mean, it's not ideal to have your ex at the ranch. And I may have needed a moment to process the news, but it doesn't change anything between us. At least, not for me."

"It doesn't change anything for me, either," I answered honestly.

"Good. Now slide over so I can warm you up better," he said slyly. Returning his grin, I scooched across the bench seat. Clay pulled me onto his lap so I could properly straddle him. He touched my cheek gently, sliding his hand to cup my chin as we looked into each other's eyes. He guided me closer, our lips meeting in a sweet embrace.

Slowly, his other hand wove behind my lower back to support me. My cowboy hat slipped off onto the floor, exposing my disheveled and tangled hair. I tried to tame the unruly mess, pulling my fingers through. Nothing helped, but it didn't matter. He wasn't paying attention to my hair, just my body on his.

The heat between us melted away any chill that settled in my bones. I leaned in, kissing him like it was the last time. Our heavy breaths fogged up the truck's windows like mist that hung over a pasture at dawn.

I rocked my hips forward in the throes of our make-out session. He moaned my name, tipping his head back as my kisses traced his neck, drifting toward his ear. A growl escaped his lips as he clutched at my backside. I could tell his desperation sent him to the edge and was taken aback when I felt warmth building inside myself. I grabbed the sides of his face and kissed him fervently.

Abruptly, he jerked away. His chest heaving as the veins in his neck popped. I was aroused, my eyes transfixed as I watched his blood pump through them. I returned to reality as the two of us caught our breath. Clay's eyes were piercing, dark, and intense.

"If we don't stop, poor Honey is gonna freeze," he teased, holding back a burning need.

I nodded in agreement, biting my bottom lip as I tried to ignore my own limits. Wrapping his strong arms around me, Clay pulled me against his chest. I slid my arms into his coat around his waist, tucking my head under his chin. I knew that this was where I wanted to be at this moment.

We held each other in the truck cab with only the sounds of our breathing and the heater filling the air. I had a wonderful feeling fluttering in my stomach, that this was the best decision ever.

But what if it wasn't?

Chapter 26

...over me.

Shane

AS THE PLANE made its final descent into Billings-Logan International Airport, I peered out my small window seat. I had to catch my breath at the sight. Levi was right, the skies alone in Montana were worth the trip. Pinks and oranges framed the sunset, giving way to the night-time blues and purples as they pushed through. An image of Kira in her pink-orange prom gown flickered through my mind, a smile spreading across my face.

The procedure for boarding wheelchair users wasn't easy. I had to relinquish my personal chair for theirs that fit down the aisle while mine went into the cargo hold. A staff member had to push me from the gate to my seat on the plane. Only then could I finally switch into my booked spot like a grown man. While it was policy, it didn't make me any less anxious that my personal chair would be damaged during the flight.

> *Hey mom just landed*
> *Hoping my wheelchair*
> *made it in one piece*
> **READ 5:02PM**

Thank you for texting me.
I'm sure it did. Call me when you
get to the ranch. Love you honey!

Deboarding was just as aggravating with all the transfers. Relief swept over me when I finally got back in my own chair again. I hadn't realized how much calmer I'd feel when it was returned to my possession. It took me a moment to adjust my sweatpants before I slipped on a hoodie. Then, I placed my arms through the holes in my backpack and wore it on my chest. Asking for directions to baggage claim, I rolled my way there.

My stomach flipped with anticipation the further I moved through the long terminal. Each section was filled with rows of black pleather seats all connected to one another. The smell of freshly baked pastries from a nearby café made my stomach rumble loudly, but I was too nervous to stop. Once at the baggage claim, I located a staff member to help carry my two bags to the lobby, where Kira and her uncle were waiting.

As we rounded the corner, I spotted her. My attention clung to the woman before me. Kira stood tall, calm, and composed. She smiled wide when we made eye contact. Her wavy chestnut hair peeked out from under her cowboy hat. Longer now, it fell just past her shoulders. Her aura of strong confidence seemed new. Or maybe it had always been there, and I never truly noticed. Either way, she was a breath of fresh air that I so desperately needed.

"Hello, Shane," she greeted. Her eyes held me like a deer in headlights. I felt my mouth turn dry under her gaze.

"I, um, hi, Kira Sk..." my tongue twisted, "You look so, uh, it's good to see you." A gentle smile formed, and my eyes darted to her lips momentarily.

"It's been a long time. I'm glad you decided to come." Hesitantly, she bent down and hugged me. I wasn't expecting her embrace, my arms trapped under her oddly. She squeezed, pressing my backpack into my trembling chest.

The man behind Kira cleared his throat. "In case anyone was wondering, I'm the uncle." His voice cut through the awkward reunion.

"Oh gosh, I'm sorry. Shane, this is my Uncle Nash. Uncle Nash, this is my, um... Shane. Shane Whitmore."

"I gathered that," he answered, extending his hand.

I gave a polite nod as we shook. "Hello, sir."

"Hello, Shane. Nash Bowman. Welcome to Montana." His handshake was exactly like Levi's. Strong and firm. "Are these all your bags? Just two?"

"Yes, sir."

He grabbed my luggage as we headed to the truck. The slushy snow made it nearly impossible to maneuver without help. Her uncle pushed me while Kira took my bags. I loathed needing assistance. Heat inched up my neck, regardless of the chill. Kira climbed into the back seat with my bags, and I hauled myself into the front. Her uncle carefully stowed my chair behind the driver's seat.

In the tight quarters of the truck, the small talk was clunky, but it passed the time and eased my nerves. The long, unpaved driveway leading to the ranch caused my stomach to lurch. Not from the jerky ride, but because reality was finally sinking in that I'd be living here for the foreseeable future.

The ranch was far larger than Levi portrayed. I hadn't realized the full scope of this place or why her uncle needed staff to live on-site. Now, I did. The sky slipped into darkness, the headlights bounced, casting eerie shadows onto the buildings. A short distance away, a myriad of lights brightly illuminated a large house and porch. The sea of brightness stuck out in the vast dark like a mirage. As we got closer, I could see that it was an older farmhouse with a porch that stretched across the entire width of the structure.

Movement caught my eye. The front door opened, and the outline of a man stepped onto the porch. Dread consumed me when the porch lights revealed a young, tanned, and muscular cowboy. He looked as if he had just walked off an old Western movie set.

Please don't be the boyfriend. Please don't be the boyfriend. Please don't—

"Looks like your boyfriend's waiting, Kira," her uncle said.

Oh, for fuck's sake! Of course it is, I inwardly groaned.

I slid out of the truck, leaning on one leg as I waited for Kira or her uncle to grab my wheelchair. But the *boyfriend* appeared with it instead.

"You must be Shane. I'm Clay Two Irons. Kira's boyfriend. It's good to meet ya," he stuck out his hand. I remained standing so I could look him in the eyes while he shook mine enthusiastically. "Welcome to Spirit Ranch! I've heard a lot about you."

Well, I haven't heard anything about you, I thought sarcastically. "Thanks."

"Hop in, I'll push you up the ramp. We just finished it yesterday. You're the first to use it," Clay boasted.

"I got it, bro. Thanks anyway," I sneered, wheeling toward the ramp myself. I glanced behind me to see him greet Kira with a kiss.

"Hey there, teacher's pet," the cowboy shmoozed.

"Hey, back." Her voice was like honey. I winced, remembering when that sweetness was directed at *me*.

I hastened to escape yet another happy couple, but the newly fallen snow made it impossible. No matter my effort, the wheels slipped.

"Hey, bro. I got you," Clay mocked, jogging over with his two functional legs.

"I don't need help," I snapped, trying fervently to roll up the incline.

"Let me—" he started.

"No!" I barked, pushing the wheels harder. My chair fishtailed as I lost control, spinning sideways and back to the bottom. "AAGGHH!"

Kira came over and placed her hand on mine, squeezing gently. She leaned in and her whispered breath tickled my skin. "It's okay. I'm here."

Immediately, I relented and allowed her to assist me. My body relaxed, anger fizzling away at those few words. But she could always do that. When we dated, she knew whether I needed to run, sit in silence, or be held. She was my refuge from the noise, the nightmares, and my mind. I'd forgotten how easily she made the world feel quiet.

That was her power over me.

Kira

I may have bitten off more than I could chew. Seeing Shane after all this time stirred feelings that I thought had long dissipated. Our reunion was familiar and awkward all rolled into one.

Uncle Nash turned the downstairs front den into a bedroom for Shane. It was on the first floor, and there was a full bath down the hall. We followed my uncle into the room as Clay brought in Shane's luggage.

"Welcome to your new home away from home," my uncle motioned around the room. This is where you'll be hanging your hat for the next several months."

"Thank you, sir," Shane replied.

"Clay and I cleared out some of the furniture, so you'd have space. Let me know if you need anything else to make it more comfortable."

"Thank you, sir."

"Now follow me." Uncle Nash led us out. "Here is your bathroom. I'm sorry it's not attached to your bedroom, but it's the best we could do."

"Thank you, sir."

"If you keep following me, this is the kitchen, dining, and great room. 'The heart of the home,' my beautiful wife used to say." Uncle Nash's voice cracked. He paused a beat, clearing his throat. "I'm sure you're famished from your travels. Let's sit and have some dinner."

We gathered at the dining table for some of my aunt's hearty chili and sourdough biscuits. Shane sat at the end of the table where there was more space, but he still had to stretch forward awkwardly to reach his bowl. The conversation during dinner stayed light, which I was thankful for. Seeing both Shane and Clay on either side of me made me squirm. The phrase "*have my cake and eat it too*" echoed in my mind.

Uncle Nash was his jovial self, entertaining us with stories and mishaps on the ranch over the years. Knowing my uncle, he did it to help take off the pressure on me.

"Shane, I want you to consider this house yours while you're here. Please use anything you like and rummage the kitchen whenever you get a hankering."

"Thank you, sir," Shane replied.

"It's Nash, son. Call me Nash."

"Yes, sir."

Uncle Nash paused, lips pressing into a thin line. "Well, it's getting late. Our days here on the ranch start early. We'll be up at 5:00 A.M., Shane. Is that too early for you?"

"No, sir."

"Okay. Just holler if you need anything."

"Yes, sir."

Uncle Nash nodded. "Goodnight, everyone." He gave a final wave before he headed upstairs to bed.

Clay and I cleared the table straightaway, like most nights. Out of the corner of my eye, I saw Shane roll down the hall. I let out a huge sigh.

"I think that went well. Don't you?" Clay asked.

"I guess, he was just so… quiet. He used to be full of life and confidence, but now he's just a shell. It's jarring." I rinsed the plate I was holding and handed it to Clay to dry.

"He only got here a few hours ago. Give him time to adjust." I tried to smile, acknowledging his comment, but I wasn't so sure. Even after the kidnapping, he still had a light in his eyes. A flicker of hope to make his dreams come true. But with that gone, all I saw was defeat.

"I'd better get back to the barracks. Tomorrow starts early," Clay said.

"Every day starts early," I mocked, rolling my eyes.

His mouth quirked upward, hands pulling me close. I stretched up on my tippy toes and placed my lips against his. He returned my kiss gently, a warm buzz spreading from my lips to my knees.

"Goodnight, teacher's pet," he said, tapping the tip of my nose. He sauntered down the hall and out the front door. I bit my bottom lip; eyes trained on him as he left. *Oh, how I loved the way he moved.*

I shook off the haze and finished cleaning the kitchen. After dimming the room, I headed to the stairway and noticed Shane's door slightly ajar, a beam of light peeking out.

I quietly knocked, slowly pushing the door open further. Shane sat on his bedside, shoulders slumped as he stared at the floor. Earlier, out of respect, I had avoided looking directly at his legs. But now, as his sweatpants hung lopsided, one leg intact and the other ending at the knee, a stark reminder of what he had lost.

When he didn't acknowledge me, I cautiously asked a question. "Do you need help?"

He didn't acknowledge me, didn't move his head. "No."

"Can I get you anything?"

There was a moment's pause, a silence of something unsaid. "No."

Maybe I should have given up, but something kept me rooted in place. "Should I leave?"

He lifted his head, finding my eyes. "No." The word was barely a whisper.

My heart fluttered, breath caught in my throat. His deep, intense stare made my body shudder. His beautiful blue eyes transported me right back to high school, mesmerizing me with memories of when we were *us*.

That was his power over me.

Chapter 27

And that...

Shane

KIRA AND I were interrupted as my phone rang. An intimate moment squandered by a helicoptering parent. I knew better than to decline my mother's call, so Kira excused herself. She paused by the doorframe, shooting me a small smile before gently closing the door behind her. To be honest, I wasn't sure why I had asked Kira to stay or what I would have even said. I frowned at Mom's impeccable timing as she bombarded me with questions about my trip.

"Sorry, Mom. Forgot to call." I threw my ball cap at the foot of the bed.

"That's okay. I took it as a good sign. Are you settled? How's the ranch? Are the skies as wonderous as Levi made it seem?"

"Yes, mom. Everything is wonderous," I rolled my eyes.

"Is something wrong?"

"No, I'm... just exhausted. It's been a long day." I ran my fingers through my matted hair.

"I know it has. Just a couple more questions, promise. I can't help but miss you already." I could hear her take a deep breath on the other end of the line. "So, what do you think of Nash?"

"He's exactly like Levi."

She paused. "Is... that a good thing?"

"I guess." *I would have thought they were twins if I didn't know otherwise.* Mom cleared her throat, and knowing her like I did, I could predict her next question. "Go ahead, ask."

"How did the reunion with Kira go?" I looked at where Kira Sky Bowman had been standing only a few moments ago, my expression falling further.

"Super great," I mocked. "Met the boyfriend too. He's a bona fide cowboy. So that's cool." My sarcasm was as thick as molasses.

"Shane—"

"It's fine, Mom. Look, I'm drained. Nash said the day starts super early so I need to get to bed."

"Okay, sweetie. Sleep well. I love you."

"Love you, too."

Sleep evaded me as I lay in this unfamiliar bed in a stranger's home. I contemplated my decision to come here, staring at the dark ceiling until a rooster crowed in the distance. Its call indicated the start of a new day. Unfortunately, the positive connotation of new beginnings was lost on me.

My mind wandered. Being close to Kira again took me back in time. Back to how easily our conversations used to flow with no forethought. Last night, I couldn't even conjure more than one word.

When we dated, our long-winded chats during our star walks covered everything from our earliest childhood recollections to our dreams for the future. Never in a million years did I ever think I would be part of her life as a client and nothing more. Bizarre how the most curated plan can transform into something unfathomable in the blink of an eye.

After fumbling around to switch on the nightstand lamp, I flung off the covers, exposing my reality. The sight of my bare leg made me flinch. I wasn't sure why I still looked, because it happened every time. In the lamp's warm glow, I spotted my suitcases sitting neatly next to the dresser across the room. Hastily, I plopped into my chair, on a mission for some clean clothes and to cover the offending appendage as quickly as possible.

Standing at the dresser, I dug through my suitcase for the deodorant and cologne I'd wrapped inside a hoodie. Once dressed, I inadvertently glanced at my image in the mirror. The reflection revealed a person I no longer recognized. A hollow man with dark, puffy circles under his eyes, and days-old scruff. *Was this how I looked to Kira?*

I rubbed at the dark circles as if they would somehow wipe away and threw on a ball cap to tame my unruly hair. Avoiding my reflection at all costs, I finished getting ready in the bathroom down the hall.

Using my phone light, I wheeled my way through the dark kitchen/dining area to the great room. I sat next to the sliding glass door overlooking a large deck and the ranch property. With no one stirring yet, I had a few moments to acclimate myself to my new surroundings.

It was quite dark outside with the tiniest sliver of light peeking out on the horizon. The moon and stars shone high in the sky like beacons of faraway worlds. I wondered if one of those worlds contained another Shane, an alternate Shane, who was happy and whole again in more ways than one.

Approaching footsteps pulled me out of my musing. I froze in place as Kira entered the kitchen, flicking on a small light in the room next to me. I couldn't help but watch her as she buzzed about.

She started brewing coffee and began breakfast with automated precision. The sweet aroma permeated the air, my stomach growling noisily. I held my gut as if I could halt its internal rumbling and salivated for a cup of hot caffeination.

While contemplating how to softly gain her attention, I accidentally backed my chair into a side table, knocking over a stack of books. They thudded onto the hardwood floor, the sound echoing loudly beneath the vaulted ceiling.

Kira yelped, turning towards the darkness where I sat cloaked, thankful she couldn't see the red of my face. "Who's there!?" she demanded.

"It's Shane."

She stumbled quickly towards my voice, turning on more lights. "What the hell are you doing sitting in the dark?"

"Watching the moon and stars. You know, since I had to be up at the butt crack of dawn."

She chuckled loudly. "I say that all the time, must have gotten it from you." I smiled at her realization.

She spun on her heels, returning to the kitchen. The sound of sizzling bacon forced a guttural growl from the pit of my stomach. "So… who do I have to kill to get some grub?" I teased in a poorly executed Southern accent.

Kira flashed a grin. "Well, dear sir, since Uncle Nash has a clear rule 'bout no killin', I guess you'll have to politely ask the very skilled and beautiful cook standing before you."

My grin stretched across my face. She quickly glanced away as she poured me a cup of coffee, a slight flush on her cheeks.

"Two creams?" she asked nonchalantly.

Still grinning, I replied, "Yup."

She busied herself as I rolled my chair to the table. Working effortlessly, she cooked two different kinds of eggs as the bacon finished on the griddle. Watching quietly, I let the memories wash over me from when she would make brunch at her parents' house.

As she placed a plate of food in front of me, I raised my eyebrow. "What's the matter?" Concern crossed her bronzed face.

"Nothing, just surprised you remembered."

"You're surprised I remembered you like three eggs over easy, runny but not too runny, with everything bagel seasoning sprinkled on top?"

I cocked my head. "Well, yeah."

"Just eat it." She smirked, rolling her eyes as my grin reappeared. She sat down across from me with her plate of scrambled eggs and squeezed a ridiculous amount of ketchup over them.

I gasped, recoiling in mock horror. "You still put that much ketchup over your whole plate?"

"Yes, why?"

"What are you, five years old?" I joked.

"Maybe," she said as she stuffed a huge bite of tomato-laden eggs into her mouth dramatically.

"Yup, definitely five years old."

"Shut up!" Her full mouth spurted bits of yellow and orange-tinged mess across the table in front of us. We both burst into laughter. The laughter startled me. I hadn't been able to genuinely do that in so long, I had almost forgotten what it felt like.

"What's so funny?" Clay sucked the air out of the room when he entered.

"Clay!" Kira exclaimed, jumping out of her seat toward him. "Good morning." She greeted, pecking him on the cheek.

The familiar scowl that often graced my face nowadays had returned. "I thought you stayed in the barracks on the far side of the ranch?" I asked, feeling prickly.

"Oh, I do. But Kira here makes me breakfast almost every morning. Well, when she's not running late," he mocked, tickling her side. She giggled, slipping away to prepare more food.

"And you just come and go whenever you want?" I asked rhetorically, stabbing my fork into my eggs.

"Yup."

"Super," I mumbled under my breath.

Clay looked very comfortable as he jumped in to help Kira. It was obvious they'd been together for a while; their movements seemed synchronized. So, what Clay had just said was true. They saw each other every morning. Green crept into the corners of my vision, making me lose my appetite.

The heaviness in my chest resumed as my heart dropped into the depths. I quietly rolled my chair to my room.

"Shane? Aren't you going to finish eating?" Kira called out.

Without looking, I hollered my response, "I'm not hungry anymore."

As I shut my bedroom door, I sat paralyzed. A million thoughts invaded my brain, completely overwhelming me. I don't know what I was thinking when I had "agreed" to come here.

Kira had a life here, and it didn't include me. It also didn't matter that we could reminisce about our past. Or that we could talk and joke together with ease. Those things were behind us. Kira needed to have the future she wanted and be with the person she deserved.

And that wasn't with me.

Kira

My gut reaction was to chase him. It was what I always did. I'm a fixer. I couldn't stand leaving things unresolved. Even if it broke my heart in the process. I thought I had *resolved* our issues when we broke up. When I moved away. When I started a new relationship. But seeing him yesterday was unsettling. It was like looking at a completely different Shane. He'd lost weight, grown out his hair, and wasn't clean-shaven. He was the direct opposite of the Shane I once lov... knew.

Making breakfast for him felt almost normal. He used to come to my house for Sunday brunch every week. My dad had protested, of course, that Sunday should be family day, but he relented, for me. I begged him to get to know Shane better. To see for himself that he was a good guy and wasn't like his brother. Until he was.

It had been two years since we'd last spent any real time together. Talked with each other. Laughed with each other. Being in such close proximity again had reopened old wounds and old joys.

Later, I headed to the barn to groom Honey. Intuitively, she knew my temperament and today was no exception. Honey let me brush her in silence and without fuss, allowing me time to center myself. That was my hope for Shane. That he could know inner peace again.

"Good afternoon, Kira!" Uncle Nash greeted.

"Good... afternoon," I responded, confused. *Where did the time go?*

"Where are the boys?"

"Clay is doing inventory, and Shane's in his room. Hiding, I guess. His mood flipped at breakfast. One minute he's fine, and then the next he shuts down."

"You know how therapy works. Time and space."

"I know. But it's hard." I fiddled with the braid I had just finished on Honey.

"Go in and try again. Show him the ranch. It'll keep you both busy. You talk while he observes. Takes the pressure off a bit."

"That's a great idea. He might consider that."

"Show him the essence of our land, our sky. Let it fill his soul. As my lovely Catori used to say: **Quiet the world to heed your spirit.** She lived by this mantra. That's why we named this place Spirit Ranch."

My uncle was right. I've always been drawn to the power of our homestead. How it held your heart in its scenic hands and kept you close. I thought about the defeated boy hiding inside the farmhouse as my feet brought me toward him. If anything could break through Shane's protective shell, this would be it.

My wonderful aunt adored horses; they were her passion. In one moment, she could tame the wildest bronco. In the next, she would assist a sweet mare usher in new life. Her compassion was a wonder. In her youth, she was a professional barrel rider. So, when she married my uncle, running the ranch with him was a natural progression of her journey.

The ranch made a difference in her life after she was diagnosed. Near the end, only five summers ago, my uncle's unwavering care was both heartwarming and heart-wrenching at the same time. *I miss you, Aunt Tori.*

Knocking quietly, I called out to him, "Shane? May I come in?" I knocked harder, trying to cajole him into answering.

"Come in." Shane sat in his chair, doomscrolling through his phone. Like gently coaxing a skittish horse, I moved delicately and deliberately toward him.

"I wanted to see if you'd like to take a tour of the ranch with me AND... before you say no, you wouldn't have to talk. I'll be the tour guide you can mute at any time," I joked.

He finally looked up from his phone. His lips quirked up slightly, and I knew I had him. Grabbing his coat, I tossed it into his lap.

The mushy snow had nearly melted, the sun shining brightly, lending an invisible energy to my bones. As we traveled in the pickup across the rutted tracks, I launched into my best tour-guide narration, pointing out every living, or non-living, thing we came across. The vast expanse of the property took us hours to cover, and somewhere along the way, the old Shane began to emerge.

He suddenly interrupted my droning. "I never would've guessed this place was this huge. Your dad really underplayed it. Or… maybe I just assumed what a ranch looked like from watching old Western movies."

I glanced over, subtly observing him as he stared out the window. He hadn't spoken since we started the ride. "It's hard to convey until you see it in person. I used to lose myself out here for hours when I was younger. It's been in my family for generations and holds a very special place in my heart."

"I can see why," he said. "I think I felt something similar in Portugal, even though I hadn't been there before my training program. Ever since that summer I spent there, it's had my heart. The city, the mountains, and especially the ocean. Everything about it was perfect…" His voice trailed off.

I waited for a beat before adding, "Sometimes, when I look across the plains of the ranch, up to where the mountains meet the sky, it reminds me of an ocean. Like the land was so magical it would allow me to see the Pacific hundreds of miles away." I smiled at the memory.

"Well, I had the real thing. The azure blue at the surf's edge kept me sane during my training schedule. Sitting in the warm sand, tasting the salt on my lips, the briny air filling my lungs. It offered a calm I still can't fully explain. Then there was the city. The culture and architecture were off the charts. Its history alone was immense."

Shane let out a soft hum, looking out towards the mountains as he continued his story. I wondered if he was visualizing that they were the ocean in Portugal. "I often found myself visiting Belém Tower. It was built in the late 15th… No, 16th century? The place could transport you back in time. I'd imagine what it had felt like when ships sailed into the harbor on the River Tagus. The views had to take their breath away."

I didn't dare interrupt him as he reminisced about Portugal. I wanted him to reveal the last couple years, but only when he was ready. After a moment, he went on. "It surprised me how interested I became in the city's history. Especially since I basically slept through those classes in high school. But being there in person?" He shook his head. "Brought a whole new meaning. Walking the same streets, touching the same buildings as people from centuries ago. It transformed me, and I needed more."

I slowed the truck as a small group of mule deer passed in front of us. I had been listening so intently that I almost hadn't seen them. Shane leaned forward to get a better look. "I made it a point to visit as many places as I could when I had my days off. Every neighborhood had something different to offer. Seems like this place does too."

He snickered, resting back against the seat. "And I visited every pub, bar, and tavern I could find. Paulo and Francisco made sure the *American* got the real tour of Lisbon. They had been on the team, at least a year or two longer, and became my official drinking buddy tour guides. Some of the situations we all got ourselves into... well, let's just say the local Policia learned our names."

The way his voice warmed as he happily described the views and his friends sounded achingly familiar. I would be lying if I said I hadn't thought about him over the years or wondered what his life looked like in Portugal. Now, hearing him speak, it was clear he had found a place that held him the way this land held me. I listened, unwilling to miss a single word.

We pulled up to the main stable after our bumpy ride. Adrenaline coursed through me, excited to share this part of my life with Shane. Introducing him to Honey meant everything. She had such a positive effect on me, and I couldn't wait for Shane to experience that magic too.

I jumped out of the truck where the bitter cold blasted my cozy, warm body. A shiver danced down my spine, causing my frame to shudder. I lugged his chair from the truck bed, and he plunked down into the seat. A familiar whistle caught my attention, and I whipped my head in its direction.

"Kira!" Clay shouted from a distance. "Wait up!" I took a few steps towards him to close the gap. Clay seemed eager to run over, and I couldn't help but think of all the disasters he might have needed me for. "I was looking for you everywhere," he said breathlessly.

"Oh, hey. Uncle Nash suggested I take Shane on a tour. We've been driving around the property."

He glanced at Shane. "That's cool. It's massive, isn't it, dude?"

Shane simply nodded his reply.

"You mentioned you were looking for me? Anything wrong?" I asked Clay.

"No, but I do have a question. Will you go to dinner with me tomorrow?" His voice almost shook.

"Go to dinner? Like in town?"

"Yes, in town," he teased. "That's what normal couples do on Valentine's Day." My eyes blinked rapidly. *Was it really Valentine's Day tomorrow?* It had totally slipped my mind. I shot a look over to Shane, then back to Clay, who was standing there expectantly. "Um…" I mumbled.

"Um?" Clay questioned.

"I'm… uh… I mean, we have a guest and—"

Clay patted Shane's shoulder. "You don't mind, do you, *bro*?"

"Nope," Shane exaggerated the "P," letting the letter pop off his tongue. He tapped his fingers on the arm of his wheelchair, body tense.

Clay swiveled his head back to me. "See? He doesn't mind if we go. What do you say, Kira?"

A bad taste formed in my mouth from his bravado in front of Shane. I hesitated before answering, "Sure, Clay." I resisted the urge to shake my head.

"Whew, you made me nervous for a minute. I thought I would have to cancel the reservations I made." He placed a hand on his chest, taking in a deep breath. "Can't wait for tomorrow."

"Me too," I squeaked out. Clay strode away grinning.

Feeling flustered from the exchange, I snuck a glance at Shane, who seemed morose. Flashes of my first date with Shane, ironically on Valentine's Day two years ago, flooded my memory. How it had turned from a spontaneous and awkward dinner date into a life-altering kiss at the river overlook. How he'd been able to warm me from the inside so quickly that I barely noticed the freezing air around us. That night I fell for another Whitmore brother against my better judgment.

I roughly shook my head to halt my memories. That was in the past, and it should stay there. Right now, Shane needed to focus on healing his body and mind. I couldn't jeopardize or confuse this process. He had to find *his own* reason to get better.

And that wasn't with me.

Chapter 28

...make it stop.

Shane

JUST KILL ME now. Watching their little love story unfold in front of my eyes made me want to lose the tiny bit of breakfast I had eaten earlier. It totally slipped my mind that Valentine's Day was tomorrow. Or maybe, I had forgotten on purpose. I didn't know and certainly didn't care.

"Sorry about that." Kira cut into my thoughts. "Let's head into the stable. I want you to meet Honey. You're gonna love her."

"How long have you been together?" The question slipped out.

"Me and Honey?" She quipped, deflecting my question. I tilted my head, waiting for her to take me seriously. She brushed a strand of hair behind her ear as we moved inside. "No, um… just a few months. Like September… uh, maybe October… fall-ish, I guess?"

I found it curious as to why she was tripping over her words, noting her wavering. "So, it's serious then?" I probed.

Her face flushed. "Um… well, I've known him a long time. But it's still kinda new. I mean, I never thought of him like that until—"

I shook my head fervently. "Never mind, it's none of my business." I inwardly scolded myself for even asking. Had it really been two years since our first date? I remembered the river lights dancing in her eyes as she looked intently into mine. How holding her made the ground shake beneath me. How my mind fought hard to protect me, only to lose to my captured heart. How kissing her radiated a warmth straight to my soul, capturing it evermore.

The intense energy between us that night showed me that I wasn't completely lost to the dark aftermath of my hostage trauma. There was still hope. Hope to find my way back from the betrayal, heartbreak, and pain. I knew then we would become more than the weird circumstances that brought us together.

Until I fucked it all up. The breakup still haunted me. Kira's words had pierced my heart; her anger permanently stung my ears. I had stayed quiet in that car when I felt like I needed to scream for her forgiveness. Scream that I loved her. *Only* her. But I didn't. And I lost her.

I followed her through the stable, my arms heavier with each rotation of my wheels. Being close to her tore at the thinly healed hole in my heart. My chest tightened, making my lungs burn.

"Shane, this is Honey. Honey, this is Shane," she said, stroking the horse's mane. The horse let out a snotty snort in return. *Gross.*

"Am I supposed to shake her hoof or something now?" I asked glibly.

"No," she said, annoyed. "But you can pat her nose."

"She just snotted everywhere. No thanks."

"Be nice." She tilted her head, pursing her lips.

"I *am* being nice."

Kira let out a long, exaggerated breath that made a visible swirl in the cold air. "Okay, you can brush her while I muck out her stall. Just move back so I can bring her out."

"She's huge. How the hell can I brush her from down here?" I exaggeratedly pointed between myself and the horse.

"Why are you in such a bad mood? You were fine at breakfast until you weren't. Then you were fine in the truck, and now you aren't!" She furrowed her brows.

"I don't need your judgment," I snapped, my face terse.

"Judgment? I was stating a fact."

"I didn't come all this way to brush horses and watch you shovel shit."

"Then why did you come here, Shane?" She placed her hands on her hips.

"For horse therapy. Your dad said it would 'change my life.'" I mocked, bringing my hands up to make air quotes.

"This is part of horse therapy, you jackass."

"That's it. I'm done!" I yelled, wheeling myself as fast as possible across the straw-strewn dirt floor.

"Oh sure, run away!" She called after me.

I spun around. "I would need two legs for that," I spat.

My heart thumped harder the closer I got to the house. I knew coming here was a mistake. There was urgency in my movement, needing to seek the refuge of my room. I fought my way up the ramp and over the home's threshold. I slammed my bedroom door shut once safely inside.

My breath gave way to a harsh gasp, fuzziness creeping into my vision. I bent my head forward and put my ice-cold hands on my face. I counted repeatedly as Dr. Collier had instructed, 1-2-3-4, 1-2-3-4, but it wasn't working. My head throbbed as I struggled to stay conscious.

Memories and reality mixed. Who was I kidding? Horse therapy was never going to give me my leg or my life back. Being around Kira hurt too much, but it was equally painful to be home back east.

And I didn't know how to make it stop.

Kira

My blood boiled over his harsh remarks. A moment of weakness, after hearing the desperation in his drunken voice on New Year's Eve, turned my world upside down. I swore that my neck suffered whiplash from his moods.

Max had warned me in advance, but of course, I thought I knew how to help Shane. The dynamics of our trio together on the ranch were trickier than I imagined, and Clay certainly didn't make it easy. I was mad. Mad at Shane. Mad at myself. Just mad.

The stress of this whole situation settled into my bones, and I needed a release. I prepared Honey, and we were off. Riding always quieted the noise for me. And right now, the noise blared loudly.

I welcomed the stinging bite of the chilly air as Honey, and I reached the property's outer fence. Involuntarily, my eyes scanned for Clay. He would be cross with me for riding in the bitter cold again, but I had bigger problems to worry about, and suddenly I knew exactly who I should search for instead.

Pulling the reins firmly, I turned Honey sharply back toward the stable. I leaned forward in the saddle as we raced across the property. Ignoring the numbness of my face, I pushed Honey harder.

Shane needed to know. His phone call had frightened me enough for me to put my life on hold for him. That I put my relationship with Clay in jeopardy to have my ex-boyfriend come for therapy. That I worked hard to leave him in my past only to invite him into my carefully curated present. I risked everything to help him, and he needed to understand that.

At the house, I tied Honey to the ramp and quickly stomped my way inside. I burst through his bedroom door, riled up and ready to give him a piece of my mind. Instead, I found him in a heap on the floor, his wheelchair toppled over.

"Shane!" I shouted with alarm, and all the anger I held momentarily vanished. I rushed to his side, pushing his chair off him as I dropped to my knees. He was panting, but his body was as limp as a rag. I gently rolled him toward me, lifting his head and shoulders into my lap. Gravity-burdened tears slipped down his cheeks.

"What happened?" I asked softly. "Are you okay?" He silently shook his head. "Where does it hurt, Shane?"

After a beat, he mumbled, "Everywhere. All the time."

I held his face, rubbing my thumb over his trembling mouth. His sad eyes drew mine, tears augmenting the blue. They always reminded me of the blue Northern Lights.

A few summers ago, I saw the rare blue and purple auroras instead of their usual pink and green. Apparently, the change occurs when the solar particles hit nitrogen instead of oxygen. But I couldn't see any light in Shane's eyes anymore. This truth tore at the thinly healed hole in my heart.

The floor creaked behind me, and I snapped my head toward the sound. Clay stood in the doorway. I snatched my hand from Shane's face, throat turning dry. When I tried to speak, the words vanished.

Clay quietly walked over, lifting the wheelchair upright. He scooped up Shane and placed him in the chair. Shane had no reaction to the transfer. Once settled, he remained eerily still, gazing ahead with a vacant expression. Clay reached down and helped me to my feet, holding my hand for a beat longer. He nodded, shooting me a tiny smile before leaving the room.

Wren suddenly crossed my mind. An odd person to focus on when I haven't thought of her in so long. But this situation with Shane gave me a new perspective. How Shane could say Wren's name instead of mine at prom made it seem like he still had feelings for her.

Because he did. But it didn't mean he wanted to be with her again or that he didn't love me. I understood that now. She was a part of his story, a distant echo of all the good things in his life, faintly calling back. I think it was happening to me now with Shane. Except, the echoes of him were deafening.

And I didn't know how to make it stop.

Chapter 29

But not...

Shane

DAYS SLIPPED BY into a week or so since my fall. At this point, I didn't know how long I'd been holed up in my room. I preferred to spend my time watching old videos of my soccer career and following the antics of my teammates on social media. I wanted to immerse myself in that world as much as possible to escape my unchanging reality, to live vicariously through them.

It was at night when my demons would find me. They chewed me up and spit me back out until dawn crested the sky. How my mind succumbed to pain, causing sleep and hunger to elude me. Holes throughout my body turned into caverns of nothingness as my energy waned. The burden inflicted upon my family, upon Kira and her family, brought me shame. Even breathing brought frustration as it reminded me that I was alive but not really living.

I had to give everyone credit. They never stopped trying to coax me out of my isolation, but I just didn't see the point. All I did was hurt the people around me. The hard truth? No amount of therapy was going to fix me.

I would never be able to follow my passions again. I would never be able to run and balance a soccer ball on the tips of my toes. To misdirect the opposing team, rushing the goal line before suddenly passing it to my teammate behind me. They'd sprint to the corner, launching a kill shot on the unsuspecting goalie.

It was my signature play, and it worked every time. Knowing it wouldn't happen again made my grief a permanent resident.

My phone rang as the screen lit up with Max's name. Hesitation influenced my finger to hover over the accept button, but my last ounce of will prevailed.

"Hey, man. What's up?" I answered, trying to sound… normal.

"Dude, I just overheard Levi talking to your mom. She's planning to fly out to the ranch tomorrow," Max warned.

My eyes widened, a sudden increase in my pulse. "What!? Why?"

"I guess Kira called her old man. Said you were depressed and wouldn't leave your room. That you basically gave up on therapy or something like that," Max explained.

I tilted my head back, a hand on my forehead. "Fuck."

"You'd better call your mom if you don't want her showing up on your doorstep tomorrow. I just thought you should know."

"Yeah. Thanks for that. I mean it."

"I've always got your back, Shane. Always."

I immediately called her after hanging up with Max. I barely waited for her to pick up the phone before my verbal attack. "What the hell, Mom!? You're coming here?" I couldn't get my teeth to unclench.

"Don't take that tone with me."

I let out a long exhale, trying to pull my energy back. "Mom, please. You don't need to come all the way out to Montana."

"I knew horse therapy was a bad idea."

"Kira was just being dramatic," I let out an exasperated sigh.

I could hear her temper flare on the other end of the line. "Shane, I have never known that girl to be dramatic. Maybe Sarah, but not Kira."

"Mom, I'm fine! It's just been hard to adjust to the ranch and being around Kira again. Okay?"

There was a pause as she contemplated my words, and I could tell she was trying to gauge how truthful I was being. "When I talked to Levi, Kira told him that you wouldn't leave your room."

I closed my eyes, attempting to hold back my anger. "Well, that's not entirely accurate." *The bathroom was down the hallway.*

"I shouldn't have pushed you to—"

"Yes, Mom. You should have. You need to get your life back. Plan your wedding! Stop putting everything on hold for me." *I did mean that sincerely.*

"But I love you."

"I know. That's why I need you to stay home. I just need… time."

She blew out a loud breath, and I knew I had convinced her. "Can you at least text or call me every few days? You haven't returned any of my messages in over a week."

"I'll do better, mom. I promise." *Always false promises.* I shook my head. "I'll text in a couple days."

"Okay. Please do, Shane."

"Say 'hi' to Mateo for me. Bye, Mom." I hung up, relieved that I was able to subvert her plans. But there was still a storm that brewed inside me. Of all the things the Bowman's could have done to piss me off? Worrying my mother was at the top of my shit list. Fueled by wrath, I made a beeline for the three sitting at the kitchen table eating dinner.

"What the hell, Kira!?" I loudly approached.

"Whoa, whoa, whoa. Take it down a notch," her uncle reasoned.

"Mind your own damn business, Nash." I spat.

"Shane!"

"Don't Shane me! You tattled on me to your dad? What the fuck!? You knew damn well he would tell my mom!" Her mouth hung open as she tried to form words. She blinked, clearly not expecting this conversation.

Clay towered over me. "I think you should go back to hiding in your room," he threatened.

"You can shut the fuck up, lover boy," I scowled as Clay lunged closer.

Kira grabbed his arm. "Clay, don't!"

Her uncle interrupted, "Okay, son. That's enough. You're in no shape to have a civil conversation. Go cool down. That's an order."

"An order?" I challenged.

"NOW!" Uncle Nash's voice bellowed, echoing off the high ceiling beams. "Before I help you there myself." Nash pointed down the hall.

With all of them ganging up on me, I yielded. Haphazardly spinning around angrily, I headed back to my bed. I slammed the door, waiting for Kira to come give me one of her lectures, but it never came. Loud chatter floated in from the kitchen. I winced, knowing I was the center of their attention, even if by my own doing. I used to like being the center of attention.

But not anymore.

Kira

The shockwaves of his behavior rippled through the three of us. To disrespect my uncle, who graciously opened his home and his beloved ranch to someone he didn't even know? I felt sick to my stomach.

"I'm so sorry, Uncle Nash. I've never seen him like this." I held my face in my hands, elbows resting on the table. Any appetite I had vanished.

"It's not your job to apologize for him. He's responsible for his own actions." Nash grumbled, bringing his mug up to his lips. It took a lot to put my uncle in a foul mood.

"Nash is right, Kira. If he talks to you that way again, I *will* deck him," Clay said, his nostrils flaring.

"You can't do that, Clay. He's in a wheelchair!" I screeched, trying not to pull out my hair from the stress. *How did a vent session with my dad turn into this?*

"Sure, as hell I can. He could be a head on a platter. I'll punch his lights out," Clay huffed as I rolled my eyes.

As the voice of reason, Uncle Nash spoke. "I think that's enough for tonight. Some good rest is what we need to calm down. Clay, you head back to the barracks. I'll see you in the morning."

"Yes, sir." Clay knew when to push back, and this was not that time.

"I'll give you both a moment," Uncle Nash said as he stood up from the table, untucking the cloth napkin at his neck before busying himself at the sink.

Clay grabbed his jacket and took my hand. He led me through the hall and out the front door. The chill of the air caught me off guard, my body shuddering. Clay folded me into his jacket against his warm, strong chest.

"I'm sorry I added to the chaos." Clay rested his chin on top of my head.

"It's not your fault. He was way out of line," I mumbled into his body.

Clay pulled back, catching my gaze. "I'm dead serious, Kira. If he speaks to you like that again, I will clock him. I don't care how many legs he has."

"I know." He squeezed me tight and pecked my forehead with a quick, soft kiss. I looked up and gave him a small smile. He leaned down and properly kissed me on the lips. It wasn't a long kiss, but it was deep and intentional.

He trotted down the porch stairs, giving a final wave goodbye. I rubbed my hands together, turning to walk back inside when I spotted a curtain shift in Shane's room. *That jerk was spying on us!* It added insult to injury, and I thundered into the house.

"How dare you!" My voice boomed.

"Don't make out with your boyfriend right in front of my window." A cocky smile spread across his face.

"I wasn't even talking about that, but I *knew* you were spying on us." I pointed my finger at him accusingly.

"I heard a noise." He shrugged.

I narrowed my eyes. "You're so full of it."

"Am I? Because your boyfriend saw me. Then kissed you to stake his claim."

"Shut up!" Fury surged through me, my hands balling into fists.

"Ask him yourself," Shane sneered.

I gritted my teeth so hard they ached. "Why are you acting like this?"

"Like what?" He tilted his head, mockingly.

"Like, you're… Sarah!" It was the worst insult I could conjure on the spot.

"Seriously, Kira?"

"Yes seriously. Bitter with a chip on your shoulder. And if the entire world isn't fawning over you, positive or negative, then you pout."

"I'm done. Get out of my room."

"Gladly." I stomped out, his door slamming for the second time that night.

***

The next morning my muscles were stiff as hell. They had gotten a full workout during my restless night. No matter how hard I tried, I couldn't turn off my brain. It was full of worry, anger, sympathy, and most of all annoyance.

Shane's rude behavior was so far from his normal that I wasn't sure whether he was truly distressed or self-sabotaging. Either way, my patience was thin.

As I made breakfast, Clay strode into the kitchen with a big smile stretched across his face. "Good morning!"

"You're in a good mood," I grumbled, wishing he could share some of it with me. "What brought that on?"

"I get to see you." He picked me up, spinning me around as my whisk dripped eggs on the floor. I light-hearted laugh escaped me, my first moment of relief since the drama last night. When he lowered me, he kissed me with a purpose. It felt much like last night's kiss when Shane pointed out what Clay had done. I soured, pulling back suddenly.

"Did you see Shane watching us from the front window last night?"

"Umm, no." Clay chewed his lip. I paused, my tongue clicking against my teeth. "Clay Two Irons, are you sure that's your answer?"

"I mean, yes?"

"Yes, you didn't see him, or yes, you did?" I narrowed my eyes.

Clay held his hands up in the air. "Kira, I was angry that he threatened you, okay? There was an opportunity to get back at him where it hurt him most. Seeing you with someone else."

I crossed my arms, creating a barrier between us. "Yelling at me isn't threatening me. I can handle myself just fine. Plus, I told you, Clay. It's been over between Shane and me for a long time now."

Clay scoffed. "I don't think he knows that."

"What are you talking about?" I asked, genuinely confused.

"*People's eyes say the words that the tongue cannot pronounce,*" Clay uttered an old Crow proverb we all learned as children. He lowered his arms, and we held each other's gaze before I turned my head to the side.

I lowered the heat on the griddle, surely burning breakfast by now. "That's not true. He's here to get therapy. To get better."

Clay shook his head, plopping down at the table. "Hey, it's an observation. Maybe I'm reading him wrong. As you said, I don't know him the way you do."

Was Clay right? His *observation* made me wonder. Back in the day, I knew Shane better than anyone. I assumed that would be the same now. That his mood swings and anger were only about losing his leg. Losing his dream. But Clay saw something entirely different.

I used to know all of Shane's tells: the way he would run obsessively when frustrated, grow quiet when he was in pain, or how he would envelop me tightly in his arms when he needed refuge from his mind. I knew what he needed, or what he was thinking, like a sixth sense.

But not anymore.

Chapter 30

...with him?

Shane

MARCH CAME SULKING in like a whimper. From my mother's threats to fly out here, to the fight with Kira a couple of weeks ago, when I caught them kissing on the porch, had been the final proverbial straw. I gave in. My old life as I knew it ceased to exist. No leg, check. No career, check. No Kira, check. The sooner I accept this, the better off I'd be. With nowhere left to run, I fell in line and began Spirit Ranch's therapy program.

Kira and I spoke only when it was related to my treatment or any tasks that I completed on autopilot. We worked with her horse on rapport, non-verbal communication, and safety. Alongside that, we practiced grounding exercises, and emotional regulation through mirroring Honey's temperament. Finally, she taught me desensitization techniques with touch, grooming, and ground-tying. But never riding.

I guess I thought I would just get on a horse and *voilà* I'm cured. How wrong I was. My treatment plan was a very structured and an arduously slow process. And that's what I did. Every day. Go to the stables, work with Honey, practice techniques, and repeat. I watched life move past me for weeks as the weather warmed and the flurry of activity on the ranch increased.

But I remained the same. Going through the motions as the hole deep within grew wider and deeper. I took my meals in my room now, Kira and Nash no longer objecting. It was better for all of us that I stayed as far away as possible.

Later, I heard the truck engine roar as it pulled up to the house. But it was a familiar voice that grabbed my full attention. I immediately rolled out onto the porch as Nash and Kira hopped out. Unable to see the figure on the other side, I strained my neck trying to make out who it was. As his tall frame and shaggy, unkempt hair came into view, everything clicked into place.

"Hey there, idiot!" Max shouted as he rounded the front of the truck.

"Max? What the hell are you doing here!?" I couldn't believe it. When had everyone planned this? More importantly, how had Max kept it a secret?

"Kira told me you were being a big baby. Figured I'd have to come out and shake some sense into you."

"I—"

"Don't even bother. I believe her one hundred percent." He winked at Kira, whose grin seemed plastered to her face.

"Of course you would." I huffed, leaning back in my wheelchair.

Max jogged up the stairs and bent down to hug me. I returned the embrace, something I needed more than I cared to admit.

"I guess we're going to be roomies. Show me this *amazing* room you never want to leave," Max mocked.

I rolled my eyes, guiding Max to the makeshift bedroom. Clay was already there, setting up a folding cot on the opposite side of the room. He strode over to Max with his hand outstretched. "You must be Max. I'm Clay Two Irons, Kira's boyfriend." His words made me tense involuntarily.

"Hey there, man. Good to meet ya. She's told me all about you."

"It's all true," Clay smirked.

"I bet it is," Max mirrored the ranch hand's expression. I could feel bile rising in the back of my throat. Clay was the enemy, and Max chatted him up like he was a long-lost bro.

Max must have been able to read whatever involuntary face I was making as he clasped my shoulder. "Don't get jealous. You're still my number one," he teased, as Clay slipped out of the room.

I waved his hand away, trying not to let the interaction dig into my mood. "You never answered my question seriously. What are you doing here?"

"Well, it was either me or your mom. I figured you'd prefer me."

"But I talked to her a while back, and we decided she wasn't coming."

"You decided. She was making different plans until I intervened and took one for the team."

"Unbelievable." I rubbed my face in disbelief.

"You're welcome," he answered in a hum.

"What I don't get is why either of you found it necessary."

"You don't think it has anything to do with your self-loathing and isolation? I'm starting to believe Kira when she says you've been acting like passive-aggressive Sarah."

"Dude, take that back." *Seriously, why did everyone keep saying that?*

"What are you going to do about it?" Max danced around me like a boxer, his hands up in a mock-fighting position.

"I'm gonna—"

"You're gonna do what, Shane? Sit in your room? Oh no. What will I do? I guess I'll have to spend more time with Kira!" he teased.

My partial smile that had been lingering fell, brows furrowing. It took all my willpower not to grit my teeth. "And there it is. The real reason you came. I get it now," I sneered.

Max paused, fists lowering as he tilted his head. "You get... what now?"

"That I'm your excuse to see Kira! Well, I hate to break it to you, buddy. You'll have to deal with Clay. I'm nowhere close to being in the picture."

He shook his head, any previous playfulness or joy in his tone squashed. "She's right. Self-absorbed to the point where you can't even see the reality in front of you. You really think I'm here just for her?"

Ire flared off my tongue, "I look reality in the face EVERY. SINGLE. DAY. Don't you dare tell me I don't."

"That's not the reality I meant, Shane." And with those last words left floating in the air, he huffed out of the room. There was a tangible ball of fire in the middle of my chest, my head throbbing. *How dare he accuse me of not seeing reality. That's all I could see.*

I wanted to go after him, give him a piece of my mind. Tell him to go home. But deep down, I knew I needed him. Max had always been able to tell me like it was, and this time was no exception. But he could've waited more than five minutes after he arrived before taking the piss out of me.

What was wrong with him?

Kira

I couldn't stop grinning. My Max. Here in Montana. It was almost too good to be true. Besides my family, he was the one person my heart ached for the most. My senior year was like a hole I couldn't climb out of after Shane and I broke up. But working at my dad's car dealership, Max and I became quick friends. Over time, Max made my heart whole again. I don't think I would have made it without him.

And now he was here. I finally had someone from Shane's past who had my back. Max may be the only person who could shake Shane out of his funk. It certainly wouldn't be me; Shane made it crystal clear that I was his therapy instructor only. He went through the motions, but I knew he regretted coming. And until he wanted to be here, he would never find himself.

Max stormed out of the house and down the front porch stairs toward me. "Uh oh. What happened?" I asked. But instead of answering, he pulled me into a tight hug.

Taken aback at first, my arms hung loosely. When he squeezed me, I wrapped my arms around him and buried my face in his chest. His heart was pounding, and I knew I needed to hug him tighter.

"I'm ready for that ranch tour now," Max mumbled into my shoulder. That was his *"I'm mad so don't ask tone"* that I remembered well.

When the truck roared to life, I shifted gears as Shane appeared at the front door. I couldn't help but pause a beat. Max placed his hand on my leg, drawing my attention to him instead of the porch.

"Let's go, Kira," Max said. I pressed the pedal, and the back tires dusted up stones behind us until the wheels finally caught traction.

The truck shimmied and swayed from all the mud-laden ruts exaggerated by winter plowing. Feeling weird in the silence, I rambled on, pointing to outbuildings and landmarks that dotted the property. He swiveled his head in the direction I instructed without uttering a word. When he spoke abruptly, I almost jumped.

"Has he been like this the whole time?"

I cleared my throat, trying to focus on the road in front of us. "Mostly."

"How have you put up with that for almost two months?"

"I'm a saint." I stuck out my tongue, trying to make Max laugh.

He smiled. "Clearly. I saw him for five minutes and wanted to punch him."

"You'll have to get in line behind Clay."

"Funny, he said something similar." Before I could ask him what that meant, he continued. "Good for Clay, though. Shane needs a good thumping."

I reached out for his hand. He took it and intertwined his fingers in mine. "What happened, Max? You were only in his room for five minutes."

"Basically, he accused me of using him as an excuse to see you."

"He's not completely wrong, is he?" I queried, grinning over at him.

"You know I'd go to the ends of the earth for you, Kira. You're my special cowgirl." He winked.

"Aww, shucks. You sure know how to make a woman blush," I exaggerated a southern drawl.

"Don't tease."

"Who's a tease?" I asked, batting my lashes.

"I missed you." He stared at me lovingly.

"I missed you too." And I squeezed his hand. He brought it to his lips and brushed a light kiss over my knuckles.

We pulled up at the house in a much better mood. Being near Max gave me strength. He helped me weather any storm, and I had a feeling that the biggest one was still looming. He jogged to my side as I turned the obnoxiously loud motor off and helped me get out by offering his hand. We started up the stairs of the porch, and like a predictable romance novel, Shane was already wheeling out the front door right on cue.

"Did you guys have a nice little lovers' rendezvous? Did Clay join in, or is he in the dark too?" His face was red and surly.

My smile faded. "I'm not even going to dignify that with an answer."

"You have no idea what you're talking about." Max pitched forward, but I kept him in place where our hands were still joined.

"Oh really? Deny that you came here to see her."

"I won't. Because that part is true." Max's grip tightened.

"I knew it." You could see the veins on Shane's neck.

"You're such an idiot, Whitmore. I came here for you, too. Although, I question that decision."

"Well, don't worry, I won't get in your wa—"

"Enough Shane! He's your best friend," I pleaded.

"And Kyle was my brother, but that didn't stop him." And with that gut punch, he spun around and into the house. Max and I literally had to close our mouths after his outburst. How could he bring Wren up again when she was ancient history? Why was he doing this? My head thudded almost as loudly as my heart.

What was wrong with him?

Chapter 31

what did...

Shane

MY BLOOD BOILED. I could see what was happening as clearly as the Montana sky. Kira and Max were together, and Clay was none the wiser. I'd been in Clay's shoes, and I knew how much it'd hurt when he finally understood. I may not like the dude, but I couldn't sit idly by while he got his heart stomped on.

I came out of my room to look for Clay when I heard a quiet chatter coming from the great room. Silently, I crept down the hall to find Kira and Max whispering and gossiping. Thick as thieves.

"We should tell him, Max," Kira said.

"Do you really think this is the right time?" Max held his knees from where they both sat on the carpet.

"Enjoying the show?" Clay's voice came from behind me, close and sharp. I hadn't even heard him approach and practically leapt out of my chair.

"What the hell? Are you trying to give me a heart attack? And right back at you, lurker!" I yelled.

His eyes flicked from me to the room in front of us, narrowing slightly. He knew very well who I had been listening to. "Well, the difference is, she's my girlfriend. Not yours."

I narrowed my eyes at Clay's retort. "I'm aware."

Alerted by our argument, Kira and Max appeared in the hall. "Caught wheelie here spying on the two of you," Clay announced, taking the opportunity to throw me under the bus. *Terrific, ableist asshole.*

"I wasn't spying, okay? I was just uh... heading to the, uh..."

"To the, uh..." Clay mocked.

"Shut the fuck up, man. You have bigger problems to deal with. Doesn't he, Kira?" I hissed, looking pointedly toward her.

"I literally have no idea what you're talking about, Shane." She shook her head, a firm frown on her face as she glanced between us all.

"About you and Max. Being together. Like together, together." Clay laughed once, sharp and humorless. The kind of laugh when you're about to rub something in someone's face. "What's so funny?" I asked Clay with a snarl. *Today was giving me the biggest migraine of my life.*

"You seriously think that's what's happening?"

"Clay—" Kira warned.

"He's not dating my girlfriend, dumbass." Clay snapped, the words tumbling out like he couldn't stop them. "He's gay." The silence that followed felt heavier than what her boyfriend had revealed. I gawked at Max. His jaw was clenched, eyes fixed on a spot on the floor.

"Clay!" Kira hissed. She stepped closer to Max, acting as a physical barrier between him and the cowboy.

Clay shrugged defensively, a curl to his lip. "He needed to know."

"It wasn't your story to share," she sniped.

"Not cool dude," Max muttered.

Snapping out of shock, I turned my ire toward Clay. "That wasn't your call to make. It was a totally shitty thing to do," I snapped, defending my best friend.

Clay dragged his hand through sweaty hair, jaw tight. "Seriously? I'm the bad guy now? Unbelievable." He didn't wait for a response before grabbing his jacket and storming out.

Kira looked over at Max, fiddling with her hair as it curled around her finger. "I'm so sorry, Max. He shouldn't have done that."

My vision tunneled onto Max. The room blurred like when I had a concussion, my eyes unfocused as hundreds of memories and conversations with Max rearranged themselves in my head.

Kira noticed. "I'll let you two talk," she said and slipped out of view.

Silence hung in the air as I tried to shake the confusion out of my brain, my shoulders dropping. I didn't know where to begin and had trouble forming a cohesive thought. *Did everyone… how long… why didn't you…* Nothing would organize into something I could say.

Max paced in front of me, walking back and forth in my silence. "Go ahead, say what's on your mind." Words eluded me. "Come on, Shane. I get that you're mad, but—"

"I'm not mad. I'm… stunned. I had no idea."

He nodded once. "No one did."

"You told others?"

"Uh, yeah," he said coyly, rubbing his temples as he moved.

My chest tightened. "Who?"

"It's not that I didn't want to tell—"

"Do Kyle and Wren know?"

"Yes, but—"

"Brody? Sarah?"

"Yes." He slowed his pacing. "But I hadn't told anyone until after you had left for Portugal."

"That's almost two years ago!" I said, aghast.

"I… know." His shoulders slumped. "I wanted to tell you so many times. But then you got hurt, and I didn't want to add another thing to your plate."

"Another thing," I echoed, pinching the bridge of my nose.

"Shane, please—"

"You didn't trust me." The words came out flat.

"That's not it." He exhaled hard. "You're the one person I wanted to tell the most. I almost mentioned it our senior year. Right before prom. I'd met this guy, but I wasn't ready. Then you needed help with Kira, and…" He trailed off, leaning against the wall. He slid down until he was sitting on the floor. "There was never a right time."

"You knew back then?" My throat burned.

"I knew in middle school, Shane." His gaze stayed on the floor. "But I couldn't admit it to myself until high school. I told my family after graduation, and eventually Kira. Over time, everyone knew."

"Except me."

He finally met my gaze; a frown firmly settled on his face. "It wasn't on purpose. You're my best friend. You're my brother. I desperately wanted to. I just… didn't know how to. I'm sorry."

The anger I'd been clinging onto cracked. He really was my brother, and my heart broke in two. A part of me was angry, he didn't trust me enough to handle the news amidst my own crises. The other half folded inward with shame. I hadn't been there for him, nor had I truly thanked him for everything he'd done. That sudden awareness was the slap in the face I needed.

"I'm the one who should be sorry. I've been so wrapped up in the Shane shit-show that I didn't notice you needed me. You risked your literal life trying to stop my kidnapping and flew to Portugal after my surgery. Now, you're here in Montana to kick my ass. I've been the worst friend, yet you always show up."

"Yeah, well." He shot me a small, crooked smile. "I've always got your back."

Emotion surged, sudden and sharp. "But I didn't always have yours. Please forgive me, Max."

"Done." He pushed up from the floor and pulled me into a hug. Two years of distance melted away in a single embrace, and we were back in each other's good graces without missing a beat.

When we pulled apart, I cleared my throat. "Clay outing you? Shitty move," I said, pivoting our focus.

"Yeah. But it ripped the band-aid off." Max dusted off his jeans.

"Did you know he knew?"

"Not for sure, but I figured Kira would tell her boyfriend."

"Her boyfriend," I muttered facetiously, rolling my eyes.

Max waggled his eyebrows. "Still not a fan?"

"I don't get a vote."

"I'm not so sure that's true." Max let his words float between us, ruffling my hair before walking off. How could he drop a bomb like that and then leave? My thoughts felt jumbled.

What did that mean?

Kira

I rushed after Clay, whom I assumed was heading to the barn. My hands curled into fists. While pissed at him for outing Max in an obvious attempt to spite Shane, I was also livid at my ex. That boy had gone off the deep end. I thought seeing Max would help, but all it did was exacerbate his poor conduct.

I rounded the corner, catching a glimpse of Clay near the stable. Picking up the pace, I hurried before my fury could dissipate. Today practically gave me whiplash from both Shane and Clay's bravado. I hadn't even noticed I was running, determined not to let him escape my wrath. I marched into Raven's stall where Clay groomed him.

"Hey!" I shouted.

"Hey, what?" Clay asked sharply, not looking up from his work.

"Max didn't deserve that. I told you that in confidence."

He scoffed. "You're mad at me now for telling the truth?" Clay sat the brush down on a nearby ledge, finally facing me directly.

"It wasn't your truth to tell."

He turned away, picking the brush back up. "Whatever." His disdainful tone grated my last nerve.

"Don't ignore me!" I bellowed.

"I have work to do."

I grabbed his arm to coerce his full attention. "Clay!"

"What?" he snapped, his face contorting in anger.

"What's going on?"

"You can't be this naïve, Kira." My face tightened, lips pressed into a thin line. He harshly freed his arm from me, pushing past me to leave the stall. "Never mind."

I followed him into the center hall, raising my voice, "You know what? I guess I am naïve, Clay. Please, share your wisdom." I gave him a mocking one-handed bow. "Explain it to me. I want to know."

"I'm not doing this." His powerful legs carried him out of the stable. I had to practically sprint to catch up. We were now in full view of the entire ranch.

"Stop!" I yelled. He turned on his heels with a menacing scowl. "Tell me. What am I being gullible about?" I pleaded through gritted teeth.

"I'm ganged up on, Kira." He took hold of both my arms, gently shaking them as if to bolster his assertion.

"Ganged up on? What do you mean? By whom?"

"The three of you!"

"What are you talking about? I am so confused by everyone today."

"You all have a history, and I'm the odd man out. How do I compete?" His voice cracked on the last word, and for the first time, I saw something raw beneath the anger. His fear. "I'm standing right here," he said quietly. "And sometimes I feel like I'm losing you."

I felt frozen in place, ambushed by his words. "Is that why you outed Max? Because you feel threatened?"

He scoffed. "You don't get it." He tried to storm off, but I clutched onto his arm again. *Have all the men in my life gone crazy today?*

"Stop walking away!" I shouted.

"I'm not! I'm trying to do my job, remember? I work here." He yanked away from my grasp.

"Why are you being like this?"

"Being like what, Kira?" He shrugged his arms, desperately throwing his hands upward.

"Like a jealous boyfriend with a bruised ego."

"Because I am, Kira!" I flinched from him as he snapped at me. "You can't see it, but I can. You haven't been the same since Shane got here. I've held my tongue these last couple of months because you swore it wouldn't change anything between us. But it has!"

"Clay—"

"Besides Valentine's Day, do you know how many times we've been alone together? Once, Kira. Once. It's almost April!"

I inhaled sharply, trying to recall if that was the truth. I couldn't. "I—" I had barely squeaked out that singular word when Clay grabbed me by the waist. He kissed me hard, too hard, banging our teeth from the force of it. Slight panic swept it as his arms coiled around me, pinning my arms to my sides. I leaned back as far as I could, trying to pry myself from his grip, my yelp stifled by his mouth enveloping mine. I struggled to untangle myself from his grasp, freeing my arms. But before I could use them to push him away, a low, menacing voice roared behind us.

"LET! HER! GO!" Shane's tone was thunder cracking on the plains. Clay released his grip, and I tumbled backwards into Shane's arms. He was standing up, balancing on one leg to catch me.

The shock on Clay's face made me whip my head around, looking at Shane. He gently held me until my feet were steady. I glanced at Max standing behind Shane's wheelchair, a proud grin on his face. Turning my head back, Clay narrowed his eyes but retreated to the stable without any further conflict.

Shane placed an intentional hand on my shoulder as Max took the cue and brought his chair over. As Shane sat, he let his hand run down my shoulder to my hand. He briefly held it before pulling away. A light blush swept over my face. My thoughts jumbled.

What did that mean?

Chapter 32

...to be.

Shane

HER HAND WAS warm and familiar, my heart picking up its pace. The shape of her palm melded perfectly with mine, and I held it a beat too long. With a flush on Kira's face, I realized that she had noticed it too. Feeling nostalgic, I finally admitted to myself that I'd missed this. That I missed her. The pressing weight on my chest shifted, the burden a little lighter.

"Bro, you were badass. I was scared of you," Max said giddily.

My focus remained on Kira. "Are you okay?"

"Yeah, but I was handling the situation," she replied.

"I know. It was a knee-jerk reaction. I won't interfere again."

"Appreciated." Kira scuffed her boot in the dirt, looking down.

Max glanced between us with incredulous eyes. "Seriously? Are we not going to talk about what just happened? He was being an absolute dick!"

"He was, but I can handle it," Kira answered confidently.

Max mocked under his breath, *"So, I guess that's a no to talking about cowboy douchebag?"*

I affirmed Kira's response. "I know you will handle it, Kira." Max rolled his eyes dramatically.

As soon as Kira left the barn, he ranted. "What the hell, Shane? *'I won't interfere again. I know you will handle it.'* Have you gone insane?"

I smirked. "Maybe a little. But now, Clay's on notice, and he knows it."

"What does that mean?" Max paced again, throwing his arms up in defeat.

"It means, I'm not going to be an idiot anymore."

I could see the pieces in Max's brain moving into place in real time as his grin widened. One could practically see every tooth. "Let's go! That's the fire I was looking for." Max shook my shoulders in excitement, spinning my chair as we made our way back to the main house.

***

The absence of Clay at the dinner table had the three of us eating in an eerie silence. It didn't take Kira's uncle long to notice.

"Where's Clay?" Nash asked.

Keeping her eyes fixed on her plate, she answered, "I'm not sure. Earlier he mentioned having a lot of work to do." She stuffed a huge bite into her mouth.

"I don't recall giving him so much to do that he couldn't stop for dinner." Nash wiped his mouth off with a napkin and grabbed his phone. "I'll text him."

"Wait!" Kira blurted, reaching for her uncle's hand. "We had a fight. He's not coming." She slowly pulled away from him.

"I see." Kira rolled her eyes. "What's with the eye rolling?" Her uncle prodded, nodding toward her.

"You sound just like my father."

"And that's a bad thing?"

"No, it's just... never mind. Can I call it a night? I'm not hungry." With a furrowed brow, Nash excused Kira, who promptly left the table. Silence returned except for the scraping of forks on our plates.

"Do you boys know what that was all about?" Nash finally asked once she was out of earshot.

"No, sir," we said in unison. We knew better than to get involved.

"Just a gentle reminder. My name is Nash." He stood up from the table with a sigh. "I trust you'll clean up the kitchen before you retire?"

"Yes, sir," we answered again in unison.

Nash walked down the hallway, muttering to himself. *"Yes, sir. No, sir. It's like talking to a wall with those two."*

I put my fork down as I heard the creak of the front door. My head snapped toward Max. "Do you think he's leaving to go find Clay?"

"Yeah, I do," Max answered confidently.

We rushed towards Kira's room upstairs, Max ascending the steps before I could even lock my chair at the foot of the staircase. I heard loud mumbling from upstairs followed by banging noises before Kira came running down.

"Shane, watch out!" Kira shouted as she tried to get past my chair. I grabbed her hand and halted her forward motion.

"Your uncle will believe your side of the story," I assured.

"That's what I'm afraid of." She pulled her hand from mine and edged her way around me.

"I'm coming with you," Max announced, hopping over the bottom railing.

"No, Max. Stay here. I mean it," she barked, hurrying out the front. We stared at each other for a moment, telepathically deciding whether we should stay or go after her. After what felt like years, I turned my chair toward the kitchen, making the decision for both of us.

He jogged to get in front of me. "Really, man?"

"She asked us to stay." Max scoffed. "I'm telling you, Max. You haven't seen her in a while. She's different here. Kira's full of strength and confidence. A whole new woman since high school. I broke her trust a long time ago, and I'm determined to get it back."

Max groaned as he dragged his feet, falling in behind me to the kitchen. Although we didn't chase after her, Kira wasn't far from my mind. Everything I had told Max was true. Kira *was* different. A mature and poised woman. I hadn't made it easy for her lately, but after what happened with Clay? Something ignited within me.

In the years since we'd broken up, I'd convinced myself that she was better off with anyone else except me. But after catching her in my arms, old emotions rose from the dead. Experiencing something other than pain was exhilarating, and I didn't want to lose that feeling. I know I'm not the man she deserves yet. But I wanted to be.

Kira

I was freaking out. When my uncle found out how my boyfriend had acted, well, let's just say: *"May the force be with Clay."* Both my dad and his brother were masters of two-word utterances laced with acknowledgement, skepticism, and judgment. But when they reprimanded someone, you knew it.

It was dark outside when I flew out the front door with only the porch light illuminating the yard. I rushed down the stairs, smacking into my uncle.

"Oof!" I exclaimed loudly. *How do I keep running into people?*

"Where are you going in such a hurry?" My uncle asked, steadying me.

I answered breathlessly with my own question. "Where are you going?"

"I was waiting for you." *Meaning he knew I was going to run out here. Great.*

"You're not talking with Clay?"

"That depends on what you tell me. But I knew it was serious when those two boys in the house clammed up tighter than a duck's backside."

Scratching heavily at my neck, I tried to soften the blow. "Clay kissed me when I didn't want him to, but it was a misunderstanding."

"How is that a misunderstanding?" Uncle Nash narrowed his eyes, a sternness about him that mimicked my dad.

"He was afraid of losing me. Or maybe he was trying to make Shane jealous. I don't know. Everyone's been acting so weird, and Clay doesn't understand that Shane isn't a threat. He has zero interest in me." *Zero interest in anything really*, I thought jokingly.

"Are you sure?" I blinked slowly. *Why ask me something like that?*

"Yeah, one hundred percent." I scratched my neck unsuccessful at quelling the itch.

"I see."

"Aagh! Could you stop that? I can't stand the two-word answers." I could practically hear my dad's voice in his tone.

"Where do you think your old man learned it from?" His mouth hitched up on one side, exposing his dimples. He genuinely looked even more like my father at that moment.

I clasped my hands together in front of me, begging. "Please don't fire Clay. This job's all he's ever wanted."

"Fire him? Nah, I plan on him running this place someday. But I will make it very clear that if he treats you or anyone on this property like that again, it will be the last thing he does. I have a lot of land; it would be very difficult to ever find a body." I acknowledged him, a nervous giggle slipping out. With that said, Uncle Nash casually strolled toward the barracks, whistling an old tune I didn't recognize. It's like he didn't have a care in the world while he was off to lecture Clay. The man didn't mince words, so it won't be a lengthy chat, but he would get his point across. Uncle Nash knew how to be scary when it mattered most.

Once back in the house, I ambled down the hall to the kitchen, where I could hear the boys. Before they were aware of my presence, I observed them while they cleaned. These two best friends picked up exactly where they left off in high school, their banter natural and easy.

"Do you think he'll fire him? Or maybe hit him? Or—"

"We'll find out soon enough," Shane said with a hum.

"Okay, Levi," Max teased in a mocking voice, resuming his dish washing.

"Hey, I'll take that as a compliment, thank you very much."

"Whatever, dude." Max handed him a plate to dry.

A smile spread across my lips just before Shane noticed me. Our eyes locked, the evening standing still. His face softened as he inhaled deeply. I saw a tiny flicker of light flash across his blue eyes, a memento of the past. For the first time since he got here, this brief twinkle cut through his darkness. My walls slipped away as I watched the Shane iceberg begin to melt in our shared and suspended pocket of time.

Max noticed me, the clock resuming. "Did Nash lay into Clay?"

"I'm not sure. He went to talk to him. I gave him my side of things, but I have no idea what Clay will say to him."

"He better tell him the truth. That he forced you to kiss him," Max blurted angrily. "We both saw it. Right, Shane?" Still dazed, Shane didn't answer; his gaze stayed locked onto me. Something definitely was different. He was different. Max interrupted the invisible tether between us. "Well, I for one hopes he kicks his ass."

Back in the moment, I announced, "It's been one hell of a day, and I'm completely beat. I'm going to bed. Remember, days on the ranch start at—"

"—the butt crack of dawn." Shane finished my sentence, snapping out of his fog. I snickered as a grin appeared on my face, wide like a Cheshire cat. His intense stare continued, holding me captive for several more moments. Max cleared his throat loudly, breaking our trance.

"Goodnight, Max," I said hastily.

Smirking, he drew out the words, "Goodnight, Kira."

"Goodnight, Shane," I tried my best to sound nonchalant.

"Goodnight, Kira Sky."

Escaping to my room, I slammed the door and leaning against it. My heart raced. The low, reverent tone of his voice reverberated in my ears. *Kira Sky. Why did he say my middle name?* He hadn't said my name like that since high school. It was what he always called me when we were together. He used to tell me that one day he would see the Montana sky I was named after. That recollection flooded my brain.

I plopped sideways on the bed, tucking a pillow under my chin. Today was the weirdest day of my life. Every interaction was like a hairpin turn on a steep mountain. Shane's turns being the craziest. He drew up feelings I thought were long gone. It unsettled me.

I had vowed to have nothing more to do with the Whitmore brothers. And at the time, I'd meant it. But here I was, living with Shane in the bedroom right below mine, at my family's ranch in Montana. Post-break-up Kira would have never seen that coming. I truly believed that we wouldn't cross paths again, let alone be friends.

But I wanted to be.

Chapter 33

A glimmer...

Shane

I HADN'T SEEN the butt crack of dawn in weeks. I had instead chosen to sleep in, but I was awake now. And I think Clay had been the impetus. Seeing him kiss Kira without her permission had my blood boiling. Until that point, I was on autopilot. But today felt like a new day. The first day. And I was ready.

I slipped out of the room delicately, although I wasn't sure why I was trying to be quiet. A rocket could shoot off, and it wouldn't be heard over Max's snoring. I sat on the front porch just as dawn broke; the air chilly as a light mist made the landscape look ominous. But it was the opposite of how I felt.

Breathing in and out purposefully, I watched the puffs of air flit away like water striders skittering on top of a pond. I held my hand to my chest and studied the rise and fall with each deep breath, allowing my beating heart to slow. Dr. Collier had shown me this quick technique in one of our sessions months ago, but I'd never tried it on my own until now. It was weirdly soothing, and for the first time in a very long time, hope emerged.

"Shane, is everything okay?" Kira asked in a hushed tone. I hadn't heard her step out onto the porch. The frame of her body glowed from the gorgeous morning colors as if she were my own personal sunrise. Her arms were tightly crossed over her torso, shielding her from the frigid morning. Strands of her hair fluttered in the breeze. Despite my earlier work to slow my heart rate, her mere presence negated those efforts. But I didn't mind.

"Yes, and good morning."

"Good morning." Her teeth chattered lightly. "I was going to start breakfast. Would you like to join me?"

I grinned. "Yeah, I'd love to." She tilted her head, looking at me curiously until I ruined the moment. "Will Clay be joining us?"

Chewing her bottom lip, she answered, "I don't know."

"You haven't spoken to him since your uncle did?"

"No," she said nervously.

Surprised, I noted her response and filed it away. "Are *you* okay?" Her eyes darted to mine. An old familiar buzzing hummed throughout my body.

Max's snoring reached a crescendo, wafting through the partially open window facing the front porch. It effectively changed the subject.

"How the hell did you get any sleep?" she asked with a light huff of a laugh, rubbing her arms for warmth.

"I got used to it over the years." Kira shook her head in disbelief.

"Well, he's lucky he has you as a roommate. I would have smothered him with a pillow already." We chuckled in unison, her eyes dashing to mine again. "I'll meet you inside," she said and quickly left.

I didn't follow her straightaway. Instead, my brain shifted to Clay. In the short time I'd known Nash, I gleaned how he chose his words carefully. That was why I found it odd that Clay hadn't come begging for forgiveness yet. I filed yet another note in the back of my mind.

Approaching the kitchen, Kira was in full breakfast mode. I took a moment to watch her movements, like a well-choreographed ballet, flitting lithely about the kitchen. I remembered when Mom was in her ballet era and took my brother and me to the city from one ballet show to the next. At that time, the beauty and emotion of it all were lost on two pre-teen boys, but I finally understood it now.

She caught me observing her, and I sheepishly cleared my throat. "Any way I can help?"

"Sure," she answered, her grin wide.

She placed the dishes onto the counter, and I lifted them to my lap. The mundane act of setting the table lifted my mood, the corners of my mouth turning upward as I placed each dish in its respective place. The task reminded me of the Sunday brunches we used to have as a couple.

It was nice to feel normal again. To feel needed. To be around Kira Sky. My smile widened. It was nice to be back in the land of the living.

A glimmer of optimism had taken hold.

Kira

Something was different with Shane. I almost didn't want to think about it for fear of jinxing it, but he looked… cheerful. And I think Clay was the impetus. Yesterday, when Shane stood and defended me, the slightest hint of his old self had risen into view. Hope welled within me.

Clay never showed up for breakfast. I leaned over to my uncle and whispered, "You didn't really *show* Clay how much land you have, did you?" His laugh boomed loudly, and I could feel a burn crawling up my neck.

The boys looked up from wolfing down their plates of food. I was so distracted I hadn't noticed that Shane had joined Max in eating his breakfast as if he were a pubescent boy again. It was nice to see him finally have an appetite after not eating much lately. "Kira and her wild imagination strike again," my uncle teased. "I may have said I had the land to hide a body, but it didn't mean it, kiddo." His laughter only strengthened.

The burn moved up, settling across my cheeks. "Then where is he!?" I asked through gritted teeth.

"He went to the Crow Fair committee meeting on the reservation. He's taking my place since I have a doctor's appointment in Billings today. You don't remember me saying this?" I shook my head no, a full-faced red-hot mess.

After taking his last bite, my uncle wiped his mouth with his napkin, dropping it onto his plate. "Listen, for a change of pace, why don't you take the boys into Laurel? Check out some of the local sights. Plus, trout are running."

"I'm not sure if they—"

"I'm in," Shane interrupted.

"Me too," Max echoed just as quickly.

"Then it's settled." He tossed me the keys to the truck. "Be gentle on the ol' bucket of bolts. Remember to—"

"Check the oil. I know." He flashed his big, dimpled grin and left the kitchen to prepare for his appointment.

I glanced at the duo by my side. Looks like I was third wheeling it today, as Max and Shane arm wrestled at the table when I briefly turned away. "I guess we're going on a field trip."

They both flashed eager grins as I rolled my eyes. Their synchronized reactions meant it was going to be an interesting day. It transported me straight back to when the three of us would do stupid things in high school.

I smiled.

***

The truck thundered to life after I had properly checked the oil. Laurel wasn't far, but it would be my luck that today would be the day I'd kill my uncle's beloved clunker. Max slipped into the backseat after stowing Shane's chair in the truck bed, leaving the seat next to me for Shane. He was quiet again but in good spirits the entire ride.

Max, however, spent the entire time switching between cracking jokes and singing off-key until our ears ached. It felt exactly like the trips our trio would take into the city or to the Jersey Shore a couple years ago. The fond memories warmed me. I remained optimistic that cheerful Shane wasn't an act, but I'd be remiss if I didn't admit I was on edge, too. As if at any moment, he might crack.

Still outside of Laurel, we headed to the river first since it was still early and many of the shops hadn't opened yet. We cut our way southwest towards the Buffalo Mirage fishing site. It was my Aunt Tori's favorite spot to fish, raft, and boat, so I knew it well. It was somewhat flat, and hopefully conducive for Shane's wheelchair to manage.

It took longer to get there than I remembered, but it could have just been my perception when being in such tight quarters with the boys. We pulled onto the gravel and crossed a little bridge. As we traveled down the long access road, we parked in the last lot closest to the river's edge. The ground would be stony until we reached the silt-laden riverbank.

At first, the wheelchair rolled smoothly over the terrain with our help but soon we lost traction and the wheelchair refused to budge. With Max holding Shane on his right side, we made our way to the water. It was difficult, but the boys were determined to get there.

The part of the river we were at was very shallow and got deeper as you moved in. Since it was early April, the freezing waters were still low from winter. Fly-fisherman stood in a line in heavy waders, perfectly spread out with mathematical precision. As the cool of the morning burned off, we watched them practice their craft.

Their movements were nimble and precise. Whipping the rods overhead caused their neon lines to dance through the air. Then the lines would finally snap straight, allowing the tied fly to fall as gently as a snowflake. My heart thrummed, fascinated to watch the rhythmic motion of the rods.

Shane's voice returned me to the moment. "Max, help me get in the water."

My head snapped toward Shane. "No way! It's freezing." His request startled me. *What the hell was he thinking?*

"Max, help me!" Shane demanded; the crack I had waited for earlier reared its head. Max looked at me helplessly as I fervently shook my head.

"Please, Max…" Shane begged.

I grabbed his arm, "No! We came to view the trout running. Not join them!"

Shane looked pleadingly at Max. With a resigned sigh, Max looped his arm around Shane, and together they entered the water.

"Max, stop!" I shouted. Max yelped from the cold, but Shane kept them moving forward. Once up to their knees, Max looked back at me.

"Shane, that's far enough!"

Shane moved in deeper, compelling Max to continue forward. Stepping into the river, I hissed under my breath, *This was insane.*

The icy water stung straight through my cowboy boots and bit mercilessly at my feet. I was about to scurry back to dry land when Shane reached out to me, encouraging me to walk toward him.

I lifted my legs high, as if that would keep the saturation at bay. The further I walked, the heavier my jeans became and the more slippery the pebbles were under my feet. Holding my arms out to my sides for balance, I slowly wobbled my way toward the pair. The water crept higher, making my legs feel like pins and needles.

Shane took my hand as I reached him, tucking me against his side. "I got you." He smiled warmly at me and for the briefest moment I forgot the cold.

He wrapped an arm across my shoulders, while I used mine to support his waist. Max grasped my forearm, keeping all three of us steady. Together.

We hobbled forward, going deeper. The frigid chill burned my skin, and I shivered. As the water reached the boys' mid-thighs, it settled at the edge of my bottom. Shane stopped abruptly. He stood frozen, mirroring our current state as he stared out into the distance.

Closer to the anglers now we could hear the pulling of line through their reels in synchronized fashion. Shane had fixed onto their movements. Suddenly, his eyes darted to the water below.

"Whoa. Did you feel that?" Shane exclaimed. The closest fisherman gave us a pointed look.

"I can't feel anything dude," Max whined.

"Feel what, Shane?" I asked.

"Fish. Lots of fish. Look at them all." Max and I turned our heads downward. Brown and Rainbow trout scattered from our movement and noise.

"Oh, shit. There's so many. I have no idea how you felt them because I can't feel anything up to my balls anymore," Max shared.

"It's wonderful!" Shane exclaimed.

"That I can't feel my balls?"

"No. That the fish are alive. That we are alive. That I'm alive!" He leaned back, looking up at the clouds as if searching for an answer to his life. Then he softly spoke, "Kira Sky."

My heart skipped the moment my name left his lips. The thudding drowned out by the surrounding stream. Max glanced over at me with a cocky smirk. It was happening. The Shane we once knew was returning to us.
A glimmer of optimism had taken hold.

Chapter 34

Apparently...

Shane

MAX WASN'T WRONG. The water froze my balls off too. But the sharp bite made me feel alive, a radiating warmth coursing throughout my body that I had never experienced before. Or maybe it was hypothermia.

This river was bliss. The refraction of light that hit the surface caused sparkles as babbling water flowed endlessly over jagged rocks, turning them into smooth, rounded pebbles. The centuries of history that formed this flawlessly constructed river were proof of a force greater than all of us.

"I'm ready," I boldly announced.

"Me too. I can't feel my toes," Kira whimpered.

"No, I mean that I'm ready to accept therapy. I'm ready to see a therapist and really put the work into your horse program." Kira tucked into my arm and looked up at me in surprise.

I tilted my head down at her and instinctively, tightened the arm draped across her shoulder. My eyes darting to her lips that suddenly had me aching to kiss them. Max cleared his throat, breaking the trance.

"Hate to interrupt, but I am *READY* to get out of this water."

The three of us hightailed our way to the shore as our wet clothes met the air. My teeth rattled aggressively as my body trembled. "I'm s-s-sorry. I didn't m-mean to give us all pneumonia."

Kira cocked her head. "I have an idea. Let's g-get to the truck." It was one hell of a time to get back, but we all happily clambered in. And when she pulled into the laundromat at Second Street and Main, we knew the plan.

I panicked at first, not quite ready to expose my partial leg to Kira yet. I glanced around the truck, looking for anything, I could use to cover myself. Finding a horse blanket in the back seat helped my nerves to settle.

We sat in our underwear while everything from our pants down dried. I kept the horse blanket securely in place covering both legs. To pass the time, we sat around and reminisced about our antics in high school.

The conversation naturally shifted to our lives during the past two years. Max working at the car dealership and Kira moving to the ranch after graduation. Then there was me, living my dream until I wasn't. The End. My breathing hitched as I felt a dark roaming inside. I instinctively reached down to rub the pain throbbing in my "Steven" knee that was no longer there.

Kira extended her hand and placed it over mine. I turned my palm, and we interlaced our fingers together. They fit perfectly. When she didn't pull her hand away, I squeezed tighter.

Taking this cue, Max excused himself from our pod of chairs. My thumb rubbed small circles on the back of hand like muscle memory. My gaze caught hers, and she grinned. Her smile was like a ray of sunshine purging the dark from my essence. Feeling bold, I decided to profess what was happening to me.

"Kira—" I started but was interrupted as her phone vibrated.

Looking like she had woken from a dream, she untwined our hands and answered the phone. "Clay?"

My chest tightened as I lost my chance to confess my feelings. With my mood dampened, I could only watch her walk away as she spoke to her boyfriend. The flannel she wore over her shirt covered most of her underwear as we sat and waited for our clothes to dry. But as she stood to speak with Clay, the flannel rose, exposing her. Fortunately, the three of us were the sole occupants of the laundromat. With my brain finally registering that Kira was half-naked, my body hummed. I quickly forced myself to turn my head, but my eyes involuntarily returned to her form.

Of course, I had known her intimately when we were dating, but this felt different. We weren't the same people as two years ago, and she certainly didn't have the same body. Her figure left me defenseless against this new revelation bouncing around my mind.

"Drool much?" Max asked, pointing out the obvious as he flopped down beside me.

I threw my hands up to my eyes, furiously rubbing them. "What am I doing?"

"You're getting her back. That's what you're doing." He squeezed my shoulder tightly.

"But she's with Clay," I groaned.

"And?" I shot Max a death glare. "That was different. Kyle and Wren went behind your back. You're taking her in front of his nose."

I scoffed, "It's still not right."

"I see how she looks at you. How she touches you. This is not one-sided."

Chewing on his words, I glanced in her direction as she walked up to us. "Is everything okay?" I asked.

Her tone was upbeat, answering with a tilt of her head. "Oh, yeah! He apologized for being a complete ass and wants to talk at home so he can properly grovel."

I blinked twice, drawing out my question. "You're... giving him another chance, Kira?"

"Of course," she said without missing a beat. The dryer chimed, and she bolted to retrieve our clothes.

I shot another death glare toward Max. "Not one-sided, my ass," I sneered, but he just rolled his eyes.

Apparently, I had gotten my signals crossed.

Kira

I had to shake myself out of a daze to answer Clay's call. I freaked out at first. It seemed like he had somehow known about my brief lapse in judgment. While holding Shane's hand, his touch had me reeling. His strength and toasty warmth had brought back tender memories. I stepped away from the boys for privacy. Clay's call was a surprise since we hadn't spoken yet.

I started cautiously, "...Hello?"

"Hey, Kira. You answered... that's a good sign. I'm hoping you'll stay on long enough for me to apologize."

"Go on." I tugged at the hem of my flannel, hoping it would help cover the tops of my thighs.

"I was an absolute asshole. I was jealous... but that really isn't an excuse."

"No, it isn't." I picked at a random sticker someone had left on the wall to occupy my nerves as we talked.

"I know."

"Did my uncle—"

"He gave me one of his famous tongue lashings, yeah. Boss got the point across. I promise."

"Uncle Nash has a way about him. It runs in the family. My dad is the same way." The corner of my mouth turned upward. It almost felt easy to talk to Clay again. I allowed myself to drop my guard.

"Weird, I never got that vibe from him when he visited."

A small huff escaped me, "You met Vacation Levi. Not Dad Levi. Trust me, they're cut from the same cloth." I glanced over at the boys sitting near the dryers, subtly trying to check in and see how they were doing. I was glad that Shane had stopped shaking.

"Mental note. Meet Dad Levi. Got it." Clay's joke fell flat.

"I'm still mad," I muttered, biting the inside of my cheek.

"You should be. But could you try to forgive me?" He begged.

"I need some time, but I'll try." A hint of guilt seeped into my answer after just having had that *moment* with Shane only minutes ago.

"That's all I'm asking for. The meetings on the rez are almost done. Can we talk more when I get home so I can properly grovel in person?"

"Okay. But I'm not home either. I'll text you as soon as we're all home."

"All?" His intonation rose.

I let out a small sigh; the cold had exhausted me. "Yeah, I'm with Shane and Max in Laurel."

"What are you doing over there?"

"Well, right now we're sitting in our underwear at the laundromat..." *Stop talking, Kira!* I screamed internally, but the word vomit kept spewing. "...waiting for our pants to dry because we all waded into the river at Buffalo Mirage."

"You waded into the freezing water? Are you all insane?" I stiffened.

"It was Shane's idea, but what really happened was—"

"Kira, if Shane asked you to jump off a bridge, would you? Never mind. I know the answer."

"Clay, it wasn't like that." I paced back and forth, blinking away a headache.

"What's it like then? Tell me. Because what it sounds like is that you're still obsessed with a guy who was in love with someone else. And here I am, right in front of you, yet you can't even see me!" he yelled.

His words halted me. A painful lump formed in my throat. He wasn't completely wrong. Old feelings of betrayal came crashing down on me like a tsunami. But this time, I was the wave of destruction.

Clay took an audible deep breath. "You've been distracted and unfocused ever since he got here. And now you tell me you're hanging out with the boys in your underwear!? How should I react to that?"

"It's not as bad as it sounds. Can we talk later when I get home?" I chewed on my thumbnail as I awaited his reply.

"I think we should. Don't you?"

"Yes. I think we *both* have a lot to say." My eyes darted toward Shane fleetingly. There was too much going on today.

"Right. Text me when you get there." He hung up, leaving me with my jaw wide open. Our conversation had my head spinning. In one little day away from each other, we certainly had loads to talk about tonight.

I glanced up to see Shane staring in my direction. I straightened up and walked confidently over to him as I knew the question that was coming.

"Is everything okay?" He asked cautiously.

"Oh, yeah. He apologized for being a complete ass and wants to talk when I get home so he can properly grovel."

"You're... giving him another chance, Kira?"

"Of course," I said without missing a beat, even though I wasn't entirely sure. The dryer chimed, and I went over to retrieve our clothes to escape his disheartened stare.

Clay was right about one thing. I'd been distracted and unfocused since Shane got here. The total opposite of the person I was here on the ranch. The Shane trickle-down effect had negatively affected Clay way more than I ever anticipated. Especially from a Whitmore brother I swore I never wanted to see.

Apparently, I had gotten my signals crossed.

Chapter 35

...was in it.

Shane

WITH OUR CLOTHES now dried, the air felt heavy as we all got dressed. Kira had to put paper towels in the bottom of her cowboy boots to absorb the moisture since she couldn't throw them in the dryer. Thankfully, her now dry socks were thick and warm. Once in the truck, our stomachs rumbled loudly from the morning's adventures.

"Hey, where can we get some authentic Montana eats? I'm starving." Max groaned, the first to break the quiet. I couldn't quite pin why, but Kira seemed off since the phone call. She stared out the windshield, squeezing the steering wheel until her knuckles turned white. "You all right?" Max probed. He shook her shoulder from the backseat. It gently jostled her to the present.

"Huh? My mind wandered for a moment. What did you need?"

"Max hungry. Max needs to eat. Max wants barbeque," he grinned, trying to lighten the mood. Kira let out a tiny snort, turning on her blinker as she moved over a lane.

"Okay, okay. I know the perfect place." Her restaurant choice didn't disappoint. It was this authentic BBQ joint stuck in between a row of shops on East Main Street. It had a tiny sign with humble décor inside. But the place was wheelchair accessible, and the food was outstanding. Their barbecue sauce struck just the right balance of smoky sweet and spicy heat. Max cleared his plate. *That guy could put away the food.* Surprisingly, I cleared mine too. I felt famished for the first time in a long while. But Kira only pushed her meal around, taking an occasional bite. It seemed like her mind was a million miles away. Mine too, honestly.

My thoughts remained at the river. How my impulsive decision to enter the frigid water had awakened my senses. The hypnotizing mix of beauty and pain. A direct allegory of my life.

I looked across the table. Max devoured his food while Kira avoided hers. These two people never gave up on me despite my jackass antics. It was a miracle that this girl was in my life again at all. I couldn't squander the gift that I'd been given. Before I left home back East, Dr. Collier had given me a list of therapists and rehabilitation places near Spirit Ranch. At the time, I couldn't have cared less. Until today.

"Can we stop at this physical therapy spot, here in Laurel, that Dr. Collier told me about before we head home?" I blurted out before my mind could stop me. "They have a department that specializes in the treatment of... amputees." The word almost got stuck in my throat.

Kira and Max stilled, their eyes trained on me as if they were gauging the ferocity of a wild animal. "Um, yeah. I know the place. Mountain Land Physical Therapy. It's literally across the street, Shane," Kira reacted first.

"It's fate. Hopefully they're open," I mused.

"You want to go now?" Max raised a brow.

"Right now. Before I lose my nerve," I said honestly.

"Are you sure?" Kira drew out the question.

"I've never been surer about anything in my life, with one exception," I declared, staring intently at Kira. She held my gaze for what seemed like an eternity. Max knocked us out of our spell as he shook my shoulder excitedly.

"That's my boy. Let's do this!"

"Okay, let's do this," Kira agreed with a small smile. She waved her hand in the air for the waitress. "Check, please."

***

The sun began to set on the drive home from Laurel. The mood in front of the truck was balanced between light and heavy. In the back, Max snored away completely carefree. Kira suggested we stay in Laurel to do some shopping after we left the physical therapy center. Max and I vetoed the idea, so she offered to take us for pizza instead. If there's one thing I remember about Kira Sky, it's that she hated pizza. This all but confirmed her avoidance going home.

As for me, I hadn't felt this light in a long time. The Mountain Land Physical Therapy program sounded perfect. Everyone was so welcoming as we toured the facility. There were people from every walk of life, yet they were all like me. An amputee, without one or more of their limbs. Being an amputee got you noticed in public. But here, I didn't stand out.

We pulled up the long, bumpy ranch drive. A palpable heavy stress emanated off Kira. I brushed the side of her cheek unexpectantly. She flinched, the steering wheel jerking the truck off the stone drive. The vehicle bounced violently until she righted it back onto the path.

Max clicked his tongue. "Geez, Shane. Your poor attempt at flirting nearly got us killed."

"I don't know what you're talking about." I snipped, my anger misplaced for being called out. Max rolled his eyes before yawning, stretching his arms out.

We parked in front of the house just as twilight between day and night hovered above us. I'll never get used to the majestic masterpieces painted across the sky every night. Levi was right. It really does change you.

Kira shot off a text and hopped out of the truck. I knew who and wished I could have been a fly on the laundromat wall, listening to their conversation. Although she seemed upbeat about the call, her demeanor afterwards said otherwise, wanting to stay in Laurel and avoid going home. Did she misdirect her emotions for her sake or for mine?

Max and I got out of the truck as Clay appeared out of thin air. I stiffened when I saw the scowl on his face. Irritation oozed off him. My first impulse was to rush over and get between them but thought better of it.

"Let's talk about this river thing," Clay harshly addressed Kira.

"It's getting late. Can we talk tomorrow?" Her voice sounded weary. *What happened to him properly groveling?*

"No, now," he snapped.

My muscles moved of their own volition as I prepared to interfere, anyway. "Don't take it out on her, Clay. It's my fault. I made her go in the water."

"And conveniently having to strip down at the laundromat to 'dry your clothes,'" he said using air quotes.

"Yes, but you need to know she only wanted to help out… a friend." I choked on the last words. Kira snapped her head toward me. Her mouth turned down, as her shoulders drooped. Her expression stabbed at my heart. I desperately wanted to tell her it wasn't true, but faking the truth was easier.

Kira turned back toward Clay. "Okay, let's talk." They headed to the barn, walking in step with each other.

Max stood directly in front of me, and I looked up at him, ready for whatever speech he was about to throw my way. "What the hell are you doing, Shane? A friend!? You know it's more than that."

"I've been 'the other guy' unknowingly before, Max. I sure as hell won't be that guy knowingly."

"People don't invite someone back into their lives when they've truly moved on. Not like this." He shoved his hands into his pockets. "Not when they're already happy and following their dreams. That had to mean something, Shane. She still made space for *you* in her life."

I had thought about that. Many times. But I always stuffed it down like I did with everything else that meant anything to me. I tried to convince myself she was only helping from a place of pity or misplaced obligation to our old lives. I couldn't comprehend that she would forgive me after all this time.

Today in the water, and holding Kira's hand at the laundromat, it made my heart pound again. It wasn't just beating to keep me alive. This time, it was a beating desire for life. It pulsated full of hope that I had long believed was gone. I could see the future.

And she was in it.

Kira

Hearing Shane say we were *just "friends"* stung. As if it wasn't annoying enough that I misread what happened at the laundromat as something more. I wasn't even sure why it hurt so much. Here I was, doing what I always did, repeating the same mistakes. Except this time, he wasn't distracted by Wren. Which only meant he really did see me as a friend, and that was... a good thing. I wanted him to come here for therapy and to heal. I wanted each of us to not interrupt each other's lives. *Didn't I?*

"Hello?" Clay derided.

"What did you say?" I blinked, realizing I had been dissociating. My vision slowly zoomed back in; I had apparently been staring intently at a crack in the wall. Today had been far too long.

"I said your name, but you were so lost in your thoughts about *him* that you didn't hear me." He rubbed his forehead.

"They weren't about him," I said. *Why did I lie to Clay?*

"Right." The ranch hand narrowed his eyes.

"Okay, they were... about him, but—" Clay scoffed loudly. "Let me finish!" I snapped. "They were about you too."

"So, this is it then? We're done?" he jeered.

"No." We may have both been surprised by my answer. "Actually, the opposite. I don't want you to feel like my second choice. I've been there. Twice. And it sucks. I honestly believed that nothing would change between us having Shane here, but somehow it did. And for that, I'm sorry."

"Uhm, I didn't... uh... think this was how our conversation was going to go tonight," Clay stammered. The hot air that had brewed under the surface seemed to melt away from him.

"You... thought we would break up?" I frowned.

"Kinda." He almost sounded embarrassed, unable to meet my gaze.

"I know we have issues that we're both working through. But I'm willing to try, Clay." I placed my hand on his cheek, and he finally met me where I stood.

"I'm willing to try too." He gently pulled me to him. I wrapped my arms around his neck, reaching up on my tippy toes. He slowly encompassed me, holding so tightly as if clinging to a lifebuoy.

Abruptly, he pulled back. "Hey, let's take a ride tomorrow. Just the two of us. Away from everything and everyone. We can talk." He asked excitedly.

Worry washed over me, and he immediately noticed my hesitation. "I... um, promised Shane I would go with him tomorrow for his consultation at Mountain Rehab. I'm sorry. Can I raincheck?"

The tension-filled muscles in his jaw flexed. "Sure," he answered through clenched teeth. After a beat he added, "I have an early morning tomorrow. I need to catch up on chores from today. Good night, Kira."

I tried to reply, "Good night," but I don't think the sound left my mouth. I watched him go, then slowly ambled to the house. My mind warred with itself over what had just occurred. *Why hadn't I promised Clay that I would spend the day with him? Ask Max to take Shane to his consultation appointment instead?*

Then I remembered my why. Shane stood at the bottom of the ramp near the house. Twinkling stars filled the sky, illuminating my path to him. His dark figure was framed by the moonlight, making him glow like my own personal constellation. My breath caught in my throat.

I reminisced about the star walks we used to take when we were in high school. We would drive to "Makeout Lake," at least that's what all the teenagers called it. We'd curl up in blankets on the ground and watch the stars while he held my hand to his chest, the other pointed out different constellations. He always said my vast star knowledge "wowed" him. But right now, I felt "wowed."

"How'd it go with Clay?" he asked, cutting through my thoughts.

Still fuzzy from the non-fight, I replied, "Good. Ish?"

He tilted his head, asking in a low voice, "Are you okay?" *That's a loaded question*, I thought. His blue eyes made my knees weak, and my body wobbled. He reached out for my arm, steadying me.

"Long day," I quipped with a shrug.

He smiled, making his dimples pop. *How many times have I traced the features of his face with my fingers? Trying to memorize every curve and angle. How I had wanted to lose myself in the blue pools of his eyes forever.* Overwhelmed by emotion, tears welled.

When he released me from his hold, both physically and emotionally, I knew I crossed a line that I had carefully drawn. He sat down in his chair, moving back up the ramp. I slowly followed, relishing the moment that was chock full of heady implications. I saw more than just my past now. I could see the future.

And he was in it.

Chapter 36

What was I...

Shane

I MISSED MAX. He'd flown home a little over a month ago. I needed more time with him than just a week. He had brought new energy to the ranch, and a breath of fresh air with his no-bullshit policy. He called it like he saw it when it came to me and everything Kira. I knew he meant well, but she was with Clay. That needed to be considered, and it negated any lingering effect of our previous life as a couple seeping into the present.

Despite Clay's jealousy, Kira had spent as much time as possible with the two of us. After the first couple days of drama, it had been nice to slow down. We hung around the ranch by day, and at night we had campfires on the back deck. It was a spacious spot perfect for gatherings and overlooked Nash's property. The perfect place to catch the sunset every evening. It had quickly become my favorite location on the ranch.

Max had taken his very first horseback riding lesson under Kira's tutelage. She taught him how to tack Honey and the best way to mount. Kira had guided him around the paddock first before the two of them took slow rides together around the pasture. He'd learned quickly, and insisted on buying a genuine cowboy hat and set of boots.

Since then, he had been insufferable with hootin' and hollering, waving his hat in the air, and using a fake drawl to speak. But that was our Max. The lovable, goofy, straight-shooting, would-die-for-you, best friend.

After Max left, Kira helped me find a new therapist, Dr. Birdingground in Laurel. She reminded me of Dr. Collier back East, making the transition to seeing her much easier on me. Since I no longer drove, Kira took me to every appointment. At my physical therapy sessions, she had been incredibly positive about their suggestions. A confidence radiated off her when she spoke passionately about how to integrate their ideas into Spirit Ranch's program. She had found her calling, but I'd be lying if I said it didn't feel like a small twist of a knife in my heart.

I also rode for the first time, with Max's encouragement. Initial nerves quickly shifted to delight. As I looked down at Max and Kira, a luxury I'd missed, a sense of calm swept over me. Kira slowly walked us around the indoor area, Max beside me. She explained that horses could sense human emotions, and with their large electromagnetic presence, they were able to synchronize both heartbeats. This encourages calmness and relaxation as well as lowering stress in humans.

Being pessimistic, I hadn't believed a horse could actually do that, but I found myself excited to get up every morning to see Honey. How this massive creature was so keenly aware of my emotions and could adjust to my needs with ease was fascinating. She was also non-judgmental, something I desperately needed with how hard I was on myself. But I was working on it.

I was out in the stable doing my normal daily routine of helping Kira groom Honey. She had gotten used to my touch and would whinny excitedly each morning I entered her stall.

The ease of this task had come in time and the trust we established allowed me to hold her braided mane to steady myself. I used this method to reach the top of her back. I may have been imagining it, but she almost seemed to bow, making the job easier on me. I patted her nose in gratitude, and she gave a happy snort. I wiped my hand on my jeans, no longer horrified at the snotty wetness she exhaled.

I heard a humming in the distance of the stable growing louder and closer. I immediately knew Kira was on her way, a grin plastered to my face.

"So, you'll never guess who just called me." Kira skipped into Honey's stall where I groomed her.

"Max," I surmised, still brushing Honey's luxurious golden mane.

"Good guess. But no, think spicier." My head snapped Kira.

"Sarah!?"

"Yup. I guess Max went to her end-of-year fashion show, and she introduced him to her friend Henri from class. Apparently, they have a date on Friday."

"Sarah does love gossip."

"Well, that's not the only news. She's working on a new fashion line with a Western slant and wants to come out to the ranch this summer. Get some inspiration, check the vibes, take some pictures." Kira counted out each request on her fingers.

"Did you say yes?"

"Does one ever say 'no' to Sarah?"

"Good point." We laughed. I loved to hear her laugh.

I gave Honey a warm pat and put the grooming supplies in the bucket. Kira grabbed it as we went to the tack room to put the supplies away.

"Are you excited about today?" Kira anticipated my reply.

"About another doctor's appointment?" I asked flippantly.

"It's the prosthetic evaluation! Max told me how much you miss playing—"

"Of course he did." Irritated, I took the grooming bucket from her and put all the items back into their place.

"Maybe this will—"

"I appreciate the positivity, but that ship has sailed." *More like it sunk,* I thought as I followed her out of the stable toward the truck.

"You don't know that."

"I do, actually, so let's get this over with." I did my well-practiced hop into the passenger side of the truck, and she put my chair on the seat behind me. As Kira got in, Clay waved from a distance. She waved back.

They were still together, but she spent most of her time with me now. Driving me to appointments and therapy sessions. Clay had been keeping a good-humored appearance, but I could sense the resentment. Lately, whenever he was around us, he acted like a bomb with a hair-trigger. As if the slightest pressure would cause him to explode. I did have some sympathy for him, since I would feel the same way if the roles were reversed.

***

"Would you like your girlfriend to stay or go during the physical part of your exam?" the doctor asked.

"Uh… " The question flustered me, yet I loved the words *your girlfriend.*

"It's okay. I can go wait in the hall," Kira offered. My breathing quickened. Was it because I wanted her to go or because I wanted her to stay?

She placed her hand on mine and moved closer to my ear. "It's okay. I'm here." The power of her presence slowed my breath.

A memory flashed in my mind of when we were together in high school. We had fallen asleep on her couch, and at some point, we'd accidentally rolled off. On the way down, I had hit my "Steven" knee on the coffee table. The searing pain, along with a dream still ruminating, had triggered a panic attack. She crawled over to me, taking my hand and whispering those same words.

"Stay," I breathed.

The doctor glanced between us. "Okay. Just sweatpants, shoe, and sock need to come off. You can keep everything else on. I'll be back in a few minutes." Then he left the room.

I picked at the skin on my thumb, realizing she had never seen me without pants since I lost my leg. Not even at the laundromat. I had kept a well-placed horse blanket on my lap the entire time. She had never seen what was left of my leg. "I want you to be prepared. It's hard to look at."

"I'm prepared," she said confidently.

Kira knelt in front of me, easing off my lone sneaker and sock. As I reached to push my pants down over my hips, I hesitated. Kira looked up at me, still kneeling. "I've seen you in your underwear before, so don't get shy on me now," she jested, trying to lighten the mood.

I managed to smile and slid my sweatpants down to my thighs, hyperconscious of the cool, stale air against my skin. The fact that she was kneeling on the speckled tile floor, and that my gnarly stump would be fully exposed, settled heavily in my chest.

Kira reached for the waistband and gently pulled the fabric the rest of the way down and off my body. When her hand brushed my thigh, just above the stump, my breath caught. A jolt of electricity shot through to my core. Kira paused, studying me, then let her fingers trace my scars, not flinching nor looking away. Just burning a trail of need as she lazily traced their lines.

My arms trembled as I held myself upright. All rational thought had disappeared. I wanted to pull her up to her feet, to kiss her, to make this moment less fragile somehow. To capture her gorgeous lips. To never let her go. Instead, the intensity overwhelmed me, and I dropped into my chair, covering my lap instinctively with a flush. I was just a boy being intimately touched by the woman that I was still in love with, after all. Leg or no leg.

She let out a small giggle, more nervous than teasing, and gathered my sweatpants. I took them from her, grateful for the barrier.

Suddenly, I heard a small knock at the door. "Fuck," I murmured.

"We need a minute," she yelled through the door before giggling loudly.

"Real funny. You know it was your fault."

"I know." She let those two little words dangle with future potential. Funny how she hated when her father did that, yet here she was. I huffed. It caused little relief to my current predicament, and I willed my body to resist its urges before the doctor came back.

***

Later, while driving home, I cut the silence with a question that had been on my mind since the appointment earlier. "Did it bother you or gross you out to see my leg like that?"

She glanced over, taking her eyes off the road for a quick second. "No. Did you think it would bother me?"

"Kinda." He squirmed in his seat, cracking his knuckles.

"I liked Before Shane, and I like After Shane. In fact, I think I like After Shane more..." Her voice trailed off.

She trained her eyes back on the road, biting her lip. It gave the impression she hadn't meant to say the last part of her statement out loud. But I liked her analogy because although I had really liked Before Kira, I liked After Kira more.

What was I going to do now?

Kira

My internal monologue screamed at me. I couldn't believe I had said that. Out loud. To him. My thoughts then wandered back to the doctor's office, where my mere touch had completely unhinged the moment. Then, in an un-Kira-like fashion, I had been so flippant about the whole situation. It was like a different me had taken over, and current me floated above, watching the whole scene play out. Maybe muscle memory snuck in from when we'd dated in high school; our intimate moments flooding back as I kneeled before him, touching him.

My mind must have wandered as I realized we had made the final turn onto the long, rocky driveway to the ranch. So lost in thought, I had driven on autopilot the entire way home. *Home,* I lamented. Where Clay would surely be waiting for me. Would he notice the obvious tension? Would he notice that the Kira he knew was changing? I looked in the rearview mirror, and I sneered at what I saw, because it was blatantly obvious.

As I shifted into park, Clay stood from the rocking chair on the porch. He jogged down the stairs, greeting me with a smile. My heart as heavy as a ton of bricks, and I feigned a smile through the dust-covered window. I hopped out and into Clay's waiting arms. He squeezed me tightly, lifting me off the ground.

"I missed you," he professed into my tousled hair. Guilt rising, I nuzzled my face into his shoulder as my answer.

He quickly let me go and headed over to help Shane, attempting to pull his wheelchair out of the bed of the truck on his own. "Hey. I got it, bro."

"Thanks, *bro*." Shane huffed. I had hoped now that the two of them could play nice. Shane had been on his somewhat best behavior around Clay recently.

"So, are you getting the new leg?" Clay asked. I tilted my head, unsure if his question was sincere.

"I need more appointments to determine the proper fit, but yeah. It looks like I will. It'll take weeks if not months before I get the actual prosthetic, though," Shane recounted, trying to remember details from the appointment.

"Of course it will," Clay muttered under his breath, but we all heard it.

"This is a good thing. Shane has time to strengthen his legs and bear weight in the prosthetic during physical therapy. But he's all mine when working on balance in horse therapy." I had tried to help diffuse the situation but had unintentionally made it worse. Clay grimaced. *Ugh, why had I said it that way?*

"Ah, here they are," Uncle Nash bellowed from the porch. Shane's mom popped out from behind him. My gaze darted to Shane, whose face froze.

"Mom?" He looked accusingly toward me, but I shook my head vehemently.

Then I heard a deep but warm voice. "There's my Kira Sky." My head snapped toward the porch like a riding crop. There was only one other person besides Shane who ever called me that.

"Dad!? What are you doing here?"

"Surprise!" Shane's mom greeted animatedly. We both stood there wide-eyed and slack-jawed.

"What's going on? An intervention?" Shane managed to ask.

"No. Of course not. We just wanted to see you," his mom said sweetly.

Nash offered an explanation. "A covert mission that I was not privy to. Apparently, Clay here reached out to Levi, and as you say, the rest is history."

I stared pointedly at Clay, who couldn't have looked prouder of himself. Kirstie rushed down the stairs and straight to Shane. Their hug was awkward and slightly strained.

Dad smiled gently. I climbed the porch stairs, and he wrapped me in the biggest bear hug. "I missed you!"

"Me too, Dad." With my face smushing against his chest, my words were muffled. "Is Mom here?"

"No, it's just me and Kirstie. Once she heard I was going, I couldn't convince her not to."

I looked up at him and asked, "Respectfully, why *did* you come?"

"Like Nash said, it was Clay's idea." Heat rushed my cheeks.

Uncle Nash announced, "I know everyone must be famished. I have some elk stew in the crockpot, and I picked up some good 'ol fashioned cornbread from the reservation today. Come on in and get you some."

Dad followed my uncle into the house. A tortured-looking Shane and his mother trailed behind them. Clay stared at me from the bottom of the stairs as I shot daggers in his direction. Taking my cue, he didn't move. Once everyone was inside, I rushed up to him and pushed Clay's chest. It wasn't hard, but it was enough to make him stumble a step.

"What the hell, Clay?"

"I thought it would make you happy." He shuffled his feet side to side.

"Do I look happy? What kind of game are you playing?" He began to say something, then bit his tongue. "Well?"

"You called Max to come out here, and I became the fourth wheel... actually, no wheel at all. And now you spend every moment driving Shane to his appointments," Clay hissed.

"You called my dad because you felt insecure?" My voice rose.

"No, I called your dad because you've lost focus. You were paying more attention to him than to the clients."

"That's a lie, and you know it." I squared my shoulders, hands on my hips.

"Is it? Because you missed your mentor session today with Misty."

Shit. That was today? I questioned myself, flummoxed. "But why is Shane's mom here?"

"She's a bonus. I didn't know she was coming until I picked up your dad."

"This is unbelievable." I half-heartedly kicked the truck tire's rim, mud flicking off my boots.

"I agree. This whole Shane thing has been unbelievable."

My eyes flashed toward him. "I'm not having the Shane argument again."

"And I'm not standing idly by anymore. Enjoy your dinner." He stormed off to the barracks.

Shock overtook me. All I had wanted was to help. Help a friend in trouble. And it had completely blown up in my face.

What was I going to do now?

Chapter 37

This wasn't...

Shane

KIRA CAME TO dinner by herself. No Clay in tow. Another note for the ever-growing file drawer in my brain. Flashing a weak smile in my direction, she sat next to her dad. My gaze drifted to Mom, who sat beside me, pushing her stew around the bowl like a toddler avoiding their peas.

I gently elbowed her, and she warily took the smallest bite of elk meat. Her face twisted into a grimace, and she made a dramatic "mmm" sound soon after. My eyes rolled as I looked at the golden goodness on my plate, I chomped down into my cornbread. I had formed a huge affinity for its flavor while here on the ranch. I rolled it over my tongue and closed my eyes, trying to soak up the sweetness and texture.

When my eyelids popped open, I noticed everyone looking in my direction. Kira's grin stretched from ear to ear. With my mouth full, I tried to explain. "It's weally dood." She burst out laughing, and the joy spread around the table.

With the proverbial ice broken, conversation flowed more easily among us. We learned of Clay's motivation for calling Levi a few weeks ago. He had shared that Kira missed her dad. Missed home. Although technically true, it wasn't exactly what happened.

After Max left, Kira had made an offhand remark that she wished she could see her family more. That living so far away was her biggest regret. With the addition of a few tears at Max's departure, it seemed that Clay had taken it upon himself to contact her dad. Kira squirmed in her seat, clearly uncomfortable with the explanation. It caught my eye. *Was there more to the "Clay's just being a nice guy" story?*

After dinner, Nash invited us to sit out on the deck. It was rarely used until Max's visit, and then the three of us had taken to hanging out there almost every night. There were Adirondack chairs in a large circle around a metal fire pit ring that sat directly in the middle. The arms of the chairs were wide enough that there was no need for side tables.

With the beauty of the spot, and good memories planted with my friends, it had become a refuge for me when the noise thundered too loudly in my head. By day, its warmth brought me energy and strength. At night, its coolness brought me calm and solace.

Since Max's departure, Kira and I continued to use the deck for nearly every sundown. We would play music, observe the stars, watch movies on her iPad, or just talk. Getting reacquainted with her felt easy and natural. It was the second chance I had always hoped for, except she was still with Clay.

We executed our normal nightly routine as everyone followed us out onto the deck. I flicked on the deck lights and loaded wood into the firepit, while she set up our chairs with blankets, drinks, and snacks. As I transferred into one of the Adirondacks, Kira lit the fire.

Noticing the eerie quiet, we realized all eyes were on us. "What's the matter?" I asked hesitantly. Nash and our parents remained motionless.

I glanced at Kira, who shrugged her shoulders. "Dad?" she queried. However, this did not break Levi's laser focus on me.

Mom finally spoke. "Um, nothing, honey. Just so happy to be here. Thank you, Nash, for your hospitality."

The corner of his mouth turned upward as he responded. "You're always welcome here, Kirstie," He motioned for her to sit, adjusting the pillow behind her back.

"Dad," Kira hissed. Levi squinted deeper before he pulled them away from me. A bit unsettled, we fidgeted in our seats as everyone shared stories. Kira twirled the ends of her hair as I obsessively cracked my knuckles. She elbowed me to stop when it grated on her last nerve.

We listened to Nash and Levi's childhood stories on the ranch and then suffered through a few embarrassing tales of Kira and me when we were young. Mom happily shared wedding updates, even running over to Kira to show her a picture of the dress like an excited teenager.

The sleeping arrangements got interesting once we proceeded into the house for the night. Nobody wanted to displace me from my room, but I insisted. Levi took my room, I would take the great room's couch, and my mom would take Kira's room. Kira took the cot to Nash's office upstairs.

Once everyone said their goodnights, I settled in on the couch. It was positioned perfectly to see out the slider door, and I let the moon and stars lull me to sleep. I was about to doze off when I heard light footsteps. Kira stood in the glow of the fridge, staring inside. She grabbed something before shutting the door.

"Kira," I whispered. She padded straight to me, with bare feet, sweatpants, and a T-shirt. The corner of my lip curved up, another memory returning from our Sunday brunches when we were dating. From her room, she would quickly hop sockless down the wooden stairs and leap into my arms to greet me. The urge to hold her again compelled me.

She sat next to me, smushing her body against mine on the edge of the couch. "Do you need some water?" She asked, holding up the bottle.

"No. I just need you." My eyes went wide as soon as the words tumbled out. *You idiot*, I scolded myself. "I didn't..."

"Mean it...?" she mumbled softly, looking down.

Oh, I meant it, my thoughts and my body screamed at me. The urge to pull her to me took over. I reached my hand up to her neck under her jawline, tangling my fingers in her hair that cascaded down her shoulder. She lifted her head, catching my eyes as her lips parted. I tenderly dragged my thumb across her mouth, and I was a goner.

Fuck it! I started to pull her mouth to mine, but just before the sweet ecstasy of a kiss, I grew a conscience. It was similar to walking through a spider web. You didn't see it until you felt the tacky webbing all around you and it made it difficult to shake off.

Snapping to our senses, she jumped up and bolted towards the hallway and up to her room. I remained still on the couch with an aching body and a more aching guilt.

Deep down, I knew that I didn't want any collateral damage. I'd been the collateral damage, and it sucked. Despite my feelings toward Clay, he didn't deserve that pain. I knew that he cared for her, so I had to do the right thing and keep my hands to myself.

This wasn't going to be easy.

Kira

The cot creaked underneath me as I leapt into it, burying my face. *What just happened?* It startled me to be so swept up in the moment that I'd almost kissed Shane. I was beginning to believe that the Whitmore brothers had some sort of supernatural power. That once their invisible tractor beam captured you, it would never let you go. It didn't matter if there was time, distance, or free will, their energy would forever hold you.

The morning came in the blink of an eye. Every single muscle in my body screamed. Between the cot, restlessness, and guilt, I knew it would be a very long day. I sat up expectantly when I heard a quiet knock at my door.

"Kira? Are you awake?" My dad's voice deflated my hope like a balloon.

"I'm awake. You can come in."

"Oh my," Dad said as he pulled over the desk chair and sat.

"I know, I know. I look terrible. I didn't sleep." I rubbed my eyes, trying to blink away the haze.

"What I see isn't sleep deprivation, my lovely awáxe. You look like you're burdened with the weight of the world. You don't have to carry it alone. I'm here." And that's all it took. I burst into tears, jumping up to hug him. I clung to him as if my life depended on it, sobbing into his chest.

"It's okay. It's going to be okay," he reassured, rocking me gently.

No matter how hard I tried, I couldn't stop crying. My tears were a sudden flash flood in the dry and desolate wasteland of my predicament. I wondered if I'd ever be able to stop.

"Clay will understand," my dad soothed.

I was so confused by his words that my sobs stuttered to a halt. "Clay will understand what?"

"That you're in love with Shane."

I leapt away from him as fast as a snake strike. "In love with S—!" I started to yell but quickly slapped my hands over my mouth. I hoped nobody downstairs heard me.

"Kira, 'People's eyes say words that the…"

"…tongue cannot pronounce.' I know." I shouted, finishing the Crow proverb my dad started. "You've been here less than a day, and sleeping for half of it. How could you have seen my eyes pronounce anything!?"

"Well, I do have a confession to make…" he said bashfully. "I may have accidentally walked in on you and Shane last night."

"WHAT?" I held out my hands at my sides in disbelief. I had to stop myself from pulling at my hair, pacing back and forth.

"I have an old bladder! I needed to use the bathroom down the hall! Then I heard talking and…"

"This is a nightmare." I flopped dramatically onto my cot, the back of my hand over my forehead.

"Kira, I already knew. Watching the two of you on the deck last night by the fire was fascinating. The way you ebbed and flowed together like you were a singular being left all of us speechless, if you recall." I did remember their awkward silence and staring, but I hadn't understood why. "Oh, and Max told me when he got home last month," my dad confessed.

"WHAT?" I shot up, screeching so loud I almost startled myself. "He told you I was in love with Shane?"

"Yes. And that Shane was in love with you."

I blinked slowly, my mind in a daze. "What am I going to do?"

"I love you, and will support any decision you make from now until forever. But the decision must be for you. Not Clay. Not Shane. For you."

I collapsed in a heap on the cot, completely drained for the day that hadn't yet begun. My dad pulled up the blanket.

"Get some rest. I'll make breakfast for the troops." He tousled my hair and left the room. I laid there, replaying a million conversations that I'd had with my dad, Max, Shane, and Clay for the last few months. It was true; my world had shifted. Shane reignited a flame I thought had burned out long ago. This entire revelation felt overwhelming, but I'd brought it upon myself.

Exhaustion took hold, and my eyelids grew heavy. My weary body and heart had hit their limit. However, one question nagged at the edge of my mind before slumber finally consumed me. How in the world would I explain these new feelings to Clay?

This wasn't going to be easy.

Chapter 38

Should I...

Shane

LEVI ALREADY IN the kitchen making breakfast without Kira concerned me. Biting my lip, I wondered if her absence was intentional. *Could she be upset that I tried to kiss her last night?* It hadn't felt one-sided, but in my lusty haze, I could have read the situation wrong.

Wanting to get back in his good graces from past transgressions, I jumped into action to help in the kitchen. Levi seemed appreciative of my gesture, but in true Bowman-style, he was a man of very few words. As I set the table, my mom shuffled into the room.

"Good morning, sweetheart," she said, bending down to kiss my forehead.

"Morning, Mom."

"Good morning, Levi. Any hot coffee?"

"Yes, ma'am." He nodded towards the just-brewed caffeinated goodness.

Mom poured herself a cup and sat next to me. "Where's Kira?" I stiffened.

"She decided to sleep in," Levi answered, giving me a quick wink. It's very unusual for Kira to *decide* to sleep in, so if Levi's wink was to make me curious about his declaration, then mission accomplished.

Oblivious to the unspoken side-commentary, Mom asked a question. "What ya'll do here on the ranch?" She used a poorly executed drawl. I cringed.

Levi answered swiftly, "Muck stalls. Always. Mucking. Stalls." His answer was laced with sarcasm.

"Well, that sounds fun," Mom said cheerfully.

"Mom, that means shoveling sh… poop."

"Oh. Never mind." She grimaced, taking another sip of her drink. I chuckled, but quickly stifled my laugh when Clay entered the room.

"Clay," Levi crowed. "Good to see ya, son. I'm sorry you couldn't come to dinner last night, but can you join us for breakfast?" Clay shot me a look.

"Nah, but thanks for the invite. I have chores that need tending, and if I don't get my chores done, then…"

"…Nash will hand you your ass in a handbasket," Levi joked.

Clay laughed. "Exactly."

Their ease with one another made me see every shade of green on the color wheel. The relationship I had with Levi always had some cracks, but with Clay it was as smooth as butter.

Clay finally turned his attention to Mom. "Good morning, Kirstie."

"Good morning," she chirped sweetly. I rolled my eyes.

"Where's Kira?" Clay directed his question toward me.

Before I could answer, Levi interjected, "She didn't sleep well last night, so…" He flipped one of the eggs in the pan.

"Misty rescheduled for today. I'll go wake Kira," Clay interrupted.

"No!" Levi said loudly, drawing our attention to him. "She needs her rest."

"But she would want—" He started before Levi cut him off.

"I said no, Clay. She had a rough night." He said tersely. *The first crack*, I thought gleefully. But I was also concerned that her "rough night" was due to my foolishness.

Clay raised his hands in defeat. "Okay. Tell her I stopped in."

"Will do," Levi mumbled without a glance as he left. Mom leaned close, placing her hand on my forearm.

"Who's Misty?" she whispered.

"Her horse therapy mentor. She advises and evaluates Kira's skills as a horse trainer and therapy teacher. It's required for her certification."

"Now that sounds fun. I hope we can watch some of that."

"Kira's amazing, Mom. Poised, kind, professional, confident. She takes my breath away." My eyes widened with my new bad habit of saying things that were meant to be internal monologue only. My gaffe garnered a quick peek from Levi.

Mom smiled. "With that glowing recommendation, I'll definitely have to watch her work today." I nodded, and heat flushed my face as I shoved a piece of bacon in my mouth.

***

"Oh, my gosh. Oh, my gosh. Oh, my gosh," Kira exclaimed nervously, rushing to the barn. I wheeled as fast as I could to keep up.

"You have plenty of prep time before Misty gets here. It'll be fine."

Her voice rose. "Fine? Fine!? I accidentally blew her off yesterday, and then I overslept today!"

"It's barely nine," I tried to catch my breath, moving around the straw-covered mess of the stable floor.

"She'll be here at ten!" she called over from behind a half-door, rushing about to get the place prepped.

"Honey, you're going to be fine." Hearing my second gaffe of the day, I inwardly groaned. *What was wrong with me today?* I cleared my throat. "I meant, Honey is a great horse. She knows what to do, and so do you."

Kira didn't seem to notice my blunder, but Clay had. He came out of nowhere again, his chin high and his brow raised. His knack for walking in at exactly the wrong moment had become an art.

Noticing she was on the edge of a freak-out, he chose not to address my slip of the tongue. "Shane's right. You and Honey know what you're doing."

"Thanks," she busily answered, making her unhappiness clear.

"Um… well, going into town," he said, but there was no answer from Kira. "Supply run. Good luck today." She was too occupied to respond, muttering to herself as she moved around a pair of saddles. Clay crossed his arms, turning to the truck to head out.

I'd be lying if I said I didn't feel bad for the guy, knowing that I was partially responsible for their discord. I'd been there before. Although the situation was not ideal, I didn't want to mess this up for Kira either.

Being on the ranch changed me for the better in every way. She gave me another chance to be in her life after she swore she never would. I wanted to right past wrongs and prove to her that she wasn't my second choice. Not even to soccer. That she had been on my mind for every passing sunrise and sunset in Portugal.

Because the truth was, it was never a choice for me. She had me the moment she awkwardly and adorably asked me to be her Valentine's date. Escaping to the other side of the world didn't change that indisputable fact. Suppressed feelings ruptured like a dormant volcano, devouring me.

Should I finally tell her?

Kira

Although my dad's visit was the result of Clay's misguided reasons, I loved every second of having him here. Watching his brotherly banter and jabbing with my uncle was hilarious. It made it easier to imagine them as little cowboys on the ranch, rolling around in the dirt and getting into mischief. I could only picture how tough they must have been to raise for my Grand-pap and Nini.

Getting reacquainted with Kirstie was also a wonderful and unexpected turn of events. She took a major interest in my training sessions and even rode a horse for the first time. My heart swelled as I guided Shane and his mother through the paddock together. He had mentioned the strain between them right until he came to the ranch. It was nice to see some of that disappear. That was the power of this place.

At the airport, saying goodbye was never easy. Seeing tears well in my dad's eyes, any man really, broke my heart into pieces. Dad thoroughly shook Shane's hand, cupping it with both of his own. It was kind of odd to see. My dad only ever did this with close friends, relatives, and his brother.

Dad gave me one more of his coveted bear hugs, where one always felt warm and safe. I'd miss that. I'd miss him. Struggling to let go, he squeezed me one last time before disentangling himself. He hurried toward the security checkpoint without looking back. I swallowed back a sob.

Shane's mom, on the other hand, openly wailed and coiled herself tightly like a vine around him. With his mom practically strangling him, it took all of Shane's might to peel her off before the dramatic scene drew onlookers.

Kirstie turned to me, wrapping her arms firmly around me. As I hugged her back, she whispered in my ear. "Shane loves you, Kira. My boys haven't always made the best decisions, but they love hard. I promise you he's the right choice. Take care of him and keep him safe." And with that little bombshell, she hustled down the corridor to join my dad. Did my dad tell her too? Or did she just guess? Had everyone known this except for me?

Standing like a statue, mouth open, Shane took my hand. I looked down at him as her words repeated in my mind. *He's the right choice*. But no pressure, right? I sighed.

The silence of the truck cab taunted me. There were so many things to say, and so many questions to ask, but it all seemed to float away and pop into nothingness. Almost home, the headlights illuminated the turn onto the long drive as our voices suddenly rang through the quiet.

"Shane..." "Kira..." we said each other's names simultaneously, roaring into comfortable laughter at the coincidence. It released the built-up tension between us.

"You go first," he extended.

"No, you." I still felt unsure how to broach the information his mother left for me. Had he mentioned something to her?

"I want to drive. I haven't driven since... before. And it's time. I know it's a crazy and stupid idea since I don't have a right leg but..."

This was not the subject matter I thought we'd be discussing tonight, but I immediately pulled over. His excited, kid-like expression had me unable to say no. I jumped out and jogged over to the passenger side.

Shane slid across the bench seat, flexing his hands over the steering wheel. It was almost as if he were trying to activate his stored muscle memory. He adjusted the mirror and tapped his left foot across the pedals, formulating a plan for how to drive with one leg.

"This is crazy, right?!" While his question was rhetorical, his beaming smile held the answer.

"The roadway to the ranch is a perfect place to try. Two things... the shifter is tight, and the brakes are soft. Other than that, it runs great."

Shane shook out his hands and gripped the steering wheel until his knuckles turned white. With his grin wide, he floored it. We both flew backward against the seat before jolting forward as he hit the brake prematurely. As our seat belts dug into our collarbones, we made a collective grunt.

"You okay? I'm really rusty." He rubbed the top of his lip, clearly embarrassed by his first try.

"I'm good," I responded. It wasn't a lie, but I was suddenly glad we weren't on the actual road.

"I guess the third thing to mention would be that the gas pedal is sensitive," Shane chuckled. After a few more attempts, he finally got the hang of it. All in all, a successful test run.

"That was amazing. Thank you, Kira for believing I could."

"I always believed you could." A thrum of emotion caught me off guard. Clearing my throat, "We can practice anytime you want."

While our adrenaline still spiked, I made a snap decision.

"See that little access road ahead?" I asked.

"Kinda," he said.

I scooted forward in the seat, trying to point it out. "Turn there. I want to show you something."

We were on the property's east side, bouncing along the pothole-laced path. The truck shuddered as it traveled, forcing me to hold on to the dashboard to reduce the rough sway. Despite the road's conditions, and claiming to be rusty, Shane handled the truck perfectly. When he put his mind to something, nothing could stop him. I was glad that he had stopped getting in his own way too.

"Pull over here." Shane did as I asked, and the truck's loud rumbles fell silent. He curiously turned his head toward me.

"What's going on?"

I grabbed the horse blanket out of the back seat, a grin on my face as I announced, "We're going on a star walk."

"Don't we need stars for that?" His question cut off when I jumped out of the truck. As I opened his driver's door, he repeated, "I asked, don't we need stars for that?"

"You'll see. Come on, slowpoke," I teased, holding out my hand. He hoisted his tall frame out of the truck and looked around. The ground was full of jagged rocks jutting out from below. Larger formations around us made small stone-like structures as tall as trees a short distance ahead. "I don't think my chair will go over any of this terrain."

"It won't. Just lean on me. It's not far." I waved my arm, encouraging him to put his weight on me. He hesitated at first but slowly agreed with the prospect of adventure.

We took our time moving across the rugged dirt toward an outcropping of rocks. "The target is those rocks ahead."

"You know I can't climb."

"Can't or won't?" I mused.

He clicked his tongue with a "*tsk*" sound under his breath, but we continued to make our way there.

Once at our destination, I threw the blanket up onto the flat rock formation that protruded out from a boulder the size of a building. I pointed to the stone at our feet, which would serve as a step. Shane looked at me with a serious side-eye, but always the adventurer, he gave it a try. He skillfully placed two hands on the waist-high rock and pulled his torso up enough to swing his lower body onto the flat spot.

"I guess *won't* is the answer," I goaded. He rolled his eyes, reaching his hand down toward me. "I've got this."

"I know," he said, still holding out his hand. I conceded. He hauled me up onto the flat surface with very little effort. I spread out the blanket next to a large stone with the perfect angle to see the sky. We leaned back like we were sitting in lounge chairs by the pool. "How did you find this place?"

"My family lived here one summer to help take care of my sick Aunt Tori. I would ride Honey every day, and when I needed refuge, I would explore their land. I got bolder and went further with each ride. I found this outcropping near dusk one day and it was the perfect spot to see the wonders of space above. This is where I saw the rare blueish-purple Northern Lights for the first time that remind me of your eyes." I clamped my mouth shut before I had another Freudian slip.

"It's gorgeous here. I can see why you and your family love this spot."

"My spot. I've never brought anyone here before. Just you." I trained my eyes on the sky to avoid looking at him when his head snapped in my direction.

Trying to justify my actions tonight, I truly believed these rocks had special powers. It had healed my woes over the years. It was a sacred place that allowed me to connect with the earth and sky on a spiritual level. I only wanted to share that feeling with Shane, and the mere fact that I did was telling.

It meant that I had never really left him in the past, despite saying I never wanted to see him again. Faking the truth was easier. But not anymore. Suppressed feelings ruptured like a dormant volcano, devouring me.

Should I finally tell him?

Chapter 39

Shane

THE DARK SKY gave way to swirls of pinks and greens with a hint of purplish blues at the edges. The Northern Lights had been a phenomenon I had wanted to experience ever since Kira mentioned that my eyes reminded her of them. Watching the colors shimmer across the sky was mesmerizing. It looked like an oil spill on water, the light striking it just right to reveal a rainbow of colors twirling beneath the surface.

Enamored, I hadn't realized that Kira had fallen silent. She was usually animated on our star walks. They held a special meaning to us and were our way of connecting on a deeper level without life's pressures. The memories alone made my hand twitch, wanting to hold hers.

"Kira? Is everything okay?"

"Do you remember our star walk at Makeout Lake two weeks before prom?" I was shocked that she chose to ask about that particular night. I cleared my throat, shifting awkwardly on the rock. That walk was a memory I repeatedly thought about the past two years. It was the night I declared my love for her despite having only been together for four months. I had never said that to anyone before. Not even to Wren, whom I had technically dated for longer. The bond Kira and I had made me the happiest I had ever been.

"Of course. Why?" I answered nervously.

"Did you really mean it? Did you really love me?" She stared up at the sky, as if the stars themselves would give her the answers she was looking for.

"Yes," I answered, surprised. "Why are you asking me that?"

"Do you know that night is tonight? The night that we laid on the blanket by the lake as you professed your love to me. Then two weeks later at prom, we were over..." Her voice quivered.

My heart ached harder than it ever had before. "Kira, what happened at prom haunts me. I still can't explain why I said her name instead of yours."

"I wasn't talking about prom. You gave up on us so easily."

I paused, partially confused. "But... you said you never wanted to see me again. Ever. I wanted to respect your wishes."

"Yes, I did. I said that... but I never thought you would." Her words danced in the cool night air. My lungs heaved, an unjustifiable response lost in my throat.

Kira continued. "I was angry and hurt. Kyle chose Wren, but you chose soccer. I watched Kyle fight for Wren even if it hurt his own brother. He fought for her, Shane. But you gave up on us. Then, after the accident, you gave up on yourself too."

The words I should have said a long time ago forced their way out of my guilty, constricted throat. "You're right. I should have fought for you. For us. I'm ashamed and have no excuse. I've thought about it so many times... if I could change one moment in my life, that would be it."

She finally turned to face me, looking deeply into my eyes. "You'd pick that moment over your accident on the field?"

"Every time." It was the truth. Kira was the one person that made me feel alive again. She was my personal Northern Lights. Her radiance freed me from the darkness. Every time.

My eyes were finally open. Trying so hard to keep everyone at a distance had been exhausting these last couple of years. I had built walls so high and strong that I never thought they could fall. However, telling the truth to her, and to myself, was exhilarating. I didn't fight for us then.

But I'm going to fight for us now.

Kira

The gravity of his words held me close. Tears tickled my face as they streaked downward. I gently rubbed them away with the back of my hand. The light that awakened in Shane at the river shone brighter, piercing pin-sized holes through my flimsy, tin heart. The boy I had once fallen in love with was now the man holding my love in front of me. But this awareness brought a new set of challenges to our dynamic at the ranch, and his name is Clay.

Shane pleaded, "I know I don't deserve it, and I definitely don't deserve you, but I'm begging for another chance to prove that I am."

Balancing two lives on my shoulders, I weighed my response carefully. Kira from two years ago would have flat out said "no." But Kira today? She was unfortunately conflicted.

"It's not that simple, Shane," I mumbled through my tears.

"I know, and I don't mean to complicate things even further. But it's always been you. There has never been anyone since you."

***

I drove us the rest of the way to the ranch after our cathartic adventure. All the beautiful things he said to me were words that I had always wanted to hear. But one small thing he mentioned still nagged in the corner of my brain. He couldn't have been serious that he said there had never been anyone else since we broke up. He had to have meant it metaphorically. It just wasn't possible. He had to have a trail of girls that he dated across Portugal.

Pulling up to the porch, both my uncle and Clay were there waiting. By the looks on their faces, they weren't happy.

"Glad to see you're still alive. We were about to send out the hounds." Uncle Nash scolded.

"Why didn't you answer your texts?" Clay's tone was fringed with both panic and anger. Realization rushed through me; we hadn't looked at our phones since leaving the airport.

"It's my fault," Shane interjected. "I asked her to let me drive the truck, which she did, on the back roads of the property. I did pretty damn well, if you ask me, and…"

I chimed in, "…then I took him to see the Northern Lights on the northeastern edge. He's never seen them before, and…"

Shane added, "…they didn't disappoint. Levi's right. Montana skies can change a person…"

"…for the better." I finished Shane's sentence again. My uncle and Clay's head stopped snapping back and forth between our incessant blabbering.

"I see," my uncle replied. There he was, Uncle Nash, with his famous two-word zinger. It was his gift.

"We lost track of time," I apologized sincerely.

"In the future, any hours long itinerary changes should be reported to me. Am I clear?" My uncle directed. I didn't blame him for worrying. There was still plenty of danger from the wildlife on our property.

"Crystal," we replied together, looking over at each other with a smile. Clay, however, was not amused.

My uncle rolled his eyes. "I'm heading to bed." As he turned to enter the house, he hollered over his shoulder, "Remember, the day starts…"

"At the butt crack of dawn." Shane and I said in unison again. We looked at each other in surprise before bursting out in a fit of laughter. It was the final straw for Clay, the man storming off the porch towards the barracks. He roughly nudged the truck on his way out.

I started to go after him, but Shane grabbed my hand. A pulse of electricity shot through my frame. "Let him cool off. He looked really upset, and I want…"

"What *do* you want, Shane?" My bold words slipped out.

He stammered, "I want… I want you to be safe." I tried to pull my hand away when he tightened his grasp. "Wait, that's not what I wanted to say." He looked at me with hunger in his eyes. "I want you, Kira. In every sense of the word."

My soul was pulled through a vortex, back to a night I held special. Where we lay on a blanket at Makeout Lake, and everything we had wanted seemed possible. My skin prickled as the memory of that night swept me away.

He said he loved me. That he was in love with me. Lost in the blue of his eyes, my heart soared. I had been working up the courage to say it for weeks, but he beat me to it. It made this moment even sweeter. Despite the whirlwind of our relationship, everything between us now felt easy, effortless. We shared our hopes and dreams, planned our future as if it were already taking shape. That was what I wanted. I wanted Shane.

"I love you too," I whispered, rolling on top of him and kissing him fully on the mouth. He wrapped his arms around me, pulling me tightly against his chest. His heart pounded wildly beneath my ear, matching my own.

I cradled his face, exploring his mouth, his tongue with a reverence that made my breath hitch. His hands roamed the length of my body before settling at my hips. His touch was slow and deliberate, sending shivers racing up my spine. My movement against him drew a low sound from his throat.

In one smooth motion, he flipped us, bracing himself above my body, his breath ragged, hunger burning in his eyes. I boldly reached down to the fly of his pants, and he gasped my name.

"Kira."

I kissed him again, unhurried and certain. But Shane hesitated when I slowly dragged his zipper down. I stilled, cupping his cheek. He leaned into my palm as I mouthed the word: I love you, Shane.

"Kira," he breathed.

"I want you, Shane. In every sense of the word." Something in him gave, and he flipped us back over, allowing me to straddle his body. I pulled the hem of his shirt up, tugging it free. I let my fingers trace the lines of his abs; his taut

stomach had always fascinated me. A low rumble reverberated through his chest as he relaxed underneath me.

When I peeled off my shirt, the cool air teased my exposed skin. Shane immediately sat up, wrapping me against him. His face tucked into my collarbone, his breath warm and steady. We stayed like that, holding each other for what seemed an eternity. As if the world might disappear if we let go.

When I finally guided his mouth back to mine, I kissed him with a tender urgency. He responded fervently, reaching behind me to unclasp my bra. His touch was gentle as his body melted into mine. I wasn't sure where he ended and I began. I just knew I wanted him in my life forever. Then and always.

I shook myself free of the memory to find Shane standing before me now, holding my hand and looking at me with the same quiet devotion. The ache of our breakup at prom, a mere two weeks after our night together, dulled at the edges. We were different people now. We had new paths to forge.

I had an answer to Shane's question. Yes, I wanted to give him another chance. I knew it would hurt Clay, and the thought weighed heavily on me. But I was going to be honest with him. Something I had not been afforded in the past. My only hope was that Clay would forgive me someday.

When I invited Shane to the ranch for therapy, he had needed help. But being here didn't just help him, it helped me too. We both needed to heal from the past. I never thought it'd be possible, and we still had a long road ahead.

But I'm going to fight for us now.

Chapter 40

...fight.

Shane

FOR THE FIRST time in years, I could see the possibilities laid out before me. I felt excited for the start of a new day. The sunrise that I now embraced brought me new energy and hope. A chance for a new life with Kira.

"You seem particularly joyful. Any reason why?" Dr. Birdingground asked.

"A lot has happened in the last couple of weeks." I could feel a grin stretch across my face as I thought of Kira.

She reached for her tablet on the side table. "Care to share?"

"Well, my relationship with Kira changed." My left leg bounced excitedly.

"In what way?" The therapist began writing notes with her stylus.

"She recently broke it off with her boyfriend and is giving me a second chance. In fact, we're headed to dinner after my session today."

"That's definitely something to be happy about. How did it go with the boyfriend? You mentioned before that he also lives on the ranch. Has there been any difficult or awkwardness with him?" She tapped the end of her stylus on the corner of her mouth.

"It's... a work in progress. But all things considered, he's handled it with maturity. I know he does it for her, but I appreciate his effort."

Dr. Birdingground jotted down a quick note. "So, you got your second chance." She smiled warmly.

"Yes. But I know it's selfish of me." My smile faded.

"It's obvious to me she feels the same about you if she's willing to break up with her boyfriend."

"I'm just worried." I started to crack my knuckles but quickly laid them flat on my arm rests.

"Worried about what exactly?" she questioned.

I rubbed the back of my neck. "That I still won't be good enough for her."

"You're a good person, Shane, despite the difficult hand you were dealt. She'll see that you're trying, and that's all that matters. It's not about being perfect; it's the willingness to try that counts."

I chuckled. "You sound like my therapist, Dr. Collier, back in New York."

She let out a soft hum. "I'll take that as a compliment."

A thought scratched at the back of my mind. "My whole life, I believed I had to be the best at everything: the best son, the best brother, the best athlete. All to compensate for my dad leaving us. I felt like I needed to be strong for my mother and brother because I was all they had. I had to be the man of the family. To make something of myself so I could support them in the future. And then, I felt like I'd fucked that up by getting hurt."

I ran my fingers through my hair and took a measured breath. "I don't know where that word vomit came from. It just spewed out of me."

"It shows you're ready for therapy. Ready to put in the work. You've put a lot of pressure on yourself to fill the space your father left in your lives, and now you're allowing yourself to process that." She set the tablet down.

"He abandoned us so easily, and he never came back. Ever." I interjected woefully. "I've always wondered why. Why hadn't he thought that I was worthy enough to stay?"

She leaned forward, "Shane, what your father did wasn't a reflection of you or your family. It was a choice rooted in his own limitations. That choice left scars, and it's okay to acknowledge the damage it caused. But you didn't become strong because he left. You became strong because you survived it, and because you chose a different path. You value commitment. You are someone who stays. You are someone who fights."

A lump formed in my throat from her words. It was as if she had given me permission to let it go. To let him go. The final weight that I had been carrying for so long lifted off my chest, allowing me to truly breathe again.

Dr. Birdingground was right. I had made it through the fire, burned but still breathing. I was alive. And I wasn't going to waste one more minute of my life.

After the session, I rushed to Kira, who sat in the waiting room. Grinning from ear to ear, she mirrored my expression. She casually walked over to me, and I stood.

Kira looked up at my face. "That must have been a great session."

"I love you, Kira. I'm in love with you." Her stunned face made me smirk. I pulled her close and kissed her. Hoping to be respectful, I hadn't kissed her since she broke up with Clay.

During the kiss, she mumbled, "Shane, everyone's watching."

"I don't care," I mumbled back, kissing her like it was the very first time.

Slow and sensual. Her body pressed against mine in the sweetest of our euphoria. She tightened her arms around me and kissed me fully; our bodies tangled with each other.

Suddenly, I heard someone clear their throat. I reluctantly broke our kiss, glancing toward the reception desk. An older woman gave us a chastised look, nodding to the door. The much younger woman beside her had her hands over her mouth, swooning at what she had just witnessed.

Kira's face flushed lobster red, and she bolted out into the hallway. I laughed, following her out of the waiting room. I fully planned on following Dr. Birdingground's wise assessment of me.

Stay and fight.

Kira

Shane's boldness shocked me. Since my breakup with Clay over two weeks ago, he had been very respectful of the situation. He made no moves on me, and we hadn't gone out on an official date until today. This morning, he asked me to dinner after his therapy session with Dr. Birdingground. I was excited to finally explore where this fresh start would take us.

But that kiss indicated full steam ahead. It took every ounce of my strength to prevent my knees from buckling. I couldn't ever recall being kissed like that by anyone, not even Shane, and I wanted more.

"What was that kiss all about?" I queried as we drove to a little saloon eatery in Billings. The food was simple but satisfying and they had live music most nights.

"To let you know I won't squander this second chance. I'll work hard to deserve you this time, and I'm not going anywhere. I'll going to stay and fight for you. For us."

I beamed. His confession solidified that I'd made the right choice. How Kirstie had predicted this weeks ago made me shake my head in disbelief.

"Just to be clear, I wasn't complaining. In fact, you've really improved your skills since high school. It must be from those Portuguese fangirls fawning all over you," I teased.

"There were no fangirls." Shane rolled his eyes.

"Okay, I meant your Portuguese girlfriends."

He tilted his head, shifting in his seat to face me. "Kira, there were no girlfriends either."

I nonchalantly tapped my fingers on the steering wheel, unable to look in his direction. "Your hook-ups?"

He shook his head, reaching over to tuck a piece of hair behind my ear. "Nope. No hook-ups either."

I furrowed my brow. "You're telling me that you didn't date anyone in Portugal? No one? How is that possible?"

"I didn't date. Anyone."

My mind raced. *He was a gorgeous professional soccer player in a country full of beautiful women.* His admission didn't make sense. It hadn't occurred to me that he wouldn't date or sleep around in Portugal. I couldn't fathom that we had been each other's first and only. I reveled in that thought.

"Kira Sky, I may have run away from my guilt, but I didn't run away from my feelings about you." He let out a soft sigh, looking down at his hands as he placed a palm on his chest. "They were always here, just under the surface, waiting for me to set them free. Despite your belief that we were a rebound relationship; it was never like that for me."

I was trying to keep my eyes on the road, but all I wanted to do was look at him. Absorb him, his words, his eyes, his heart. He continued when I didn't reply. "Yes, the circumstances of us being together were… unconventional, but being with you is real to me. My love for you was real then and it's real now. This may be my second chance, but you were never my second choice."

Feeling speechless, dismay gnawed at my thoughts. All the misconceptions that occurred between us were astounding. How had we let teenage angst and drama cloud our judgment? My judgment. It all felt incomprehensible.

Dinner was laced with anticipation for what our second chance could mean. That somehow, we made our way back to each other. Thwarting barriers that plagued us mentally and physically. This simple act of sharing a meal together with no attachments and no misdirection felt refreshing. Our cards were on the table, and we were both all in.

On the ride home, quiet contentment warmed the inside of the cab while the sun warmed the outside. I loved that there was still light shining late in the evening as summer approached.

I tapped my fingers in rhythm with the radio before glancing at Shane. "Hey, when we get back, do you want to go on a sunset ride around the property with me?" I asked on a whim.

"I only know how to ride in big circles around the arena. Are you sure I'm ready to ride in straight lines?" he asked, mocking himself.

I shook my head. "Very funny. It's part of…"

"…therapy. I know. I know." He smiled so wide his dimples popped.

I smirked. "Poor Shane, having to be patient."

"Oh, don't worry. I know how to be patient." He winked seductively. I shook my head at his lusty innuendo.

"What I meant is you'll be fine if you ride Honey since she basically rides herself. I'll ride Copper." His sultry smile and waggling eyebrows forced an eye roll from me. One date and the old Shane Whitmore showed up.

We went to the stable and began prepping the horses. Honey whinnied excitedly as we saddled her, and Copper let out a happy grunt when I placed the blanket over him. I enjoyed riding Copper when I got the chance. His steady, tolerant temperament was ideal for a therapy horse, despite having been a mischievous gelding that often escaped to roam the pasture. Deep down, I understood Copper's innate desire to roam this beautiful landscape.

Ever since I explained to Shane how riding horses simulated walking on two legs, because horses had a similar pelvis structure, he wanted to ride every day. Usually, Clay helped him mount, but that was no longer an option. Lately, Shane and I have practiced with just the two of us. He used a footstool to get himself higher. Then, holding the saddle horn, he'd use his upper body strength as I pushed his backside until he could right himself and find balance. It wasn't perfect, but we got better at it every day.

After riding for about half an hour, we edged along the fence line on the far part of the property. Shane managed Honey expertly. His natural ability made it look as if he had been riding his entire life. To see him share my passion was thrilling. A picture of my future flashed before my eyes. We were living together and running the therapy program as a team. He'd become a living testimonial, making our ranch the number-one destination for patients to heal their minds, bodies, and spirits. A dream with Shane in it. Our calling.

Looking up, I noticed on our travels that the night sky began to darken. It's funny how fast time moved when one enjoyed being in the moment.

"Hey, we should probably—" Before I could finish speaking, I was interrupted by an ear-piercing, high-pitched squeal. Copper flinched, brushing his hoof into the ground assertively. That's when I noticed movement. A jackrabbit struggled in the barbed wire near one of the fence posts. Immediately, I hopped off the horse, gently patting his nose twice before investigating.

"What's going on?" Shane asked, doing his best to circle Honey back to Copper and me.

"Looks like a jackrabbit got stuck. It'll only take me a moment to release him." I strode over slowly with my hands out, speaking in a soft voice. "Hey there, little guy. It's okay." I squatted next to the rabbit, adjusting my gloves as I reached out. It kicked its back leg wildly, twitched, and then, except for its wild darting eyes, the jackrabbit stilled.

"Is it alive?" Shane asked. I looked at Honey as she stiffened, letting out a heavy snort as her ears snapped forward.

"Honey, girl. What's wrong?" I said calmly to comfort her as a crisp rattling sound set off alarm bells in my head. Before I could react, a searing pain stabbed into my right forearm. I fell back onto the ground, clutching my arm, a scream tore from my throat.

"Kira!" Shane shouted. Fumbling with Honey's reins, he moved to dismount.

"No! Don't come over here. Back away. I got bitten by a rattlesnake."

"Where is it?" He asked, trying to stabilize himself on a nervous Honey.

"I don't know. But I need to get to the hospital, NOW!"

Standing up, I lost my balance slightly. I wobbled over to Copper, who had moved a safe distance away after sensing danger. The snake had bitten me on my right arm, my dominant one, and it hurt like hell.

"What do I do?" he asked, panicked.

Since time was of the essence, I made several desperate attempts to remount Copper. I almost had it when I slid off again. Feeling woozy, I stumbled backward right into Shane's arms. When had he gotten off his horse?

"I told you to stay... on the h..." My vision clouded as everything went black.

As I woke up a moment later, Shane yelled loudly on the phone for help. I lay on the ground, fluttering in and out of consciousness. Abruptly, he appeared again, hovering over me. His mouth moved, but no sound met my ears. A foggy halo formed around my vision as if I peered through the wrong end of a pair of binoculars. He seemed to repeat the same words over again. Before the dark shrouded my awareness, I finally understood him.

Stay and fight.

Chapter 41

Shane

EVERYTHING HAD HAPPENED so fast. The fear in Clay's voice over the phone scared me. He confirmed what Kira had said before she fell unconscious, that she needed medical help immediately. Clay told me to put her on the back of Honey and send her to the stable. Honey knew the way and would be easily directed to take Kira there. He said he would take care of things on his end and drive the truck to intercept them.

I hung up the phone and assessed my surroundings. With the sun almost set, I hurried my pace. Scooping up Kira's limp body while balancing on one leg was a feat of its own, but my adrenaline fueled me. I placed her on the saddle and draped her over the horn. Once secured, I slapped Honey on the rump and sent her cantering.

I stood watching Honey disappear into the distance with my Kira. Her life hung in the balance of a therapy mare. My chest heaved. I bent forward before the gasps could escape my lungs, whistling for Copper to come to me. Still skittish, he hesitated at first but then joined me at my side.

Copper stood taller than Honey, and any attempts I made to hop to his saddle were futile. As dusk deepened into night, I pulled out my phone light to search for any large rock I could use as a step. When I found the right one, mounting Copper was made easier. I splayed across the saddle at first but soon righted myself in the seat. I commanded Copper to start the trek toward home. Toward Kira.

It seemed like forever before I caught up with Honey as she steadily and gently trotted forward. She was an amazing horse. So cautious with her helpless rider as she went toward the stables. Consumed by night. I used the distant glow of the lights as a lighthouse to guide us safely home. Except it felt like there was no real safety, only dread.

As the soft, steady clomping of horse hooves on the ground droned on, my mind spiraled. The full gravity of the situation was sealed when I had heard Clay's panic. How he'd shot out succinct instructions like an ER doctor dealing with a trauma patient, using words like: *urgent, critical,* and *anti-venom.* I couldn't lose her now. I'd just gotten her back. *What cruel twist of fate would allow me to survive mental and physical trauma only to lose the person I loved?* It seemed so impossible that I almost couldn't believe it.

The frenetic pace of my breathing picked up. Staving off a possible panic attack, I took deep, controlled breaths, counting in time. Kira moaned quietly, de-escalating my growing fear. Still breathing was good. She attempted to pick up her head but just as quickly slumped over again.

Then, in the distance, I heard a truck horn blaring. Bright headlights bobbed in front of us. I frantically waved my arms to gain their attention. When the lights flashed, I let out a sigh of relief.

The truck skidded to a stop. Clay leapt out first and came running straight for Kira. "Kira!" he shouted, shaking her gently, stirring a soft groan in response. Clay carried her to the back seat of the truck as Nash stepped out of the front passenger side and approached me on my horse.

"Thank you, Shane, for reacting so quickly. Leave the horses. We'll collect them tomorrow. We must get her to Billings immediately."

"Yes, si... I mean, Nash." Nash shot me a quick smile as he helped lower myself from Copper. I got in the truck's backseat and carefully laid Kira's head on my lap. Clay drove as if he'd just seen the checkered flag while rounding the final lap at the Indy 500. Nash hung onto the dashboard for his dear life but remained silent.

We got to the hospital just over an hour after Kira's snake bite. The doctors sounded encouraging with how quickly we got her there since Nash had called the hospital ahead of time. The team met us when we arrived. "You made it here in record time Mr. Bowman. We have the anti-venom ready. She will be in good hands." The emergency doctor stated.

Once they rushed her into the emergency room, all we could do was wait. Wait for any type of news or updates. In a waiting room where, as Nash would say, *time moved like slow elk.*

I sat in a borrowed hospital wheelchair, mine having been left in the stables when we saddled up. While unable to physically pace, my mind wandered. Waiting made me sympathize with my poor mother. What she had gone through after my accident and surgeries in Portugal. It must have been brutal. Being a patient experiencing pain and procedures was difficult, but waiting and having no control was harder.

After what felt like an eternity, we finally got an update.

"Mr. Bowman?" The emergency doctor from earlier called out.

"Yes, I'm here. How is my niece?" Clay and I moved closer to hear.

"She's responding as she should. You getting her here so quickly made a huge difference. She's resting and we'll have a wound care specialist come in to assess the damage soon. But all things considered, she was very lucky the strike was on her arm." The tension I held dissipated.

"Much obliged, doctor. What happens now?" Nash inquired.

"We'll admit her to the hospital for a few days to monitor the wound and pain management."

Immediately following the news, Nash went outside to call Levi back with the good report. Clay sank into a seat and put his face into his hands. His shoulders shook. I wasn't sure if consoling him would be helpful or a hindrance.

However, Kira would want me to try. Clay was an important part of her life; therefore, he was now important to me. I went over and placed a comforting hand on his shoulder. For a moment, he didn't move, then abruptly he sprang up and hugged me. Taken aback by his actions, I froze.

"Thank you for saving her. For putting aside our differences and trusting me to get help. Thank you for loving her that much." Then, just as quickly, he let me go and rushed outside.

I could feel myself blinking heavily as if waking up from a dream. *Was this his way of calling a truce for the sake of our beloved Kira?* I couldn't fault him for loving her. Her pure soul was warm, kind and unconditional and I had no ill will toward Clay. I was confident that someday we'd be friends because of her. That was the invincible power of my Kira Sky.

The adrenaline that had coursed through my body the past few hours was now edged out by exhaustion. Dr. Birdingground and I would have a lot to talk about in our next session. But for now, my Kira would recover, which filled me with joy. Dreams and reality. It was a fine line and delicate balance.

"Before Shane" may have been living for the dream, but "After Shane" only wanted reality. I had misdirected my feelings and the truth for so long that I had stopped recognizing myself. But Kira saw me, the real me, and she had restored my hope. I could see clearly now.

Kira *was* my dream, my reality, my home, and my future.

Kira

It had taken a while to get back to normal after my rattlesnake encounter. And I was still mad at myself for not being more careful that night, especially since I knew better. I should have listened to my horses and assessed the situation before sticking my hands anywhere near that rabbit in the dim light of the day.

Prairie rattlers weren't aggressive, but they would defend themselves, and I'd encroached on their meal. After being hospitalized for several days, it had taken me more than two weeks to regain a significant portion of my strength. I still felt fatigued, but I improved daily.

My entire family had flown out to help me recover. I loved having them here despite the circumstances. It took time to get used to the new dynamic on the ranch between myself, Shane and Clay. Oddly, Clay had made it so much easier. He had been acting differently toward us since that night. Doting yet not overstepping. Clay made a genuine effort, and it hadn't gone unnoticed.

Dad took a sip of lemonade as we sat on the front porch rocking chairs. "The more you give, the more good things will come to you," my dad nonchalantly dropped that little nugget of wisdom out of the blue.

"Who are you referring to with your Crow proverb?" I asked.

"I was going to say Clay, but I guess it could be Shane too."

We had just returned from the airport. Mom and Zach had flown home. Ironically, for soccer camp this summer. Shane had surprised us when he'd offered advice, tips, and techniques that Zach could use as a striker for his team. The same position as Shane. Talking about soccer lit up his face, making his blue eyes sparkle. I was so proud of him for all the progress he had made on his healing journey. Thinking about soccer again was a huge step forward.

I responded to Dad, "I think you're right. I can see that in both of them."

"See what in both of whom?" Uncle Nash asked, sinking into the cushioned wicker couch next to us.

"The boys. The effort. The reason," Dad cryptically stated to my uncle, who nodded in full agreement. I shook my head as I observed the exact same person, but in two different bodies.

Leaving them to chat, I ambled my way to the stable, now strong enough to ride. My mentor Misty was coming later today and said we'd take things slow. She had been so kind and understanding with everything that had intruded my life as of late.

"Hey there, teacher's…um… I mean, Kira," Clay stammered. "I heard that you're strong enough to ride."

"Like they say, '*If you fall off a horse and get bitten by a rattlesnake, you just get right back on,*'" I chuckled.

Clay shook his head. "You're starting to sound like the old men sitting over at the house. You better watch your company."

"You take that back," I teased. We both laughed. I liked having the ease of our friendship return.

"Well, I'm glad you're feeling better."

"Thank you, Clay." I smiled.

Clay pointed a thumb over his shoulder. "By the way, he's in the paddock. Riding again. I'm not sure he'll need to pick up his prosthetic leg anymore since he's always on a horse," he snorted at his own joke. I giggled. Seeing glimmers of the old Clay warmed my heart.

As I entered the paddock, Shane rode past on Honey. The two of them dashed expertly in big figure eights before they galloped the short length of the fenced area. His new favorite move.

He noticed me and gave an excited wave. I loved how he looked at me. How unabashed he was now. Two years ago, our broken hearts had merged. Full of teen angst, drama, and attraction. But now? Our love was vibrant, intense, ethereal, and freeing. It was like the Northern Lights. Our molecules collided together, emitting the most excruciatingly colorful light. And I loved him.

"Hello, my beautiful Kira Sky," Shane greeted me as he slid off the horse. I slipped my arms around him to feel his closeness, nuzzling my face into his chest to feel his beating heart.

"Hello, my handsome Shane," I said, no longer embarrassed by anyone who saw us in our numerous embraces on the ranch. Shane tilted my head upwards and held me with his hypnotic gaze.

"Kira, I love my life here with you. I found the real me again. The confident, hardworking, driven Shane. And when I get my new leg, I know I'll be unstoppable. It's all because of you. You're my solace. My home."

Tears threatened to escape my eyes. "Welcome back, Shane."

"It's good to be back," he responded, wiping away the singular tear that slid down my cheek. "Diiawachisshik, Kira Sky."

I grinned. "I love you too, Shane."

We sealed our affirmation of love with an all-consuming, passionate kiss. My Shane was fighting for us and fighting to get his life back. My whole existence soared with the possibilities of our life together. Dreams and reality. It was a fine line and delicate balance. But I could see clearly now.

Shane was my dream, my reality, my home, and my future.

About the Author

I consider myself a conscious dreamer and have always relished living in my imagination. I'm an avid fan of all types of storytelling, and it brings me joy every time I get to take a happy book DETour into those worlds. Thank you to all my loyal readers who drive me to write and publish. I sincerely hope you love the ride as much as I enjoy being the driver!

Now, a few acknowledgments: Thank you again to my team at Tempered Ink for all their hard work with editing, cover art, my website, and a MILLION other book-related tasks. Thank you doesn't truly convey my gratitude for your assistance and friendship! I am endlessly appreciative of your tireless support with all my literary works. Thank you to my family for their continued support and enthusiasm with all my writing ventures. Lastly, thank you to all the friends, family, and beta readers for their invaluable input, feedback and suggestions about the story, my writing, research, cover, and title to make my book even better: Julie, Debbie, Nancy, Brandi, Amy, and Wayne. I value all your time and efforts to make this a better story.

Jennifer Conklin is an award-winning author and former special education teacher. She resides in New York with her husband, their youngest son (Electrical Engineer), and two adorable fur-babies. Their older son, his wife, and their infant daughter live nearby, making her a VERY happy Mom and Grandma!

Check out my other books:

Fine Line Series (YA Novel Series)
*PRETEND- Book 1

The Adventure Above Series (Children's Book Series)
*SHE WHO WALKS ABOVE THE TREES- Book 1
*SHE WHO SWIMS ABOVE THE SEAS- Book 2
*SHE WHO FLOATS ABOVE THE BREEZE- Book 3

Visit me at:
www.jenniferconklinauthor.com
or www.happydetours.com
Facebook & Instagram: @jenniferconklinauthor